A DEATH AT
TIPPITT POND

A DEATH AT
TIPPITT POND

SUSAN VAN KIRK

Encircle Publications, LLC
Farmington, Maine U.S.A.

Paperback ISBN 13: 978-1-948338-64-6
E-book ISBN 13: 978-1-948338-65-3
Kindle ISBN 13: 978-1-948338-66-0

Library of Congress Control Number: 2019940492

Editor: Cynthia Brackett-Vincent
Book design: Eddie Vincent
Cover design by Deirdre Wait
Cover photographs: front photograph © Felix Russell, Unsplash.com; back photograph © Getty Images

Published by: Encircle Publications, LLC
PO Box 187
Farmington, ME 04938

Visit: http://encirclepub.com

Sign up for Encircle Publications newsletter and specials
http://eepurl.com/cs8taP

Printed in U.S.A.

Acknowledgments

Because I'm a former teacher, I rely on the help of experts and friends. Blood spatter, guns, and detective work were never in my high school curriculum.

I am grateful to the following people who helped with the details:

• Tammy Wolbers, currently vice president at Bank of New York Mellon, who really does live in New York.

• My partner in mystery reading and amazing genealogist, Eileen Owens, for help with the genealogy procedures.

• Charles Fry and Scott Spitzer for their expertise in the art of creating beautiful furniture.

• Rick Sayre, former head librarian at Hewes Library, Monmouth College.

• Andrew Doyle, Warren County state's attorney.

• Detective Ian Lawler of the Des Moines, Iowa, Police Department for advice on weaponry.

As always, I am grateful and indebted to my editor, Lourdes Venard of Comma Sense Editing, for her editorial wizardry, her publishing advice, and her friendship.

Finally, thank you to my intelligent, well-read friends, Jan DeYoung, Hallie Lemon, and Eileen Owens, who encourage me and who search-and-destroy my errors.

Chapter One

Shading her eyes from the morning sun with her hand, Elizabeth Russell stared up at the roof of Tippitt House with an anxious ache in her gut. In this small Midwestern town, she was pulled in opposite directions. Should she fly back to her New York home, leaving this mystery behind, or should she wait and appease her curiosity despite her uneasiness?

Frozen with indecision, she studied the massive Tudor home that rose three stories. The sun reflected off the slate roof as well as the finials on the gable points. It was a Queen Anne Tudor, its patterned bricks laid in headers and stretchers. She'd learned the process while researching an English manor. Some bricks were laid with their ends forward while others were laid with their sides forward, exhibiting a pattern called a Flemish Brick bond. She briefly saw a woman staring from the darkness of a bay window, then disappearing.

Well, Beth thought, taking a deep breath. Standing here examining brick patterns is not going to give me any answers. I'm simply putting off the inevitable.

Feigning confidence, she marched across the street, checking both ways. Unlike New York City, she wasn't likely to get hit by a car. Sweet Iron, Illinois, population 15,000, had little morning traffic in either direction. Climbing the stairs, she was about to push on the doorbell when the door opened, and the woman she'd seen in the window a moment earlier was looking into Beth's eyes with interest. She was thin, maybe a runner, Beth thought, her brown hair blunt-cut, framing her long face perfectly. Her facial features

1

were symmetrical, her smile a little too wide for her narrow face.

"Good morning, Ms. Russell," the woman said with a smile. "I'm Molly Grayson. I've been keeping an eye on the house for Janet Landry and, more recently, for Mr. Hatcher." She put her hand out, and Beth shook it firmly. "Unfortunately, Mr. Hatcher has been delayed, but only momentarily. He asked to have you wait in the living room. I laid a fire so it's warm."

"Nice to meet you—Molly, was it?"

"Yes. Here, let me take your coat. Follow me."

Once Beth was seated, the Grayson woman indicated a silver tea service on the coffee table. "Help yourself. I'm sure he will be here shortly." Then she left, quietly pulling the exquisite pocket doors shut behind her.

Beth sat back, ignoring the tea and concentrating on the ache in her stomach. Ever since she could remember, she had been plagued by anxiety. This situation was no different. Her thoughts went back to the investigator who had found her at the New York City Public Library. Besides giving her a plane ticket and expenses to come to this little town, he'd piqued her curiosity with this ridiculous story about being heir to an inheritance from some family named Tippitt. She was between projects, so she decided to check out this fiction. Why not? It had cost her nothing. Now her uneasiness made her sorry she had come.

She glanced around the living room—beautifully crafted furniture, a baby grand piano, heavy drapes over the windows, and walls filled with gilded frames surrounding massive paintings. It was so quiet, except for an occasional crackle from the fireplace, that Beth felt like a patient waiting in a room for her doctor to give her bad news. Glancing at the tea things, she pursed her lips and thought about her day yesterday in the small town. Beth had kept an initial appointment with this efficient but stuffy lawyer, Remington Hatcher.

She had felt a sudden desire to flee even then. Entering by the front door of the law office, Beth had seen an empty waiting room except for a man in a sportscoat and slacks. His dark hair was brushed back in a slight wave with only enough silver to be attractive. He had a small scar on his left cheek near his ear. Beth might have missed it entirely, but he was turned toward the window light. He was about Beth's age, and she could see he sported a shoulder holster. When he saw her noticing the slight bulge in his jacket, he explained he was a detective with the Sweet Iron Police Department.

"Kyle Warner, ma'am," he intoned quietly. "I'm here to take DNA to the lab if I'm needed. This is my day off, and Mr. Hatcher wanted to ensure the validity of the sample."

"How do you do," she said, holding out her hand. "I'm Beth Russell, but I suppose you may already know that."

"Yes, ma'am, I do."

Beth felt the color in her face rise and she shook her head. Moving to New York City, she had fled her small hometown where everyone knew everyone else's business. She took another glance at Kyle Warner as he sat down and thought he was good-looking in a rugged sort of way. Turning, she stepped over to a desk where a middle-aged woman, dressed in a brown suit with a white blouse, was standing at attention. Her smile was pleasant, her manner efficient, her hand outstretched. "Good morning, Ms. Russell. I'm Harriet Newman, Mr. Hatcher's assistant. If you'll have a seat, I'll see if Mr. Hatcher is ready for you."

Beth shook her hand and, turning, eyed the clock as she sat down. 9:50 a.m. She could still catch a plane home in the afternoon.

"Mr. Hatcher will see you now, Ms. Russell," said the assistant. Beth followed her into an office with thick, dark blue carpet and wood everywhere. Two leather chairs sat in front of the desk.

A short man stood up, forty or forty-five with dark hair—a little gray at the temples—and looked at Beth expectantly. He must have been five-foot-seven and carried maybe twenty extra pounds.

"Good morning, Ms. Russell," he said, stretching out his hand.

"Good morning to you, Mr. Hatcher." She shook his hand, and he gestured that Beth might sit in a leather chair. As he walked behind the desk, Beth watched him take an antibiotic wipe from the top drawer and sweep it across the hand she had just shaken.

"Cold and flu season," he said. "Can't be too careful." He sat behind his desk, a lone folder occupying an otherwise pristine surface. No papers, no other folders, bare. He must be super-wizard

3

organized, Beth thought.

Taking two pens out of his desk drawer, he lined them up side-by-side, meticulously making sure they were parallel. Then he looked at Beth, a cordial tone to his voice. "I trust your flight went well and everything was in order at the bed-and-breakfast. I hope you're comfortable there."

"I am, indeed." She stared right at him, her fists tightened on her lap. "I appreciate the trouble you've taken sending an investigator with this story about a lost heir, but I doubt very much that I'm the person you're trying to find."

Hatcher licked dry lips and looked up. "That remains to be seen." He clasped his hands together, setting them on the folder. "I am mainly concerned, Ms. Russell, with discharging my fiduciary duty as executor of the estate of my client, Janet Tippitt Landry. She left quite explicit instructions." He lightly tapped a finger on the desktop. "Frankly, I am not sure I even believe this missing child theory. No records exist about a child being born, but Janet Landry was definite about her desire to find a baby she remembered. Depending on our discussion, I have been advised of two separate directions for disbursement of the Tippitt estate. So, this is where we are."

Beth leaned forward in her chair, figuring she should end this quickly and mercifully. "I may as well begin by telling you I grew up in Spring Harbor, New York, with two parents who certainly existed, a birth certificate, and any number of records to show I am the adult child of Robert and Laurel Russell. So, I'm confused. Why would you associate me with a family I've never heard of in a place I've never been?" She sat back in her chair, crossing her legs.

"My investigator. It has taken him several months to find you, and, unfortunately, Janet died during that period. She tried hard to survive her cancer to meet this elusive niece, but it wasn't to be."

Beth took in a breath, feeling her anxiety again, and said, "I figure I'll listen to you—since you're willing to throw so much money into a free trip for me when I'm between research projects—then I'll return to New York City and my real life. I'm simply curious, as I said, about the context of this whole mysterious family."

Hatcher opened the folder on his desk and said, "Would you like to know a bit about the Tippitt family? I can give you some information if you'd like."

"Sure." She settled back in her chair, watching as the lawyer pulled the cap from an expensive gold pen and cleared his throat. Beth studied him. He glanced down at the first page, turned it over, and began talking while his pen tip touched various spots on the next page. Precise, she thought.

"I wasn't present, Ms. Russell, when this situation with an out-of-wedlock birth allegedly took place. I can explain that the Tippitt family has been a driving force in the history of Sweet Iron for several generations. You might have noticed the college and the various venues named for the generous donations of the family."

"I did on my way into town." She nodded, trying to hide her impatience, but a jiggling leg put a lie to that.

"Of course, the local library has books about the history of the town, and the Tippitts have been highly involved since Sweet Iron's founding. I inherited their legal affairs from my uncle, who was an attorney and a friend of Judge Tippitt's."

"Oh, he was a judge?"

"Yes." He nodded solemnly. "Judge Tippitt has been gone now twenty-six years, and his wife, Joellen, twenty-one. Their only surviving child was Janet Tippitt Landry, who died a few weeks ago at age seventy-four. She had a younger brother and sister who predeceased her."

Beth looked down at her hands in her lap. "So many early deaths. I'm sorry for the family."

He hesitated, his facial expression approving her scruples. "That is kind of you." He shuffled another page and resumed. "If I describe the three siblings, maybe it will help you understand. Janet was the oldest. She married Neal Landry, who sold real estate in the Fort Worth area. They didn't have any children. Neal died some time ago, and since Janet was the only surviving child, she returned to the family home."

After the lawyer paused, Beth said, "Was that her house, or maybe the family's house, I saw down the street from the bed-and-

5

breakfast?"

"Yes, Tippitt House. It's in the historical section of town. I believe the house dates to the mid-1800s."

She moved forward in her chair, her voice becoming animated. "I figured that was the case. I'm a historical researcher and genealogist, you see. It must have been built fairly soon after the founding of the town."

"Correct. Much of it was preserved even after the deaths of the siblings." He put his head down and returned to his notes. "After Janet came Jeff, the judge's only son. Unfortunately, he was killed in 1967 in Vietnam. Helicopter pilot. It was quite a blow for the family, from what I've been told, since he was the presumptive heir, continuing the family name. The youngest child, Melanie, who was six years younger than Jeff, took his death very hard. I am told they were close."

"I can see why Janet Landry was trying to find this mysterious heir, since I imagine they want to keep the family's estate intact."

He looked up at her, nodding. "The focus of our little chat would be the last child, Melanie. From what I have heard—I have, of course, seen photographs—she was quite stunning. Blond, like you. It was her eyes, however, that were the cause of great interest. You see, she had green eyes, and each had little gold flecks in the irises." He paused, and added, "Much like yours."

Hatcher waited, considering her eyes, and silence filled the space between them.

Beth's body suddenly went still. Her whole life people had remarked upon her unique eyes. She hadn't given a thought to their origin, since she knew so little about either of her parents' families. Suddenly, Beth heard someone clear his throat and realized she had been sitting in silence while Remington Hatcher waited.

He cleared his throat once again, saying, "You know, Ms. Russell, all of this took place a long time ago. Jeff Tippitt has been gone forty-nine years, and Melanie, forty-five. It was all a long, long time ago. Only people in their sixties or older could remember what happened back then, I'd imagine."

"You're probably right," Beth said, in a quiet voice. She looked down at her hands in her lap and saw they were trembling again. Seconds went by in silence. Deep down, Beth had always known something was wrong. She could remember a conversation with her well-meaning friend, Gabrielle, who said, "But I have grandparents and aunts and uncles and four brothers and three sisters and nieces and nephews too numerous to mention. At last count, I think that overwhelms your zero. Don't you find that strange?" It was true her parents kept her close to home. No history. No relatives. If she were honest, even she found it strange.

A ghost of a kindly expression passed over Remington Hatcher's face and he said, "I doubt we will find this missing baby, now adult. If she were alive today, she'd be forty-seven years old."

Beth raised her eyes. "I'm forty-seven. Forty-eight next April."

She saw his face suddenly transformed by shock, as if he were finding it difficult to believe her last words. He turned several pages of papers in his folder and began searching for something. Finally, his pen lighted on a spot on one of the pages. He looked up.

"When, exactly, is your next birthday, Ms. Russell?"

"April 10."

He stared at her, and his voice began to take on a more mellow tone. "I believe maybe we should consider a DNA test."

"Why?"

"The baby Janet Landry remembers was born on April 10, 1969. She was quite definite about the date. She was in attendance, you see."

Beth stared at him as if he were speaking a different language. She tried to say something, but the words stuck in her throat. Taking a deep breath and finding her voice, she asked, "What were the circumstances surrounding this baby's birth, Mr. Hatcher?"

He pressed his lips together and said, "I can't tell you more until we determine identity. I believe I've already said too much. If you are the Tippitt niece, I am prepared to give you a great deal of information, but we will have to establish your identity first. A simple DNA test. We have DNA to match from Janet, as well as a lock of the alleged baby's hair."

By now Beth's researcher instincts were kicking in, and she

considered reasons they could abandon this whole ridiculous story. "I thought DNA results took a long time to complete. I seem to remember some of the more dramatic legal cases in the news had to wait weeks, maybe months, to determine the results."

"That is where we are in a sweet spot. Not far from here is a private lab, and Tippitt money has been set aside to pay the cost of the test if we have a candidate with a reasonable background. In addition, a new DNA test is now out which takes approximately four hours to match," said the lawyer.

She sat forward in her chair, a gasp leaving her lips. "Four hours? You have to be kidding!"

"No, Ms. Russell. We could resolve this whole situation quite quickly. We would know later today, or, possibly, by tomorrow morning."

Beth brought a shaky hand to her forehead pushing back her hair.

"However, we would have to have your permission to swab your mouth."

Beth slowly assembled her chaotic thoughts. "This is all impossible, Mr. Hatcher. My parents were present at my birth. Never did anyone question I was anything but their child. My mother had me quite late in life—she was forty-two. But they told me they never gave up hoping they might have a child while she was still able to do so. I find it difficult to believe these parents I loved and cherished lied to me about this fundamental information."

Hatcher pushed back his chair and stood up, walking around the desk. He didn't touch Beth on the shoulder or put out his hand, but he did say in a somewhat empathetic tone, "Maybe we should see if you are that heir."

She had played that first meeting with Hatcher back and forth in her mind, restlessly tossing and turning all night. As soon as her eyes got heavy, her brain kicked in, keeping sleep just beyond her reach.

That was yesterday. Now, as Beth sat in the Tippitt living room, she thought about pouring a cup of tea after all, but she was afraid her hands would shake too much. Into the silence came Molly Grayson's voice, a distant murmur from behind the pocket doors.

Remington Hatcher must be here, she thought as she listened to the sound of the front door closing. Hmm, she thought. His voice sounds quite optimistic.

Chapter Two

The pocket doors opened, and Hatcher walked into the living room nodding with approval at the fire burning in the huge fireplace. Beth rose and shook his proffered hand, then sat down as he placed his briefcase on the sofa across from her. She noticed he had even remembered his antibiotic wipes.

He began. "Well, Ms. Russell—Elizabeth, if I may call you that—we meet again."

Beth swallowed and thought, first names. If he is into calling me by my first name, the DNA must have come back a positive. How could that be? She tried to keep her face neutral as she began to consider what that might mean. Her anxiety beat a drum in her middle.

"Here, let me pour you some tea," he said, and he began arranging teacups and saucers, napkins, sugar and spoons.

After he had handed Beth a cup of tea and poured one for himself, he sat back and said, "I hope you slept well last night, Ms. Russell."

"Not really, I'm afraid. Please, Mr. Hatcher. I think we should get on with what news you may have."

He set down his teacup and said, "Remington. Please call me Remington. Very well." He turned, opened his briefcase on the sofa, pulling out numerous packets of papers. "Well, Elizabeth, the tests came back all positive. I am afraid there can be no doubt. 'Afraid' is an improper word here. 'Delighted' would be correct." This was followed by a pregnant pause on both their parts. The silence was broken by Remington's awkward words. "I am sure my investigator must be gloating since I didn't really believe you existed. But here you are."

"I don't quite know what to say Mr.—uh, Remington—because I never imagined I had two sets of parents." She tried to ignore her churning insides, tried to think of something else to say, but no words came out, leaving a silence hanging in the air.

"I believe it is obvious that Janet Landry was correct, and her story about being there when you were born was evidently true. Finding you, after all this time, has been like the old needle and haystack cliché." He set his own teacup down, took out a handkerchief, and wiped his mouth as if he were done drinking tea and prepared for a serious discussion. "Now that the results are in—and they are totally substantiated after three identical tests—I must warn you that your life is about to change forever."

Beth thought the lawyer was being overly melodramatic, but it soon dawned on her that maybe he was correct. "I don't want all this—this house, that is. I just want to go back to New York City and go on with my life. I was perfectly satisfied with being plain Beth Russell, researcher."

Hatcher clasped his hands together, pausing before he spoke. "I'm afraid it's too late for that. And, 'plain' you are not. It's hard to know what to call you, how to think of you. You're not Elizabeth Tippitt since you're legally Elizabeth Russell. But, no matter what the name, you are the inheritor of a substantial estate belonging to the Tippitt family." He once again wiped his mouth with a handkerchief, and Beth figured it was a nervous habit. "I—ah—I will be more than happy to clarify all this for you. Then, if you'd like, I can assist you with the burden of dealing with the paperwork and legalities." He waited for Beth to respond.

Beth set her teacup down and leaned forward, rubbing her hands. "I don't quite know what to say, Mr. Hatcher—Remington. This is all a bit overwhelming. It's as if, overnight, I must get used to a whole new identity, one that includes people I've never known in my life, and one that involves people I thought I knew."

"I detect a tiny bit of bitterness in your voice, Elizabeth. I'm sure your adopted parents had reasons of their own for keeping the story of your birth secret. What those were we'll never know."

She slowly nodded her head.

"So," he said, turning to his folders and packets and giving Beth a crisp nod. "I keep saying, 'substantial estate.' Now that you are the legal heir, I need to unravel what that is." He had several packets of papers that he arranged in neat piles to his side on the sofa as he finished speaking about each area of her holdings. "First, of course, you own this house. It is a historical Tudor home that the family originally built in the 1800s. I assure you it has been kept in pristine condition. These are the keys," he said, handing her a keyring with several keys on it. "The house and car keys are on this ring. I believe other keys you might need are in the kitchen hanging on the inside of one of the cabinet doors." He sat back down, trying to figure out where he had stopped reading while Beth studied each of the keys. "You also own a great deal of acreage north of the city, some of it farmed by tenants, and some of it timberland. I realize you may not know much about agriculture, but we have people here in town who can help you with that."

Beth smiled and said, "No. A farmer I'm not."

He looked back at her with a slight smile and moved on. "You have a portfolio of stocks and bonds managed by a firm in Chicago, a vehicle owned by Janet, and an apartment in Chicago she often used because she liked to attend the opera or the theater."

Beth's breathing began to constrict. Whatever was she getting into?

"You also have a house in Fort Worth, Texas, where Janet and Neal used to live. Of course, you could always put that on the market. It would bring an excellent price, maybe two million."

At that casual remark, Beth started taking quiet, deep breaths, but Hatcher didn't notice. He laid aside several packets of papers and turned to her with a serious demeanor. Beth could tell more advice was forthcoming.

"Janet was prominent on many boards in Sweet Iron, and people knew her. They will undoubtedly be curious about you. Take some time, catch your breath, and deal with those people a few at a time. I might mention that discretion would probably be a good idea. Midwesterners are naturally curious and want to know what's happening. The Tippitt family tended to be leaders in the community, but seldom gossipers."

"Mr., uh, Remington," Beth said, her voice trembling slightly, her hand twisting the chain of her necklace. "When you put this—these holdings—together, how 'substantial' is this inheritance?"

He looked in the air over her head as if he were adding up sums. Then he brought his gaze down. "Oh, I'd say well over fifty million dollars. Again, I will say this to you: I know it is a bit overwhelming at first, but I am sure you will grow accustomed to it. I'm at your service if I can help you. The Tippitt family has trusted me with their legal matters for some time."

She stared at him for a full minute unable to say anything. Her skin tingled, her heart raced, and a fluttery feeling had taken over her chest. "I believe it is good, Remington, that I am not a fainting type of woman. Could you pour more tea in my cup, please?" Beth asked, her hand trembling only slightly on the saucer. She thought of asking for something stronger, but a glance at Hatcher said "inappropriate" at 10 a.m. "Now that we have established that I'm someone I didn't know I was, could I ask you questions about these biological parents?" she asked as he poured the tea.

"Certainly," he said, handing her the teacup and saucer.

She looked straight at Hatcher, her voice filled with a resolve she only pretended to have. "I want to know about this adoption and what happened to these Tippitt people who gave me away."

"Certainly," he repeated. "Your mother, Melanie, was sixteen when she became pregnant with you. I don't need to tell you what a stir this caused in the Tippitt family. This was the late 1960s. Having a child out of wedlock was not a desirable situation, especially for a family whose stature was well-known in the community. My understanding—from Janet—was that the judge arranged for a private adoption by another family. He evidently met your adopted father at legal conferences where Mr. Russell confided to the judge that he and his wife had not been able to have children. Naturally, the judge thought he could solve two problems with one adoption."

She looked down at her teacup and said quietly, "Good to know I was a problem-solver even then."

"Perhaps I put that a bit—roughly," Hatcher said, licking his dry lips and reaching for his tea. After taking a deep swallow, he continued. "I meant only that your adoption was a decision meant to spare the family from unsavory gossip. Furthermore, Melanie Tippitt was only sixteen, not even of legal age, or what we call the age of consent."

"Why do I have a birth certificate with my name and my adopted parents' names? I haven't come across this kind of situation in my genealogy work."

"Unlike today, adoptions were closed back then. When a baby was adopted, the original birth certificate was sealed. Sometimes destroyed. My understanding is that your original certificate was expunged, and a new certificate issued with the names of your adopted parents. The laws have changed considerably, but you can probably see why discretion was important. That, I might remind you, was also before the law changed to allow legal abortions."

This was piling insult on to injury, Beth thought. "Now that's a lovely idea."

Her irony was lost on Hatcher who was organizing the paper packets into a neat pile. She looked up at him. "What happened to my biological mother? Who was my father? Where is he?"

He hesitated, wiping his forehead again. "That is not such a happy story. Your mother died at Tippitt Pond on July 20, 1971. She had been there with a group of her friends. She was nineteen at the time, home from college for the summer."

"Nineteen? How did that happen? How did she die when she was so young?"

"I'm not sure. As I said, I wasn't here. My understanding is that an investigation ensued, and a young man named Brian Nash was found guilty of murder. He spent time in prison, then disappeared. His parents had left town years earlier after the scandal. In any case, it was all a long time ago, Elizabeth. Sometimes it's best to let the past be the past."

"Why did he kill my mother?"

"I don't know."

She paused, thinking.

"What was he to her?"

He hesitated. "A better question might be, 'What was he to you?'"

It took several moments before the truth dawned on her face. "My father."

Chapter Three

S o.
  There it was.

The irrefutable fact. Melanie Tippitt did exist.

Beth Russell, genealogist, stared at her computer screen and read the lines out loud, whispering, her lips barely moving.

"Melanie Tippitt. Age 19. Date of Death: July 20, 1971. Cause of Death: blunt impact to head/cerebral contusion. Manner of death: homicide. Birthplace: Sweet Iron, Illinois. Date of Birth: April 10, 1952. Parents: Emerson Tippitt and Joellen Dawes Tippitt."

Beth locked her eyes on the word "homicide" until her focus began to cloud. Closing her eyes, she leaned her forehead on her hand and thought, Melanie Tippitt, a woman I never knew. But she had known me. DNA doesn't lie. I had rested, first floating, then tightly swaddled in her womb. How could she give me away? Why couldn't she wait— not die—before I found her?

My biological mother murdered. Why would my father kill someone with whom he'd had a child? She stared out the window of the dining room at Tippitt House. This can't be the end of the story. What happened that day at Tippitt Pond? Picking up her cell, she tapped on the calendar. I have at least until mid-February before I must be in New York. I need to find out what happened here back in 1971. That shouldn't be too difficult. Hatcher said to leave the past alone, but he underestimates my curiosity.

Melanie Tippitt would have been sixty-four if she were still alive, Beth thought. She stopped leaning her head on her hand, her elbow resting on the cool walnut surface of the desk in the dining room at

Tippitt House. Sitting back in her chair, she took a deep, calming breath.

"And I alone survive," she whispered. She picked up her pen, jotted down the dates on the Tippitt family tree she'd constructed, logged the information into her new folder, and made sure she typed the source of the information in correctly. Only then did she close the cover of her laptop, sitting at the dining room table in a house she now owned. Correction: A huge house she now owned.

That is why I love genealogy, she thought. It's like being Sherlock Holmes. I gather evidence, keep track of it, make assumptions and connections, and eventually create an entire story of a family. Starting today, I'm going to find out what happened to my biological parents.

She would use her skills to discover a family she never knew existed, a family who had silently sent her away. What harm could it do if I checked this out? They're all dead or gone by now.

My first entry in the genealogical data. Only the beginning of many mysteries to solve. I'll spread out significantly from my biological parents, beginning with Melanie Tippitt's family.

My family.

She felt a growing ache in her stomach. Anxiety.

Here I am, she thought, with two sets of parents, one set who had a daughter they didn't want, and the other set who raised me as if I were their own. But I wasn't their own, and they never told me. Beth began to search her memory for corroborating details.

Her mind had nagged her all morning with a fluttering thought she couldn't quite nab in her net. It had begun as soon as Hatcher mentioned her eyes.

On the morning of the day she died, Beth's mother, suffering from dementia, had looked at her daughter and said the strangest thing. Beth had forgotten it because at the time she figured her mother's mind was wandering, as always. That morning, Laurel Russell's mind had rummaged through the past and present for several years. But—as her mother would say—Beth heard the footsteps of someone walking over her grave. She shivered as she recalled Laurel Russell's conversation with Beth's already-dead father: "But, Bob. I don't know what we'll say—how to explain—people will wonder, won't they? She's ours, isn't she? No one can take her from us, right? But how to explain the strange color of her eyes?"

Chapter Four

A fter looking up Melanie Tippitt, Beth decided to check out the
back of the house and get a glass of water in the kitchen, a room
she discovered was filled with every gadget and appliance known to
chefs. A set of sliding glass doors led from the kitchen into a massive
back yard and a three-car garage whose doors were open. She could
see the back of Janet Landry's silver BMW parked inside.

Stepping outside to explore the grounds on the unseasonably warm
winter day, she punched up her cell phone to call her best friend,
Gabrielle Martinez. Gabby was in Florida for the Christmas season
with her husband, Anthony, their two teenagers, and extended family.
Normally, she lived in New York City, and she and Beth met quite
often for lunch with two other friends, Alyssa and Sarah, who were
also off seeing extended families for Christmas. Gabby knew Beth
had gone to the Midwest on this hare-brained adventure, and she had
pushed Beth to go, figuring it was a free trip and it couldn't hurt to
listen to some lawyer's cockamamie story.

Beth explained what she had found out, occasionally punctuating
her description with a laugh, sometimes a tear, and often with well-
chosen swear words. She wandered around the backyard of Tippitt
House in circles, using sweeping arm gestures and stamping her foot.

"...and I don't know who to be angrier with, Gabby—my mother,
who gave me away, my father, who was evidently a murderer who
left my mother in the lurch—pregnant at sixteen—or my adopted
parents, who didn't have the decency to tell me I was someone else's
child. No wonder I never had a past. I can't believe how livid I am
with all of them. My past life sounds like a giant soap opera," Beth

said, sticking her left hand in her pocket to keep it warm. "Oh, we mustn't forget my father went to prison for somehow killing my mother."

"You don't really know the entire story, do you?" said Gabby, trying to be reasonable. "I mean your biological parents. They aren't around to explain what their motives were in all of that."

Beth paused briefly before replying. "Well, it's clear to me. My mother obviously didn't want me, and my father was a statutory rapist. Today he'd be on some sexual predator list, although they'd have to find him first. He took off after he got out of prison. *Prison.* Did I say that? Amazing." Her arm flew out again. "One of my parents went to prison for murder. It's not something I'd drop into casual conversation."

"My guess is you wouldn't have to mention it back there in Sweet Iron. Probably everyone knows." Gabby hesitated. "What are you going to do?"

"The first thing I'd like to do is find a decent bagel." She listened to Gabby laughing on the other end of the phone.

"I suppose they don't have delis either in these small Midwest towns," said Gabby.

"Haven't checked yet, but I wouldn't put money on it." Beth yanked her wool scarf tighter around her neck. "I have been giving this a great deal of thought, Gabby. I am going to hightail it out of here as fast as I can. I'll have the lawyer, who seems to be my lawyer now, liquidate the assets, sell the house, and transfer it all to New York City to my bank. For now, I'm going to move my things from the bed-and-breakfast to the family digs and deal with the entanglements. It will take time to wrap up the details. Then I'll be back to my home in Sea Cliff." She kicked some more leaves.

"Does this mean you won't have to work ever again?" Gabby whistled. "What an inheritance! Think about how it could free you to live without deadlines. You could go to the library and get books to read for fun. Or, you could keep your job but hire a research assistant to do your research for your author-clients. You could travel all over the world, but this time you wouldn't have to take notes for authors. Or, better yet, you could start your own genealogy business just for

20

fun." Beth smiled as she heard Gabby chuckle again on the other end of the line.

She used her foot to push some dead leaves and twigs around on the ground. "I hadn't really thought very far ahead. It's a little overwhelming. I guess we'll see." She took a deep breath and considered how tired she was. It was barely early afternoon. "I'll figure it out."

"And you haven't mentioned Chad."

"Chad. Well, we are no longer a couple."

Silence. "So, I guess it was wise not to move in with him, right?"

Beth paused a moment. Then she asked, "Gabby, is there something wrong with me?"

"No, of course not. Why would you say such a thing?"

"Here we are, forty-something years old, and you, Sarah, and Alyssa are all married, have kids, and all is well. Me, I just seem to pick one loser after another."

"Nothing is wrong with you. He just wasn't the right one," Gabby said. "I don't think he ever put you first in anything. When you love someone, you're supposed to put him first and vice-versa. For some reason, you never get the vice-versa. I didn't say anything because I knew you'd figure it out."

Thinking about beautiful Gabby with long, dark hair, married twenty years to perfect Anthony, Beth said, "I think all the good ones are taken. I missed them in the prime of my life, and now it's too late. And, as you know, I always compare them to Richard."

"Not sure I see any comparison there," said Gabby. "Besides, you were blessed with a strong sense of right and wrong. One of the things I admire about you is your concern for what's just. Not sure Chad was into that or any real understanding of morals. I know that sometimes you find it hard to trust people, and sometimes you shouldn't. I can understand that after, well, after what happened back when you lived in Chelsea."

Beth thought for a moment but let that topic drop.

Suddenly, Gabby said, "I gotta go. Jacob is trying to drown his sister. Talk to you soon. Keep your eyes wide open and trust no one."

Beth laughed. "You got it. Okay. Bye."

She nestled her phone in her coat pocket and shuffled up the steps into the kitchen. Looking back through the sliding doors, Beth imagined how perfect the gardens would appear in the summer. The Tippitt family undoubtedly had their own gardener. Make that gardeners, plural. She decided to go to the bed-and-breakfast and pick up her belongings. "Car keys. Purse. Lock the sliding doors. Out the front with the keys to my new house. The keys to my new house," Beth repeated. "I have to admit that phrase has a lovely ring to it."

The front doorbell rang, stopping her in her tracks.

Beth could see a woman with her face pressed against the window of the outside door. She looked about fifteen years older than Beth and had light brown hair with blond streaks. It was all piled up on top of her head with a few wisps pulled out on either side. Long, dangling earrings clinked against the glass window as she tried to see in. Beth opened the door, watching the woman step back a few paces. Up closer, the stranger had an expensive coat, perfect makeup, red lipstick, amazingly high, spike heels, and a leather skirt peeking out from the folds of her coat. Beth decided, on closer inspection, that the woman was older than she first appeared. She looked lopsided, a large tote pulling her right side down.

"Good afternoon. Can I help you?" Beth asked.

Pulling a business card out of her tote, the woman said, "Hi. Are you Elizabeth?"

"Yes."

"I'm Elisha Davis of Foster-Davis Realtors. Could I come in and have a few minutes of your time?"

"I was just leaving—"

"Oh, this will only take a few minutes. I know you're in a hurry to put this white elephant on the market and get back to the East Coast, so I thought I'd stop by. I'll cut to the bottom line. I own the biggest realty company in town. I would love to sell your house for you and take the responsibility off your shoulders." She stared past Beth and into the foyer. "Okay if I come in?"

"Yes, I suppose so."

The woman's stiletto heels clicked across the tile floor of the entrance and echoed right into the large foyer that organized the various wings of the house. "I almost listed this house once for Janet, but then she changed her mind. It needs the right buyer, of course," Elisha continued, gazing around and moving toward the living room. Beth followed her as the real estate agent forged her way across the floor and into the carpeted living room where her shoes, thankfully, stopped their annoying clatter. She turned to Beth. "Oh, just call me Elisha."

Beth considered telling the woman to call her "Beth," but something about Elisha Davis annoyed her.

"Well, Elisha—"

"Oh, my dear, my dear. This will be a nightmare to clean out." She gestured wildly with her arms. "The family has been here so long, you see, that the place is stuffed with antiques and bric-a-brac. My, my, my... just a nightmare." Elisha Davis never stopped moving. Beth watched as she circled the room, gazing at the chandelier while pulling off her coat. She threw it over a chair, dropped the tote bag, and examined the drapes like she was measuring them. Somehow Beth felt as if she had been found wanting.

"Well, Elisha—"

"Ah." The real estate agent pulled off her gloves, flinging them onto the chair also, and asked, "Have you gone through the house? Do you have any idea what is in this monstrous castle?"

"Well, no, but I—"

Suddenly, the Davis woman grabbed her by the arm, saying, "Let's start upstairs. I haven't seen all the rooms, although I did visit Janet when she was ill." Elisha literally dragged Beth up the huge front staircase without even holding on to the intricately carved mahogany railing as she teetered in her ridiculously high heels. What a great sense of balance, thought Beth.

"I suppose it might be a good idea to see what is in the house," Beth offered.

Elisha flung open the first bedroom door. "Oh, this would be Jeff's. Egad. It's like a museum to the Vietnam War. They must have left it this way after he died. His mother, you know, was a very sentimental person. Oh, I guess Joellen would have been your grandmother, right?"

Beth was too busy looking around the room at all the artifacts from a different time—photographs of soldiers in Vietnam, a khaki helmet, old magazines and posters. Her eyes opened wide as she stood in the entrance.

Elisha sniffed. "Perfectly wasted. Why didn't they clear most of this out? They have an attic with plenty of space for these old rags and souvenirs." She shook her head. "Well, let's see what is next."

Beth was examining a paperback book by the bed, but she reluctantly followed Elisha Davis into the next bedroom.

"This was Janet's. Her room is good-sized, and most of her clothes were sent to Goodwill, so at least it won't be quite as difficult to deal with."

Beth walked over to a small table with a lace doily on it and stared at three framed photographs, picking up each one. Janet and her husband on their wedding day. The second was maybe Janet's parents. The woman in the photo had silver hair pulled straight back from her oval face. Joellen Tippitt was beautiful by any standard with those much-envied high cheekbones. The man had a stern visage, his blue eyes direct and cold, his mouth surrounded by full, fleshy lips. Both were dressed exquisitely, as if they were leaving at any moment for the opera.

Last, she saw a photo of Jeff and Melanie as teenagers. Beth studied her mother's face. It was beautiful, her skin tones lovely, and she shared the bow of her lips with Beth. Then, of course, the eyes—maybe she, too, had to deal with the stares. In a teenager, those eyes looked sultry. As Beth was studying the photos, she realized Elisha had moved on to the next room. She heard a huge gasp from the hallway. Beth followed in the direction of the gasp and saw the woman standing in the doorway of the next bedroom, her eyes staring into the room.

"Oh, my God," the Davis woman said. She turned in a circle, her arms reaching up. "How insane. They left Melanie's room like a time capsule of the late sixties, too." Elisha shook her head back and forth, and Beth wasn't sure if she imagined the real estate agent's face had turned as white as a sheet. "Unbelievable. Even her favorite perfume." Beth watched her pick up a bottle of perfume from the chest of drawers beside the bed, studying the label. "Chantilly. Ugh. We all wore that foul-smelling stuff. I'm sure it doesn't get better with age."

Beth said, "Maybe looking at my mother's possessions will help me understand who she was."

Elisha ignored Beth, her shrill voice rising with each new discovery. "This is like another museum. All of her things." She opened the closet. Another gasp. "Oh, my God, her clothes." Her hands moved over the clothing, brushing past bell-bottom jeans, a CPO jacket, and a peasant skirt. The closet was jam-packed with clothing that had belonged to Melanie. This time Elisha Davis dropped onto the bed, speechless. She put one hand to her throat. "I remember when Melanie bought the navy CPO jacket. It was her favorite, and we picked it up downtown in a secondhand shop. How excited she was."

"What was my mother like?" asked Beth. "Were you friends?"

"Best friends. She was beautiful. Melanie had that kind of perfect good looks that drew guys' eyes to her immediately."

"But what was she like?" Beth asked, an encouraging tone to her voice.

Elisha looked down at the bedspread and one hand traced circles on the material. "Fun. That's how I remember her. She was always up for an adventure, knew the latest dance craze, and could make the most mundane conversation interesting. I think it was her eyes. Like yours. Men simply fell for them."

Beth hesitated, then asked, "Does that mean she was promiscuous?"

Elisha looked up indignantly. "What a question to ask! No. She was a one-man woman, despite her charm and beauty."

"What was your favorite memory of her?"

The real estate agent rolled her eyes. "That would be tough. I have so many. Let me think." She stared across the room at the chest of drawers and Beth waited patiently. "The night she became the queen of the May Dance. Our sophomore year. She wore the most beautiful pink formal with white elbow-length gloves and a glittery tiara. Afterward, we sat on the football field bleachers, our shoes kicked off, and talked about where our lives would go." Elisha sighed. "She wanted to travel to the Far East—India, I think. She loved history, geography, travel. She told me she wanted to graduate from college and go see the world. Me, I thought I'd marry a handsome man and live happily ever after. You know, typical teenage stuff. Silly. But I believed she'd make her dream come true—she was that kind of person. She lived a charmed life." She looked down again at her hands in her lap. "Funny how life never quite turns out the way you think it will."

For a moment Beth thought she saw tears in the corner of Elisha Davis's eyes. She just remained silent. Finally, a steely resolve returned to Elisha's face. She said quietly, "Well, it was a long, long time ago."

Beth looked around, blinking, at the room her mother had occupied when she was a teenager. A book—Erich Segal's *Love Story*—lay on the table beside her bed, a bookmark in it as if Melanie were going to return and finish reading it. A jewelry box occupied the top of a chest of drawers. Beth walked over and opened it. A little ballerina figure rose from somewhere in the box while a melody began to play. Enchanted, Beth touched a necklace with multicolored beads. Letting it slither through her fingers, she suddenly felt a warmth to them, as if they were alive, and she quickly dropped them back into the box. Melanie's teenage life was frozen in this room, never to go on.

Finally, the real estate agent found her voice again. "See. This is what I mean. Melanie's room will take forever to clean out. Who will want these old relics anyway? Maybe a history museum? I'll bet the cedar chest is crammed to the top. Believe me, Elizabeth, you're much smarter to simply put this in my hands, and I'll take care of everything." Elisha took one last look around the room, brushing her hands together as if she were getting rid of the lot.

"I think I may want to go through my mother's belongings a bit," Beth said. "After all, they were my mother's."

"Well, suit yourself." She glanced at Beth, scanning her features. "You do—look like her, you know. But you also favor the darker side. Your father's genes, I suspect. It's the shape of your nose." She paused, and then grabbed Beth's hand again. "Okay. The parent's room is pretty much cleaned out, but I haven't seen the attic. Let's

26

check it." She looked up at the high ceiling dramatically. "Please, God, let it not be packed wall-to-wall."

Elisha easily found the narrow set of stairs leading up to the attic. Beth followed behind her, hearing every squeak of the floorboards and watching Elisha teeter on her spindly high heels. However did she walk on those? Beth watched as the agent reached the attic door, pulling it open with both hands. Then one hand snaked around the walls on either side, trying to find a light switch. Suddenly, a light came on—not exactly a flood of light—but Beth could see the cavernous attic room through the doorway. What she saw was daunting.

Boxes and objects jammed every inch of space, broken only by narrow pathways between various groupings. They were all clearly labeled, so someone must have been very organized. Beth and Elisha walked around the small paths between boxes. As she slowly ambled, carefully looking at the boxes, Beth noted various labels: "Vinyl record albums, Fort Worth, Jeff, Mom & Dad, genealogy, family history, Tippitt House papers." A dress form sat forlornly in the middle of the boxes. Beth also saw a couple of cedar chests— maybe they held old fur coats, or blankets. Several boxes were labeled "Trip to Europe."

Beth wasn't paying much attention to Elisha as she walked around, examining the labels. On the far side from the door were several boxes Beth spied with a shock. "Family—Civil War" and "Underground RR" were sitting among several groupings. Beth could feel her researcher adrenaline kicking in and her love of history and genealogy.

She was back in eighth grade again and her history teacher, Mr. Keever, began the Civil War unit with his wonderful words designed for idealistic teenagers: "Long, long ago, in the southern colonies of this country, was a culture that is the closest we will ever come to having landed aristocracy like the British. Wealthy families, who owned hundreds of acres of land, lived like kings and queens in huge mansions and held great balls to socialize. The wives ordered satin gowns from Europe, and the husbands rode out on sleek, perfectly groomed horses to inspect their kingdoms..." Of course, she also learned that year about slavery, and how that civilization came at a terrible price. That was the year—at age thirteen—that she read *Gone with the Wind*, crying in her bedroom in the wee hours when the saintly Melanie died. She was hooked on history from that moment on, whether fact or fiction.

Beth refocused and glanced back toward the door just in time to notice Elisha crouched over a box that said "Melanie" on it. It was in a corner as if someone had moved it away from the other family boxes. Elisha was about to pull the flaps on the box open.

"Oh, don't, please," Beth said. "I might want to go through these boxes with historical significance. My mother's things, well, they might be personal."

Elisha reluctantly slid the flap back down and straightened up, brushing the dust from her hands. "Sorry. I wondered why this box was up here in a separate spot and not down in her room."

"Beats me. Maybe it's legal papers."

"I suppose you're right. You can see what I mean," Elisha said, "about having to go through all this and get rid of it. It's going to be a nightmare. Might as well back up a truck with a dumpster and throw everything down from a window."

Beth's eyes scanned the attic, lighting on the boxes with the Civil War labels. She felt as if an angel and a devil were sitting on each of her shoulders. *Huckleberry Finn* revisited. The good angel said, "Go back to New York City. Leave this to other people to sort out. You'll have plenty to interest you in your next research assignment after you get home." Then, the devil said, "What is in those boxes? Civil War? Underground Railroad? If you leave now, you'll never know. Stay a while and find out." She blew out a long stream of air.

"You know, Elisha, I think I'll grab this box that says, 'Underground Railroad' and take it downstairs. I'm curious about how that topic might connect to the Tippitts."

Elisha was stationed at the door, cell phone in hand. "I'm sure it's nothing. Old houses. Junk." She scrolled on her phone to a new page and said, "Why don't I get your phone number, Elizabeth? We can plan for this house to go on the market. It may take a while because it is going to need someone with deep pockets and a love of old houses to buy it. I can handle it all for you."

Where had she heard that before? Oh, Remington, the lawyer. Why was everyone so anxious to handle all the details for her and get her on her way? She decided in a split second. "Elisha, I appreciate your concern, as well as your willingness to take on this undoubtedly gargantuan task. Let me get back to you. I need some time to think about this. You'll be the first to know if I decide to put the house on the market. I promise."

The real estate agent stood at the doorway with her mouth hanging open and her eyes filled with disbelief.

Chapter Five

After saving her new family's possessions from the fast-moving, heirloom-destroying Elisha, Melanie once again combed databases for the Tippitt family. It was time to round up the immediate family. *I think I'll begin with the Tippitts, from Melanie and her sibs, through her parents*, she thought. *It's a small step, but I have no idea what research dead-ends I might find.*

She had called Hatcher's office and spoken with his assistant, Harriet Newman. Harriet was able to give Beth some of the dates. After that, the most consistent records she thought she would find in her search were marriage records because the Illinois State Archives listed marriages from 1763 to 1900. Unfortunately, her grandparents were married after that.

The judge was born on January 15, 1919, and her grandmother, Joellen Dawes, was born April 21, 1920. Harriet had those dates, as well as their death years in 1990 and 1995. Thank goodness the lawyer's office knew those. The State of Illinois had passed legislation in 1843 and 1877, stating that county clerks had to record birth and death dates. They failed, however, to pass any enforcement. In 1915, another law was passed with incentives to record dates. The records became more consistent after that. But still, even in her grandmother's day, children were often born at home and no record was officially kept. *A family bible would be nice*, thought Beth. *Maybe one exists since I haven't been through everything in the attic. I'd guess my birth will not be recorded in that book.*

It was a start. She logged into a genealogy website and found the page where her grandparent's marriage license was recorded:

Emerson Tippitt and Joellen Dawes, married First Presbyterian Church, McClendan County, on May 23, 1943.

The marriage license confirmed both their birth dates. Once she found that, she could use the same database to find her aunt and uncle.

Janet Joellen Tippitt was born in Sweet Iron on February 23, 1946 and died October 5, 2015. At least she'd left home. If she'd had kids, I would have some cousins, thought Beth. Then she found Jefferson Webster Tippitt—my uncle, she thought. His date of birth was June 5, 1948. He only lived nineteen years. Did he have colic or learn to walk early? Did he graduate first in his class? She mused. Did he fall in love? I guess I'll never know. He occupied parts of the world and lived in this house for most of his nineteen years, and the people who could tell me those things are gone.

She looked at her entries, satisfied, and closed the computer program. It's a start, she thought. She was beginning to understand why people might love their adopted parents, but still long to know who accompanied them through those nine months and held them first in their arms.

Family: Tippitt

Husband: Emerson Tippitt
Born: 15 Jan. 1919   in: Sweet Iron, Illinois
Married: 23 May 1943   in: Sweet Iron, Illinois
Died: 20 Jan. 1990   in: Sweet Iron, Illinois

Wife: Joellen Dawes
Born: 21 April 1920   in: Chicago, Illinois
Died: 30 Dec. 1995   in: Sweet Iron, Illinois

CHILDREN
1 Daughter: Janet Joellen Tippitt
Born: 23 Feb. 1946   in: Sweet Iron, Illinois
Married: 23 Feb. 1968   in: Sweet Iron, Illinois
Died: 5 Oct. 2015   in: Sweet Iron, Illinois
Spouse: Neil Landry

2 Son: Jefferson Webster Tippitt
Born: 5 June 1948   in: Sweet Iron, Illinois
Died: 6 June 1967   in: near Ben Suc, Vietnam

3 Daughter: Melanie Anne Tippitt
Born: 7 Oct. 1952 in: Sweet Iron, Illinois
Died: 20 July 1971 in: Sweet Iron, Illinois

Chapter Six

Thursday morning Beth sat in what she was beginning to think of as her kitchen in a warm bathrobe eating a bowl of oatmeal with blueberries and an English muffin piled with orange marmalade. She had slept quite well despite the visit yesterday from the daunting Elisha Davis. Thinking about the many rooms she hadn't explored yet, Beth took another bite of oatmeal and looked around the kitchen. My house, she thought. The appliances sparkled, the granite counters were cleared of odds and ends, and the floor was a neutral-colored tile above which a barely detectible cool draft lingered. Old houses. Cold air, leaky, huge. My New York apartment would fit about five times into this house. No, more like seven. And I own this place!

She was about to load her dishes in the dishwasher when she heard a tentative tapping on the glass doors. Turning around, Beth saw the woman who had been in the house yesterday with Remington. Molly, wasn't it? Molly something. The woman was holding two cardboard cups of coffee in a carrying tray. She pointed to one, then to Beth, and smiled.

Beth let her in through the sliding door.

"Thought you might want a little company. You know, strange town, no one you know, and all. I figured coffee might help," said Molly. "I'm Molly. Molly Grayson."

"I think I will call you lifesaver," Beth replied. "I couldn't figure out where the coffeemaker was, or even if they had one. I considered getting dressed and going to find a Starbucks."

Molly set the tray down on the table and took off her coat, laying it over a kitchen chair. "We have a couple Starbucks." She pulled the

33

coffee cups out of the tray, setting one in front of Beth. Taking the lid off, Beth inhaled the coffee fumes deeply.

"You know, I knew about the strange eyes in your family. I guess your 'new' family," said Molly. "I had heard of your, ah, mother's. I'm told they only show up on the female side and not in every generation. Remington mentioned that. Me, I'm not a genetics expert." She laughed. "I have a lot of curiosity."

"Oh," Beth said, pouring half-and-half into her coffee. She hesitated a moment. "Molly, could I ask you what you do, I mean, for a living? House-sit for people?"

Molly sputtered into laughter as she stirred her coffee with a spoon Beth had fished out of a drawer. "Sure. That's easy. I'm head librarian at McClendan College. Right now, the college is on break, but I still need to catch up on paperwork today."

Beth laughed softly. "Really? How funny. Research and genealogy are what I do for a living."

Molly set her spoon down and looked up. "I think Remington might have mentioned that, too."

"I'm a little hesitant to ask personal questions, you know. The city is a much larger universe than Sweet Iron. In the city, you'd never tell me your last name, only your first. It's what I'm used to. People are more reserved."

"Ah, afraid you're in a small town now. I grew up in the suburbs, University of Iowa for an English major and University of Illinois for library science degrees. Worked in a couple of other colleges before here."

"How long have you been here?"

"Since 2000. Met my husband, Charlie, twenty-five years ago. One kid—Charlie Jr., in Portland, Oregon." She paused. "So, sounds like you have had quite a shock."

Beth took a sip of her coffee. "Now that's getting right to the point."

"Sorry, that's me. I need social skills. Charlie's a no-nonsense, cut-to-the-point kind of guy. He's rubbed off on me."

"I think you're refreshingly direct," said Beth. "Since you've lived here a decade and a half, maybe you can tell me why on earth anyone would name a town 'Sweet Iron'?"

"It will take a three-minute history lesson. I just happen to know the answer to that one."

"Love history," said Beth, settling back in her chair. "Carry on."

"I did a talk on this recently, so here goes. A group of families in the 1830s left Pennsylvania and founded Sweet Iron in the new, young state of Illinois. The prominent leader in the settling of the town was Thomas Johannes Bergmann. His family had settled in Pennsylvania in the 1700s and were associated with some of the first iron works in the colony. They made their fortunes in iron, and by the early 1800s, the demand for iron products in places like Philadelphia was phenomenal.

"Eventually, however, the work of the iron foundries peaked, and conflicts became more commonplace between the owners and workers. Bergmann could see the writing on the wall. Unions had formed among the workers, and he foresaw more strikes, more strife.

"However, this Thomas Bergmann was a visionary. Adventurous and looking for a new challenge, he decided to move his family to the wilderness of the state of Illinois and found a settlement. He brought his wife, Maria Catherine Sweet Bergmann, five children, and a handful of like-minded families, and they settled in this area in the 1830s. Iron had been his life, and it had brought his predecessors a fortune. When he began considering a name for this little settlement, he decided on a combination of 'iron' and his wife's family name. So, we have Sweet Iron. He was a profitable steward of the family money, and he knew there were new possibilities in settling the wilderness.

"One of his friends was a minister and another a teacher. They saw the opportunity to charter a school, later becoming a college. The minister's name was McClendan; thus, McClendan College. And that was the beginning of this little town of Sweet Iron. You can, of course, read a lot more about it at my library. The Tippitt family, by the way, came in the second group of settlers, but they soon became prominent members of the town. One of them started the newspaper we still have today."

"Very interesting," said Beth. "You are positively a font of information, Molly Grayson."

Molly rechecked the heat of her coffee, found it fine, and took several sips. "So, I hear you are a researcher who works with authors. That must be fascinating. When did you start doing that?"

"Shortly after grad school in New York. I was a fact-checker for a while with a New York magazine. That gave me some valuable contacts, as did my professors from grad school. Took a while, but eventually I got more jobs researching and could afford to simply do that. Now I can pick and choose projects. Believe me, some authors are easier to work with than others."

"What are they like, these authors?"

"Oh, some are real prima donnas, others are grateful. Some are amazingly thoughtful, others are direct and abrupt. Some give me an area of time to research, others want specific information. Often, after they receive my requested work, they will get back to me because they are writing and need some specific fact."

Molly leaned on her palm, her elbow on the table. "That sounds like such an amazing job—to be able to find out about different periods of time and actually get paid well for it."

"I love what I do," said Beth. "History has always fascinated me."

"What have you been doing lately?"

Beth laughed. "Women's work! I've been investigating the lives of women during the late 1800s for an author. Here are some interesting facts: ninety-five percent of married women in that time stayed home with books and magazines about how to do various domestic chores—their highest calling, of course. They wore corsets that put twenty-two pounds of pressure on their internal organs, resulting in collapsed lungs, displaced livers, and fractured ribs. Nice, huh? Makes you appreciate living now."

"I should think so!" said Molly.

They were talking as if they had known each other for years, thought Beth. How strange to find a friend in the middle of the country who seemed so like herself in many ways. Similar passions, similar work. She decided to take a chance.

"Molly, I know this is changing the subject, but do you know much about the Tippitt family?"

"Mostly bits and pieces I've picked up through conversation."

"I'm planning to do some research. Maybe we can talk because we're simpatico. We both like libraries, books, and research. I love genealogy, too."

Molly was silent for a moment. "I would have been five when Melanie Tippitt died, but I didn't live here then. What I know I've only heard around town on occasion, but mainly I read the stories in the newspaper database at the library because I was curious." She paused and appeared to be thinking about her next words.

She said, "We don't know each other enough to offer advice, but I'm going to offer it anyway. Kindly. That's the key word." She smiled, and Beth could see she was working hard to be tactful. "My bet is you may be upsetting the applecart by showing up here unannounced. Some people still live here who remember what happened way back when, and they may not all be happy you're here. From what I read in the local newspapers we have on microfilm at work, the Nash trial was quite a sensation for a small town like this. While the Tippitt family is down to the very end—you—other people were there the day your mother died. I would say, 'tread lightly'."

"Why? What would anyone have to be angry about? It sounds like my father, Brian Nash, confessed to the murder and did his time."

"I'm not so sure it was as simple as that. People still talk about it on occasion. Some important people in the area were involved."

Beth nodded her head slowly. "I see."

"Another thing that happens in small towns is people talk. If you start investigating the past by asking questions, you'll be feeding the rumor mill in town. Small towns have tangled threads, hidden relationships. People don't forget. In fact, they hang on to misunderstandings, wrong ideas, and often incorrect information."

"I grew up in a small town. I understand how it works."

"That's a good start," Molly Grayson said, giggling to lighten the mood. "Plus, you might stop by my library to see all the research possibilities we have available. I think you'd be surprised. We're a one-stop-shop for anything you might want to research."

"I will take you up on using your library," said Beth. "If it has a coffee shop, that would be a bonus."

"It does, with the most splendiferous coffee."

Beth smiled, her voice light and bubbly as she said, "Sounds like

37

a plan. I have a few other things to deal with first, but I'll get around to seeing your library. Thanks. You've already warmed my heart when it comes to hating small towns. A little bit. I want to do some snooping into my biological parents' histories. As long as I'm here while the lawyer untangles things, I would like to know more about the past. My adopted parents had no pasts. Well, not known by me."

"Hmm," said Molly. "*Quietly* is the key word."

"I will take your advice. Quietly. Right now, the college is on break, and I'd guess no one will notice me snooping around," said Beth. Suddenly, a thought came into her head. "Speaking of snooping, I have a box to open that might interest you too."

"A surprise? Any clues about it?"

"Sweet Iron. Mid-1800s," said Beth.

"Let's see. Lead-up to the Civil War... Sweet Iron, did you say?"

"Come with me." They both walked to the dining room, where Beth had left the box from the attic that was labeled 'Underground Railroad' on her dining room table. "This was in the attic. What do you think might be in it?"

"Do you know? Did you already look?" Molly asked.

"No. I brought it down and figured I'd check it out today. I'm savoring the suspense. Want to look with me?"

"Oh, oh, oh," Molly exclaimed, rubbing her hands together in anticipation.

Beth unsealed the tape across the flaps of the box and began taking items out. She named things as she pulled them out and handed them to Molly. "Articles from William Lloyd Garrison's *Liberator*; an 1850 copy of the *Western Citizen*, a Chicago abolitionist newspaper; an appeal from the *Pennsylvania Freeman* for donations to their abolition society; and a sermon from a Presbyterian minister on the evils of slavery." She glanced at the headline. "It looks like this lecture was given here in Sweet Iron."

"This is amazing," said Molly. "Some of these would probably be better preserved in the archives at the college."

Beth hardly seemed to hear her because she was so engrossed. "Here's an account of the Lincoln/Douglas debate on October 7, in Galesburg. Fifteen thousand attended, according to the byline. It appears to be from the *Sweet Iron Sentinel*. I had forgotten how close we are to so many centers of abolitionist activity."

Molly reached into the box next while Beth was looking at the clipping. "Here's another newspaper clipping from the *Sentinel* about the Presbyterian Women's Sewing Circle holding a bazaar to raise money 'for the cause'."

Beth reached in and her hand found a hardcover ledger. "I wonder what this was used for?" She began opening pages and discovered it was an account ledger with information about payments, cargo, and initials. "Molly! It looks like the Tippitts may have been involved with the Underground Railroad. This appears to be an account book with entries and dates. Think how valuable this must be!"

Molly looked at one of the pages. "Hmmm... After all, we are in the middle of the western end of the conductor stations. Look, here's a map of routes: Missouri into Illinois and various routes through counties that look like they lead through Sweet Iron and up to Princeton and the Great Lakes."

"And here's a train schedule," said Beth. "This whole area of Illinois was crisscrossed with train tracks back then."

"Oh, my gosh," said Molly. "Look at this. Not too many of these exist, and some are rumored to be in the new National Museum of African-American History they're building in Washington, D.C. It's a certificate of freedom. It must have been carried by this man, Amos Washington." She looked at it, her voice softening into reverence.

Beth examined it. "Unbelievable. And to think these things have been sitting in the attic of this house for over a century." A good reason not to sell this house quite so quickly, thought Beth. What would Elisha Davis do with such valuable objects? Probably throw them out.

Molly looked at her watch. "I hate this! Gotta go. If I don't get these reports done today, I'm going to be in serious trouble with several people at the college." She looked at Beth. "What are you going to do with all this?"

Glancing at the various items spread out across the table, Beth said, "I think I'll take some time to look it over, package it up, put it in the attic again until I figure out what I'm doing with the house, and then I'll decide where to put it. A lot hinges on what I'm going to do with this house. Still thinking about that problem."

"Keep the college in mind. Most of the founders and trustees were involved in the abolitionist movement. We could make it a lovely permanent home, and scholars would come here to study these artifacts." She smiled. "Whenever you decide to check out the past of the Tippitts, I'll have a spot for you to research. But for now, I must be off."

They walked back out through the kitchen, where Molly grabbed her coat. She turned to Beth. "I'm glad—really glad you decided to come back our direction. Hope you consider staying longer. We have so much history all around us in this area that you could stay busy a long time. Thanks, Beth, for letting me help open your surprise."

"You're welcome. The feeling is mutual—it's so much fun to talk to someone who loves history like I do. Get going. Your reports are waiting."

Chapter Seven

Later that morning, once she had showered and dressed, Beth's curiosity got the better of her, especially after looking at the 1800s in Sweet Iron, and she decided to explore what she thought of as "the museum bedrooms." It seemed weird to think "uncle" or "mother," since they were blood relatives she never knew. She felt like she was trespassing in the personal lives of strangers, but no one was here to say "no."

She stopped in Jeff Tippitt's doorway. Maybe she could get a sense of who he was from his things. Beth stood perfectly still, capturing the layout of the bedroom, her hand pressing her chest. His desk had a photograph and a few objects strewn across a writing pad.

Walking over to his desk, she picked up a photograph, examining his features and attempting to see anything of herself in the young, unlined face. His hair was shorn in a crewcut. No long ponytail for Jeff Tippitt. He was dressed in a flak jacket, green clothing, and the various belts and pockets of a soldier. He had posed in front of a helicopter with all kinds of graffiti painted on it and the requisite pin-up girl. Dark glasses hid his eyes, but his smile was much like Melanie's, with a bow to his upper lip almost hidden under a struggling moustache. He was definitely a Tippitt. His skin was tanned from time in Vietnam, and his body had the scrawniness of a nineteen-year-old. She had forgotten Vietnam was a young person's war. I wonder what he thought that day as he stood there, his dog tags around his neck reflecting the sunlight. Did he think he was invincible? Did he figure he would come home to his sisters and his parents? Was it an adventure?

She lingered over his face for a moment, then gently set the photo back on the desk. The desk pad held a set of dog tags, a religious medal, and a cigarette lighter, its inscription rubbed off. A black-and-white photo of a group of soldiers, its corners torn, its surface filled with lines from too much folding, lay next to the dog tags. Maybe this was his unit, or perhaps they were other helicopter pilots. They were just kids, their arms around each other's shoulders, several smoking, out on an adventure. How many of them made it home alive, she wondered, unlike Jeff Tippitt?

Her eyes fell across a high school class ring and some folded, wrinkled money that was obviously Vietnamese. A dog-eared, much-read copy of *Catch-22* was partly on top of the paper money. Those must have been objects the army sent his parents. His "personal effects."

Beth turned toward the book shelf, focusing on an army hat of camouflage material, a strap around it holding four bullets in a perfect row. Objects had been glued to it, most of them too faded to recognize. But on one side was the circular peace symbol of the sixties. A couple of *Life Magazines* sat next to it, their covers filled with photos of soldiers in Vietnam.

The book shelf held tightly packed copies of both hardcover and paperback books. Beth scanned the titles on the spines. His interests ran to things military. No *Autobiography of Malcolm X* or *Herzog*.

A wooden box, its glass top revealing a flag folded into a triangle, rested on the chest of drawers. A corner of the box held a metal rectangle with Jeff's name, army unit, and the date and location of his death. When his parents and sisters left the cemetery with this flag, pain and grief must have walked on either side of them. Beth wondered what they thought of him going off volunteering like that to the jungle when he was young. Did they argue with him? Were they proud? He must have been confident and fearless to be in Vietnam flying a helicopter when he was only nineteen. Sadly, he must not have been there very long. She sighed, feeling an ache in her throat.

Beth turned back, examining all the objects of his life, so little to describe who he was. Her uncle... and now she was over twice his age. At a loss for words, she left Jeff's room, looking back briefly over her shoulder. It felt strange knowing she was related to this boy she'd never met. Her uncle.

Walking toward Melanie's room, Beth thought about her mother's relationship to Jeff. She knew Melanie was much younger than her older sister, and Janet was already out of the house by the time of Jeff's death. Melanie would have been fifteen when Jeff died—a year before she got pregnant.

She walked over to a window, pushed back the curtains, and let in the sunlight. Just as she was about to turn around, her eyes caught a glimpse of someone standing in the trees across the street staring at her house. At first, she thought she was imagining it. But no, he was still there, unmoving. Too tall to be Detective Kyle. She was curious about why anyone would watch her house. Still he stood there, perfectly still.

She opened the curtains on a second window, and the motion caused the watcher to look up. Then she saw him back up into the trees as if he knew he'd been seen, and he disappeared into the woods. How odd, thought Beth.

She opened the curtains on the third window, scattering the gloom she had sensed in Jeff's room. Melanie's bedroom was larger than Jeff's, perhaps the result of being the last child in the house. She opened the closet doors. Clothing from the late sixties and early seventies hung on metal hangers, tightly packed between some shelves on either side holding purses, headbands, and shoes.

On the left end of the closet, Beth turned dresses with white Peter Pan collars and cuffs toward her, leaving plaid mini-skirts, their pleats hanging crookedly from disuse. A tailored black suit hung in the far corner. Their sizes were all terribly small.

In the main part of the closet she found bright colors surrounded by layers of hippie clothing, a style Melanie must have shifted to in the early seventies. Wild colors and polka dots, vintage vests and pants, geometric patterns and the peasant look crowded out the older clothing. Beth pulled out a filmy dress that was crazy-short with daisies in a border around the skirt. It was also amazingly small. A brown suede vest with fringe at the bottom hung lopsidedly on a hanger adorned with many silk scarves of various colors. That might be a beaded headband curled around the top of the hanger, Beth thought. Several tie-dyed shirts accompanied a shift with a miniskirt made of faded yellow. Sucking in a deep breath, Beth thought, my mother was a fashionista! What a different world and time that was! What amazing excess, but what fun.

Bringing a shaky hand to her forehead, Beth backed up and sat down on the bed. She was lightheaded and could sense her mother after touching these clothes. She was so beautiful, so young, so full of life. She had dreams ahead of her, as the Davis woman had said.

After taking some deep breaths, Beth rose again and closed the doors, turning next to the chest of drawers. On top, along with the jewelry box, a plastic tray held all kinds of jewelry in every shape and size. Wildly colorful geometric shapes, clusters of plastic flowers, chunky bangles, and pop art necklaces that described that chaotic decade of excess. Two or three beaded headbands snaked through the necklaces.

She opened the top drawer of a chest and saw scribbled notes about nothing important. One said, "Sam, I—" but the rest of the note was torn off. At least she could have left some love letters, Beth thought. I wonder who Sam is. Honestly. Wouldn't you think I could find pressed flowers or love letters? Nothing.

The second drawer contained 45-rpm records in paper sleeves. She picked up a small handful. "Yesterday," by the Beatles; "Stop! In the Name of Love," The Supremes; "This is Dedicated to the One I Love," the Mamas and the Papas; "Bridge Over Troubled Waters," Simon and Garfunkel; and "Only the Good Die Young," Billy Joel. The irony of the last song didn't escape Beth. Melanie was up on the pop hits of the day. Beth wondered how many times she listened to these, lying on her bed in this room.

She pulled out two or three other drawers but found little of interest. Then she turned, noticing the cedar chest at the end of the bed. I'll bet it's a hope chest, she thought. She had read about those in her research. She guessed it was full of dishtowels and bedsheets Melanie had planned to use when she got married. Of course, that didn't happen. Beth took a long, embroidered white doily from the top of the chest and moved her hand across the finish. It was flawless.

Such craftsmanship. The surface was perfectly smooth, the wood finely matched. How lovely. Her family obviously could afford only the best. Beth got down on her knees and pushed on the button that opened the cedar chest. Immediately, the smell of old clothing and cedar assailed her nose, and she sneezed three times. Even the dust was old.

A light pink blanket was pushed in around the edges to keep everything safe. Beth held the ends of the blanket, lifting it up and placing it gently on the foot of the bed. Examining the chest, she saw a couple of well-used teddy bears, perhaps childhood companions. She laid them down on the floor and pulled out what at first, looked like a photograph album, but turned out to be a scrapbook. Melanie or her mother had glued various objects onto the pages. Ah, here were the pressed flowers, Beth thought. Corsages from prom, programs from plays or concerts, a high school graduation program from her junior year. She decided to take the scrapbook downstairs and look it over that night.

The other book was a photograph album, its black-and-white pictures positioned with photo corners whose glue had long since dried. They looked like photos of Melanie and her friends from about junior high forward. Eventually, they were faded color photos toward the end. She laid it aside with the scrapbook.

She moved a layer of dishtowels and saw several notebooks, the three-ring binder kind she'd used in school. Opening the top one, Beth found notes from what appeared to be a physics class. Turning the pages, she saw several totally blank pages. On the next page was a brief note to Brian. That would be to my father, your murderer, Beth thought. She laid aside the notebooks and felt around the bottom of the chest. Nothing else.

After repacking everything but the scrapbook and photo album, she was about to get up from the floor when her hand brushed something on the outside of the chest, sticking out near the bottom right corner. It would help if I had more light, she thought. Beth remembered the small flashlight in Janet's bedroom drawer. Fetching it, she got down on the floor in front of the hope chest and examined it. It was a double heart, one in front of the other, but slightly off center so you could see the outline of the second heart. They had been added on, probably glued to the chest. In the front heart were the initials, M and T and the number, 68. Melanie Tippitt, thought Beth. The carving was so intricate, so perfect that once more Beth marveled at the workmanship. It must have been the year it was made: 1968. She traced the letters and numbers with her fingers and thought that whoever made this hope chest was a veritable craftsman.

Should she sell this house and let Elisha destroy these items that represented two lives? On the other hand, what would be the purpose of keeping all this clothing and these artifacts of two lives gone long ago?

After Beth had replaced the contents of the chest and piled up her finds to take downstairs, she turned to the dressing table and the Chantilly perfume Elisha Davis had pointed out. A dusting powder box sat next to a half-empty, mostly dried-up bottle of Chantilly body lotion on the dressing table.

Let's see how awful this smelled, Beth thought. She sprayed a little of the perfume into the air. The fragrance was strong and powdery, with a scent of orange blossoms and lemon. Maybe a hint of vanilla too, Beth mused. She closed her eyes, taking in the aroma. Over her came a softness, a tenderness, a comfort as if she never need worry about anything ever again. Her whole body relaxed. It was hard to describe: a feeling of euphoria, lightness, peace. Joy spread through her, and her breathing slowed down. It was the sense of being held in someone's arms, safe, cared for, and loved.

Chapter Eight

That evening, Beth sat in Janet Landry's king-sized bed thinking about the attic. She considered Elisha's announcement that she would throw out those boxes through an attic window into a dumpster. Beth munched on an apple and shook her head. This family might have historical records that need to be saved, she thought. They could even be valuable. Before she did anything, she should examine the records in those boxes. This meant she would have to move slowly about selling this house. She didn't know half of what was in it. And the house, Beth thought, looking around. Its history from the 1800s should be amazing. What if someone bought it after she left, just to tear it down and put a modern monstrosity in its place?

Beth set the apple core down on a dessert plate she had precariously balanced on her knees, wiping off her hands with a napkin and moving the plate. She glanced at the photo album on a chair but would have to get out of bed to get it. So, picking up one of Melanie's notebooks lying on the bed, she pulled up her knees and set the notebook on them. Before she began reading it, however, she thought about how quiet it was. When she first lived in the Chelsea neighborhood of New York City, she'd hear police and fire sirens all night. It was hard to get used to the round-the-clock noise. After she moved to the quiet neighborhood of Sea Cliff, the nights were so much better. Now, she was in round-the-clock quiet. She didn't even hear any cars on the street. Maybe she should buy a small fan.

She opened the notebook and tried to determine whether it was high school or college. The first page had notes about Wordsworth, and they began with a date: August 23, 1968. That would have been

47

the fall before Melanie had me the next April. Melanie probably didn't even know she was pregnant. Beth read several pages of English notes, sometimes interrupted by things Melanie needed to remember like, "Meet Shelly after school—Sandrin's." Hmm... maybe Sandrin's was a place in town, she thought.

Beth skipped through more pages of notes from high school classes, and, after several blank pages following an entry in October, she saw something that stopped her cold: two lists, one of them girls' names and one of them boys'. Her mouth fell open. Three names were circled on each list as if Melanie had made up her mind what to name the tiny baby who would finally be called "Elizabeth." Me, Beth thought. She knew about me and was thinking about my name. Beth felt a shiver go through her. Back then, Melanie must have been scared, Beth thought, but still, she was making plans for me. Several names were crossed out, but the six that were circled were Brian Jr., Paul, Anthony, Sarah, Grace, and—oh, my gosh—Elizabeth. Tears welled up in her eyes. My mother was planning for me. I ended up with one of her names. She wiped the tears from her face and managed to smile. A joyful smile.

Her eyes were tired from trying to decipher the squiggly lines of handwriting. Well, she thought. Tomorrow is soon enough to read more. She dropped the notebook on the floor, checked her cell phone for messages, laid her glasses on the bedside table, and turned off the lamp next to the bed. It was so quiet. Was she going to be able to sleep in this ridiculously silent town? Her eyes blinked closed as she sank into the covers.

*****

Her eyes blinked open and looked at the bedside clock: 2:25. Why was she suddenly awake? At first, she was in that hazy stage between sleeping and waking. She sat up in bed recognizing the fragrance of Chantilly in her bedroom. How? Her heart racing, Beth held her breath, staring all around in the dark, and a sudden warmth surged through her, a comforting feeling causing her to relax. She stared into the darkness, whispering, "Melanie?" The fragrance grew stronger. Pulling the covers back, Beth tiptoed out of the room and over to her mother's room. She could see from a dim light she'd left on in the hallway that the bottle of perfume was still sitting where she'd left it, the lid tightly secured.

Going back to Janet's bedroom, she gasped when the light next to her bed clicked on. Beth pushed off the light switch on the bedside table and touched the other side of the switch, clicking it back on. She knew she hadn't turned this on when she woke up just now. She sat up on the bed, picked up the notebook she'd dropped on the floor, and a black-and-white photo fell out from the middle of the pages. She reached down, picked up the photograph, and set it on the bedside table.

Beth let out a sigh and climbed under the covers. She was settled in when her bedside lamp came on again. "Melanie?" she whispered, "Time to stop playing. I need to get some sleep," she said in a quiet voice. She turned off the lamp, moved onto her side, and heard the furnace fan kick off. That's probably what woke her up. Pulling the comforter up to her neck, she closed her eyes and... heard a noise.

Beth sat up. Cocking her head to the side, she listened again, concentrating so hard she was holding her breath. Then it was silent. I must be imagining things. Perfume, lights coming on by themselves. Sounds like I'm sleepwalking. She pinched her arm. No, I'm awake. She took a few deep breaths. Nothing. She lay down again, but she was more and more awake. Maybe a cup of hot tea would help. But before she got up, Beth heard another unusual sound. Standing up, she crept over to her doorway, gripping the doorframe, her knuckles white. She prayed the floorboards didn't creak. Beth listened intently, leaning forward. Soft noises like a person doing something quietly, almost stealthily, came from below. Someone was downstairs. Her heart pounding, Beth licked her dry lips and held on to the doorframe as if her life depended on it. Did I forget to lock the doors? she wondered.

She leaned over the upstairs banister but could see nothing in the darkness. Slowly her eyes adjusted. Since the stairway overlooked the front foyer, light from the street lamps outside came through the door windows. No one was in the foyer.

The sound began again, and now Beth knew she wasn't imagining it. In fact, as she heard it, the Chantilly fragrance immediately became more powerful, as if her mother were saying, "Yes, someone is here. Danger!" Clinging to the upstairs banister to make herself small, Beth crept down the stairs, one at a time, her fingers griping the banister so tightly she had to force them to move forward. At the bottom landing she found four light switches on the wall, pushed all of them, and the overhead light in the front foyer blazed on. The sudden light was blinding, and she gasped and felt her legs begin to shake. The front door was standing wide open, cold air streaming in. No one was in the foyer, but she sensed someone in the house. Where were they? She hesitated. Then she cleared her throat and called out in a loud voice, "Whoever you are, I have a gun and I'm an expert shot. Get out of my house! I'm calling 9-1-1!"

Beth heard nothing, perhaps a pause while the intruder grasped her intent. A dark figure came barreling out from the living room off to her right, dressed in black, a ski mask over his downturned head. He didn't expect to see Beth there, and he sped past her, knocking her onto the lower stair steps. The intruder barely looked back at her and then raced through the front door carrying an object under his arm. Angered, Beth screamed, got up, and charged after him, despite the pain in her hip from falling on the steps. How dare someone come into Tippitt House—*my* house, she unexpectedly thought. By the time she raced out the front door, a car sped off, its taillights all Beth could see. She didn't have her contact lenses in or her glasses on, so she couldn't begin to see that license plate. She gave a long low sigh and stood in the doorway shivering, briefly staring in the direction of the vanished car, her shoulders sagging.

Why would anyone break into my house? she wondered. Beth checked the door and didn't see any signs of someone using a crowbar or trying to force the lock. She would have heard it, even asleep, as quiet as this place was. She closed the door, locking it—as if locking it would help—and closed the inside door, locking it also. She started to turn but changed her mind and went into the dining room, dragging out a chair to put under the inside door handle.

Plodding back upstairs, she looked for her cell phone. Strangely, she didn't smell Chantilly anywhere. Had she imagined that? Her room was in darkness, no light on beside the bed. Sitting down on the bed, she realized she had broken into a sweat. Her fingers were shaking so much she could barely pick up her phone. Wiping her forehead, Beth shakily dialed 9-1-1.

Chapter Nine

"Here," said Detective Kyle Warner, laying a crocheted quilt from the living room sofa over Beth's shoulders. "You're in shock. This should stop the shaking." He looked around. "Sugar helps, too. Do you drink coffee? Tea?"

"Coffee," she said. "I guess Janet didn't drink the stuff since I only found the coffeepot this afternoon, hidden away in a lower cupboard. I haven't had time to check out where everything is in the house. In fact, I've not seen all of it yet." She realized her teeth had stopped chattering.

"Coffee?"

"In the refrigerator."

"Ah, I see."

As he busied himself making coffee, Beth watched him silently. He was about her age and dressed more casually than she'd expect. Well, she undoubtedly got him out of bed, Beth surmised from the somewhat-combed state of his dark hair. His badge was fastened to a belt on his jeans, and those were topped with a gray sweatshirt that said "SIPD" in small letters near his left shoulder. She studied his face. When she had seen him at the lawyer's office she hadn't paid much attention. His face was nice-looking, but like he'd seen plenty of difficulties in his life, attested to by lines across his forehead. A dark brown-tinged-with-red moustache and barely-there beard added to the rugged look. The tiny scar on his cheek was less visible tonight. Unlike other men his age, he still sported a full head of dark brown hair with a little silver threaded through, obviously styled by someone, but not tonight. When he turned around, she noticed his eyes were green. No gold flecks. Only green.

He moved confidently, knew how to make coffee, and didn't have on a wedding ring. Now that she was calmer, she speculated about his "situation." Her nerves were less jangled, and she knew her heart had returned to a normal rate since it wasn't pounding in her head. Too soon to find out anything about whether he was married or single. Beth, she thought, pay attention to business.

He sat down across from her and took out a pen and his notebook as the coffee dripped into the carafe in the silent kitchen. "Well," he began. "I guess our little town isn't being very friendly after all, Ms. Russell. I suppose someone might want to get in here because they figure it's empty between Janet Landry's death and another person taking over the house."

"I think you can call me Beth, especially since I'm sitting here in front of a stranger in my pajamas and bathrobe." She saw the corners of his mouth rise slightly, and then he went back to his notepad. "I didn't see that the front door had any signs of someone breaking in," she added, hoping he would at least think she wasn't crazy.

He nodded, all business. "You're right, which begs the question, who might have keys to the house?"

"You got me there. I've only been here a couple of days. I've met my lawyer, Elisha Davis the real estate agent, and Molly Grayson. That's about it. Oh, and the Bingleys, who own the bed-and-breakfast."

"Well, Ms. Russell—Beth—someone or maybe several people have keys. The locks are older versions, and they've been here quite a long time. I'd suggest, first, that you have the locks changed. I know an honest locksmith, and I can call him for you in the morning if that's all right." He jotted a note in his notebook.

"Yes, I'd appreciate it." She pushed the afghan off her shoulders onto the chair and stood up to retrieve some coffee cups, sugar, and cream. "I know the house has valuable objects in it, but I can't figure out why anyone would want to show up in the middle of the night and steal my mother's scrapbook."

He stood up too, and moved over to the counter, putting the

objects she'd retrieved on the kitchen table. Then he sat down again. "I know this question won't help, but do you know if anything else is missing?"

She thought a moment. "No."

Just then they were interrupted by the fingerprint technician, shaking his head at the detective and leaving to go home.

While she poured two cups of coffee, the detective asked, "So this was your mother's scrapbook?"

Beth noted the earnest look on his face. "I suppose that's what I should call her. I've been saying 'Melanie' for lack of a better idea. Since the DNA test came back, I'm getting used to the idea that I have a biological mother who lived in this house until she died. Yes, I'd brought the scrapbook downstairs from her bedroom since I found it in the chest at the foot of her bed." She returned the carafe to the coffeemaker. "I thought it might hold clues about who Melanie was. I wanted to get—I guess—a sense of her. It isn't every day you find out your mother isn't really your mother, and some teenager a thousand miles away bore you decades ago and gave you up. I suppose I was trying to find out who she was."

The detective took a sip of his coffee, setting it down and holding it between his square-shaped fingers. "Makes sense. I believe the better question might be, why would they steal a scrapbook that is relatively worthless to anyone else compared to other things more valuable?"

Her eyes narrowed. "Maybe if I'd looked more closely at the scrapbook I would know about the contents. I think it was from her last two years of high school. I remember corsages, ribbons, programs for high school events. I only glanced at it briefly. I also found a couple of notebooks from high school classes. I was reading one before I fell asleep. It was typical teenage stuff."

"I'd imagine this scrapbook would contain events in the past shortly before her death. On the other hand, you surprised this intruder, and maybe he picked up the first thing he saw and took off."

"You may be right. That makes more sense." She stood up and moved to the coffeemaker, pouring a little more coffee into her cup, and turning to refill his. As she did, she noticed a light scent of cologne. Hmmm, nice. Sandalwood. A frown crossed her face, and she touched the crown of her hair, realizing she had gotten out of bed, had no makeup on, and her hair was probably going every which direction. Oh, well. Too late to worry about that now.

She sat down again and said, "A strange thing happened on Thursday, late in the morning."

He looked up from his notebook curiously. "Strange how?"

"A man—he was watching this house from the woods across the street."

Now she had his undivided attention.

"How could you tell he was watching your house?

"I opened the upstairs curtains, saw him, and when he saw the movement he stepped back into the shadows."

"What did he look like?" the detective asked.

"It was quite a distance to see him. Hmm..." She took another sip of coffee. "He was tall and thin with a hood up over his head. I couldn't see his face at all."

"Why do you say 'his' face?"

"That's a good question. It was something about the way he moved when he backed into the trees. More like a man might. It's hard to explain."

"Well," he said, "I'll go across the street and check the area out in the morning when it's light. Of course, by now the snow has melted again. May not find much."

"It gave me a scary feeling to think he was watching the house. Kind of like someone peeping in the window. Made my skin crawl."

He looked up and said, "If you see him again, let me know."

She moved her saucer over, the coffee gone, and considered what he might say about her parents.

"Detective Warner, what do you know about my parents, Melanie Tippitt and Brian Nash?"

He stirred a little more cream in his coffee, and Beth figured he was trying to decide what to say. "Not much," he said. "When your mother died, I wasn't here, and besides I was still in diapers. Over the years, I've picked up bits and pieces since the town is small and people talk. Guess it was a huge event. From what I've heard, the trial was half over, and Nash decided to change his plea to guilty. He ended up going to prison but would have gotten out long ago." He took another sip of coffee. "Once his probation was over, no one saw him again. I doubt it would have been easy to come back to this town. I understand your mother was well-liked."

Beth looked down at her coffee cup and didn't say anything. It was quiet for a moment.

"The case was closed," the detective said.

Biting her lip, Beth folded her hands on the table and thought about what to say next. "I think Molly Grayson at the college told me some people in the town still remembered them."

"Probably true."

Beth thought, how easy he is to talk to. What a thoughtful listener.

"Did you know your parents growing up, Detective Warner?"

"Sure. They raised three of us in a small town near Milwaukee."

"You're lucky. I thought I knew my parents, but they turned out to be the people who raised me. I don't know why I'm telling you this. Since I came here, I've felt as if Melanie has been moving me, keeping an eye on me, watching over me. I know it sounds crazy, and I've always been a logical, find-the-answer kind of person. This is a new experience. On the other hand, I always wondered, growing up, if something was a little off, not quite right. I believe it would be a kindness for people to let me know what my parents were like, despite my mother's untimely ending."

"Might be some attorneys still around, a newspaper editor—Abigail Sandstrom—and a few grownups who were teenagers back then. I'll check the file and see who the public defender was. You may want to consider, however, if you really want to know."

Beth stared straight into his eyes. "Oh, I do, no matter what I find."

"I thought you were going back to New York City."

She cleared the dishes from the table, setting them down in the sink. "I am. But I have a break before I start a new research project, so I certainly have time to do a bit of digging of my own." She turned around and stood, her back against the sink. "I have to say, Detective, I'm worried about all of this. A break-in and a man watching the house. I had a—a difficult experience years ago, and since then I've always kept a gun nearby for protection. I'm feeling—I'm feeling scared right now. I don't like that because I usually feel like my life is under control." As she said those words she thought about her Glock locked up in her apartment on Long Island—safe, quiet, sleepy Long Island. "I'm an excellent shot, but right now I'm the target, and I have no way to defend myself."

He stared at her face, and she imagined her expression said it all—a woman alone, no protection, and unknown people watching and breaking in. Then he said, "Could I ask—I mean, could you tell me why you feel a need to be an expert shot? You live in a relatively crime-free area."

She sat down again, took a breath, and said, quietly, "Not sure I could tell you without shaking again."

He stood up, walked over, and laid the afghan back on her shoulders, saying, "Try me."

She hadn't relived it in years. Only Gabby knew what happened. Certainly not her mother. Beth looked at the detective's face. It was relaxed, open, expectant.

She took another deep breath and hesitated. "I've been fine living on Long Island. Even commuting into the city is easy and safe. When I first got out of grad school in New York City, I rented an apartment in Chelsea because it was what I could afford. I knew it would take some time to build up a clientele, even though my grad school professors did what they could to give me an introduction into the world of authors. I was twenty-six when—when it happened."

Beth paused and looked down thoughtfully. Warner patiently waited for her to continue. He set his pen down and sat back in his chair.

"I got a job part-time in a small gas station with a grocery store. It supplemented my income and was a few blocks from my apartment. I—I knew a lot of the customers because they were regulars. One was an older retired lady who came in each week to buy one or two lottery tickets. She'd been widowed five years earlier and was barely able to live on her social security check. She was always cheerful and just spent a few dollars on tickets. Her—her name was Nancy." She paused again, thinking about the lady, a ghost of a smile passed over her face.

"Was?"

"Was." She looked up and sniffled. Taking a tissue out of her pocket, she blew her nose. "It's difficult to talk about her."

"I understand. You don't have to."

"One night—January 23—I was working, and two men came in wearing ski masks that covered their faces. I was the lone clerk, and Nancy and another older man were in the store. I remember thinking it was a mild evening, weather-wise, for late January in New York. Stupid how my mind selects facts like that to remember. One of the men moved over to the grocery aisles, and the other walked toward me..." Suddenly, she stopped talking, tears in her eyes. "I'm sorry. I can still see this."

Warner's face softened, and he said, "You don't have to tell me this. I was simply curious."

"I keep thinking if I say it, it will get easier. You're the second person I've told this to. I keep thinking that. Easier. But, you see, I wasn't used to sudden anger, and it was terrifying. The robber who went down the aisles, he—he shot them both. Why? I have never understood that." Now tears were cascading down her face. "Nancy—she—she died. Instantly. The other person—the man—was badly wounded." She wiped her face with a tissue.

"Where were you during all of this? Where was the second robber?" He said it gently, and Beth didn't feel he was pressing her. She took several deep breaths but didn't look up at his face.

Her voice came out slowly, haltingly. "He came to the counter and yelled at me to hand over the money from the register." She paused. "So—so I did. I opened the drawer and took out the bills. I think it was about $150. Then he looked at me and yelled at the other man to—to—to lock the door."

She stopped talking and felt the fear again, the memory attached deeply in her thoughts.

"I didn't know what to do. In that second, I looked at his eyes in the holes of the ski mask, and I knew. I knew.

"I began to back away, but I had nowhere to go behind the counter. I sensed he was smiling. He—He put his heavy hand partly over my mouth and grabbed my blouse.

"I think I must have closed my eyes. I could hear a woman screaming, and then I realized it was me... or else it was the sirens. His partner yelled at him to get out the back door. He hesitated, and then put a hand on my throat so I couldn't breathe. He whispered, 'I'll be back to finish this,' and then he was gone."

Silence. Her breathing was all she could hear. She was shaking again and pulled the afghan over her shoulders.

The detective waited. Then he said softly, "I'm sorry. I can't imagine." Silence again. "Did they catch them?"

She shook her head slowly back and forth, feeling the energy drain from her whole body. "I sometimes have nightmares. I can see his eyes."

"I can understand why you'd feel so vulnerable."

She wiped her eyes and her face and took a deep breath. "I'm—I'm not used to such anger, such terror." Then she paused. "I guess a regular customer who walked past the store had seen the robbery going on and called the police. I am so—so thankful. But it was too late for Nancy—totally innocent of anything. Just being in the wrong place. The other customer—he survived."

Beth was breathing easier now. She pulled the afghan a little tighter around her shoulders. "Years earlier, my father had taught me to shoot. After my parents died, I sold his gun collection, but I went out the next day and bought a handgun. After the—the incident—I quit that job and found another until I was able to support myself." She looked directly at Kyle Warner. "There. Story ends." She cleared her throat. "I—I guess it's important to me that you not think of me as a crazy, paranoid woman. When I heard someone in the house, I think my anger overcame my fear. That someone would break into this house, a house that I feel some responsibility for, well, I—I didn't think. I just went down the stairs."

It was silent in the kitchen—an uncomfortable silence. Such a raw, emotional memory to tell a perfect stranger. She wasn't sure what to say next. He broke the silence.

"That definitely answers the question about why you feel afraid after these incidents since you came here. I understand. I get it." He took a business card and pen out of his pocket, writing his cell phone number on the back. "Here," he said, handing it to her. "You can reach me on this phone. Anytime, night or day. I'll call a locksmith in the morning and send him over. I'll also have a cruiser go by a few times during the night—what's left of it." He smiled and added, "I doubt whoever it was will be back tonight. It will take me a while to look up those murder case files, but I'll get back to you."

Beth followed him out to the front door, thanking him for arriving so quickly. She watched him walk down the sidewalk, thinking about how easy it was to talk with him. Kind of like Richard, so long ago.

After he'd left, Beth locked the doors again and turned off the lights as she walked up the stairs. She hadn't told him about the perfume or the light going on. He'd really think she was crazy, at least crazier than he might already think. If she were smart, she'd go back to New York City tomorrow, but something told her to hang around. A voice inside her said, *Beth, you have research to do.*

Chapter Ten

The following morning, Beth was somewhere between sleeping and waking when she was rudely jolted by the front doorbell. A brief look at the bedside clock shocked her into rolling out of bed and throwing on clothes.

"I haven't slept until nine o'clock in forever," Beth thought with alarm, and then remembered how late she'd been up because of the break-in. Pulling up socks, she ran her hand through her hair and hustled down the main stairway. Hope it isn't the detective again, she thought. He already saw me at my worst. When she reached the inside door, she spied a man, his face to the glass, his hand across his forehead, attempting to see if anyone was inside.

"Coming," she said, pulling the chair out from under the door handle while unlocking the compromised lock. Beth unlocked the outer door and saw a short, middle-aged man, a toolbox in his hand. He was almost as wide as he was tall, with a round, childish face that resembled a cherub.

"Locksmith." He looked at his work order. "Are you Tippitt? Elizabeth?" He spoke with an accent, broken up by pauses. Perhaps Italian, Beth thought.

"Not exactly. I'm Elizabeth Russell, but this is the Tippitt house, and I need to have the locks changed. Detective Warner must have sent you."

"That would be I," he said, taking off his hat. "Antonio Caleca." Glancing at her, he added, "Is this a—uh—proper time for the locks?"

"Absolutely," Beth said. "You're here so quickly. When I lived in New York City, I'd have to wait a week and worry about another burglary the whole time I was waiting. Amazing, Mr. Caleca. Thank you so much for coming." She stretched out her arm and shook his hand, a wide grin on her face.

"All doors?" he asked, looking beyond her into the foyer.

"All of the outside doors," Beth said. "I, well, I don't know how many that is. I haven't been here long enough to check out all the entry doors."

The locksmith said, "I will check, count, fix. You leave it to Antonio. Lady like you should not be afraid. I will begin here with this door. New locks, keys, no problem."

"Thank you again," Beth said. "I'll go fix coffee—do you drink coffee?"

"Coffee, yes, but I have had enough this morning. Don't want shaky hands while I work, you see," he said, holding out a perfectly still hand.

She smiled at him, thinking what a charming man he was. If this were New York City, she'd have to see at least three forms of identification to make sure he was from the company she called. Somehow this seemed too easy.

He looked at her expectantly, adding, "You go make coffee. I'll be fine counting doors, fixing, working around you." He put his toolbox on the porch floor and began pulling out tools. Parked at the curb was his truck with "C and F Locksmiths" on the side.

A half hour later, showered and feeling better, Beth stood at the front window staring out, her coffee cup in her hand. Four squirrels were chasing each other up the tree trunks, in and out of the neighboring yards. She laughed out loud at the antics of the squirrels, especially as she watched a baby trying to keep up with the adults. Mr. Caleca had finished the front door and was working out in the kitchen.

Once done, he handed her a set of keys. "These are the same," he said. "They fit all locks, all doors. Come, try one." She followed him to the front door and tried out the new locks.

"Perfect," she said.

"Now, you have six keys, three doors. If you have boyfriend," he said and winked, "you can give him a key. Other keys you can keep in case you lose one, maybe two."

"Thank you, Mr. Caleca. You do fine work and quickly. Please leave me a bill—"

"Call me Antonio. Please. I will send, pretty lady. US mail. You keep my business card. I fix anything," he said, tipping his hat and turning to walk back to the truck.

Well, thought Beth. Charming guy. She glanced at the card. She should put this in a drawer in the kitchen. Whoever buys the house may need his help.

She walked back to the kitchen and was putting the breakfast dishes in the dishwasher when she heard her phone's ringtone. It was Elisha Davis calling about the house.

"I haven't decided yet, Elisha, but if last night is any indication, people are dying to get into my house. You shouldn't have any trouble." Beth pushed her hair off her forehead.

"What do you mean?"

"Someone broke in last night." Beth heard a pause on the other end of the phone.

"Oh my God! Did they damage anything?" Beth held her phone out from her ear.

"No. It's fine." She's guarding her investment, Beth thought.

"Did you call the police?" asked Elisha.

"Yes. They came out and checked for fingerprints."

"And—"

"Nothing. Whoever it was wore gloves. No prints. However, I talked to a detective and had the locks changed this morning."

"That's good. Maybe this house is more trouble than it's worth since you're planning to go back to New York," said Elisha.

Beth paused a moment. "You're probably right, but I'm still learning about its history, and that of the people who lived here. I have time before I start working again, so I'll stick around for a while."

"I wouldn't wait too long. Lots of papers to sign to get the ball rolling. You have my number once you decide."

"Yes." Beth tried to remember what she was going to ask the quirky real estate agent. Then it came back to her. "Elisha, have you ever heard any stories of ghosts haunting this house?"

Silence. Then, "Ghosts? You're kidding, right?"

"No."

"Not that I've heard of. The Georgian colonial a couple of blocks over, yes. Your house, no. Have you seen ghosts?"

"No, at least not seen."

"For goodness' sake, don't talk to anyone else in town about ghosts. I'll never get your house sold."

Beth smiled as she pushed "end" on the phone. That should give her something to worry about, she mused. What next, she wondered as she saw a short, stocky fellow in a mail uniform walking up the front walk. Man, life is exciting in small towns, she thought to herself.

"Morning," he said. "You Elizabeth Russell?"

"I am. I can't believe you have mail for me. I'm only here for a short time, and no one knows I'm here"—she looked at his name on his jacket—"Emmett." He had a ruddy complexion and a handlebar moustache. Beth hadn't seen one of those except in the movies. It curled perfectly on either side of his nose. Amazing.

Emmett leaned on the doorframe. "I heard you were here from New York. Must be quite a change. Whereabouts in New York?"

Ah, small towns, she thought. It was just easier to say, "The big city."

"New York City?"

She laughed. "That's the one. On Long Island, actually."

He pulled a thick envelope out of his mailbag. "Did you know New York City, counting the boroughs, has 177 zip codes plus one for the World Trade Center, a number which has been retired? Sweet Iron— one zip code. Must be awful quiet for you."

"It certainly is." She narrowed her eyes and checked the envelope in his hand. "Is that for me?"

"It is, but I can't give it to you."

"What? Why?"

"You don't officially live at this address. But I can give you a form to fill out and return to the post office so you can have your mail delivered here." He searched through his mailbag for a paper.

Beth scratched her head. "Does this mean you would have to forward that envelope to my address in New York?"

"S'pose to. However, seeing as how you seem like the Elizabeth

Russell with the funny eyes everyone's talking about, I think I can give it to you." He handed her the envelope, and she saw it was from Hatcher, Liggett and Finley. "They're right. You have green eyes with gold dots in them. That's strange."

She tossed the envelope on the table in the foyer, folded her arms, and said, "You aren't the first one to tell me, Emmett. Thank you for my mail."

"Here," he said, handing her a small paper. "You need to fill this out so I can deliver your mail here."

"How long will it take for this to become official?"

"Oh, 'bout four weeks."

"I'll probably be gone by then."

"Gone?"

"Back to New York City."

"Why would you want to do that?"

Now she chuckled. "You may have a point. It is friendly here." When I'm not being broken into in the middle of the night, she thought. "Thanks, Emmett. I'll look forward to seeing you tomorrow."

"Tomorrow," he said plodding back down the stairs. "New Year's Eve. The next day you'll just have to do without me."

Beth was still smiling as she closed both the doors and turned the locks. She heard her phone ring in her jeans pocket. What a busy day I'm having, Beth thought. I don't get these many calls or visits in New York.

It was Detective Warner. He asked if the locks were done and told her the public defender who took Brian Nash's case was still in Sweet Iron.

"His name is Ken Muir, and when I checked, I found out he volunteers at the senior center on Tiffany Court in the afternoons. It's only about three blocks from your house, due west. You could easily walk it, and the weather's mild today. Might give you an idea of what's around your house, at least to the west."

"Fantastic. Thank you so much, Detective Warner."

"Kyle."

"Right, Kyle." She checked her watch. It was already afternoon. "I'll head over there. Thank you again for having the locks done. I feel safer now. In Sea Cliff, I'm in an apartment with security, and, of course, a gun. Didn't think I'd worry about that back here."

"Fair enough. I know this is a small town, but even a town of 15,000 has its share of crime. You're still wise to lock the doors."

"Absolutely. Point taken."

As she was making her bed, Beth saw a photograph on the bedside table. She glanced at the chair and saw the notebook she had started on last night. She remembered the photo falling out of the pages. It was a color photo, badly faded, of two people on a beach. She recognized Melanie, who might have been in college. It only showed her from the shoulders up, and she appeared to have a swim suit on. Next to her was a guy, smiling, who had his arm around her shoulders. He had light hair and sunglasses perched on top of his head, and a plain gold necklace circled his neck. His round face held light eyes and a patrician nose. Both Melanie and the guy were smiling and tanned. She turned the photo over and saw "1971 Memorial Day" written in blue ink. No names. Could this be her father? she wondered. He has light hair, like Melanie, and recessive genes for light-colored eyes. She stuck it in her pocket, figuring the former public defender could tell her.

Chapter Eleven

Beth left the house, carefully locking the front door with her new key. Now, she thought, no one has a key but me. Much safer, more secure. She had thrown on rolled-cuff jeans—her favorites— and a long-sleeved blue waffle shirt with a white quilted vest. In her walking shoes, it was a short jaunt to go three blocks west. As she moved along, she noticed the yellowed lawns, no longer covered by snow, and here and there a snowman, mostly melted, or a fort, its walls all but melted. Christmas decorations were on full display, their lights off for now. How different than the city neighborhoods. The houses were not alike. No cookie cutter patterns. No apartment buildings. Large yards. Space between houses, much more than two feet.

Beth tried to imagine what this neighborhood would look like in the spring with leaves on the trees, green grass, and bushes and flowers in full bloom. More like Spring Harbor, she mused, but maybe a little wealthier than my old hometown.

It was indeed only three blocks. Beth thought the senior center building could have been something else originally, and then repurposed for this use. It looked like perhaps it had been a neighborhood store in a former life with large windows in the front. She walked in and asked for Ken Muir at the front desk.

"Right now, he's teaching a fitness class for seniors," said the young woman at the desk. "If you go over to that window you can watch the last five minutes. You'll see the door to go in once he's done."

Beth moved across the front desk area and looked through a large glass window with several others who were evidently waiting for the class to end. She saw a white-haired older man dressed in a T-shirt, sweatpants, and stylish kicks, leading the class. Faintly, music from the sixties and seventies came through the glass. After a few minutes, the music stopped, and the man put a towel around his neck and began conversing with several other people. They all laughed, and he pulled off his glasses, wiping them on his towel. To think he knew my father, Beth thought. As the group began to disperse, Beth walked through a doorway and approached the older man, who appeared to be in remarkable shape. He must be at least in his seventies, Beth guessed. He's sure-footed and moves so smoothly, she thought.

She introduced herself and shook his hand.

"Do I know you, Beth Russell?" He looked curiously at her eyes.

"Well, no," she said, smiling back. "But you did know my biological father. He was Brian Nash."

Muir's mouth dropped in shock, and he simply stared at her face. "I'll be. You know, he said he had a child back then, but I guess that thought went right out of my memory. I can see the resemblance to Melanie Tippitt. Yes, you are certainly their daughter." He shifted the towel off his neck and said, "What can I do for you?"

"I'd like to talk with you about my parents and Melanie Tippitt's 1971 murder case."

He thought for a moment, saying nothing. He let out a long sigh. "I guess I can talk with you, but even though that was a lifetime ago, you realize I have to be cautious about what I say. He was a client, after all."

"Sure, I understand. I imagine the newspapers tell most of the story, and I haven't gotten to those yet. I thought you might be able to add the shading, the atmosphere."

"Why don't we go out to the little snack bar past the front desk and sit down? I could use something to drink after all this." He looked down at his shirt. "Pardon me for the sweaty workout clothes."

In a few minutes, they were seated at the snack bar on the other side of the building, Muir with a bottle of water and an energy bar, Beth with coffee.

As he unwrapped the energy bar, Muir said, "If you don't mind my asking, do you have some reason for bringing all of this up again? After all, it's been forty-five years or more."

Beth adopted a decisive tone. "Mr. Muir, you don't know me. I just found out my biological parents were Melanie and Brian. Before that, I lived comfortably for forty-seven years believing I was someone else. I think, for my own curiosity, it would be good to know who my parents were, especially since one of them killed the other."

He stared at her, took a swig of water, and said, "Is that what you think?"

"He confessed, didn't he? From what I hear, he went to prison. What else am I to think?"

"The Nash trial is not simple at all. I can tell you the published facts I know, information you could probably read in the papers."

"The newspapers won't tell me what you thought after talking with Brian Nash. I don't even know what he looks like. I have this photo that was in a notebook of my mother's. Is this my father?"

He studied the photograph and laid it down on the table. "No, this is a young Sam Conklin. He was dating your mother that summer. He's still around town, and in fact is a big man in town these days. I'm sure he'd talk to you. No, your father was darker—dark brown hair and eyes, kind of an olive complexion, and nothing like Sam."

"What was he like, my father?"

"Let's see. What to tell you," he said, pausing. "When I took on his case, he was still screwed up from drugs, alcohol, and what we now know as PTSD. He had flashbacks, nightmares, and hallucinations about the time he did in Vietnam. He was working on getting clean. I admired him for that. Of course, he was scared, and in way over his head."

"What do you mean?"

"The town. The town was divided. You must understand, this was quite early in my career. I was, maybe, thirty-two or thirty-three. Judge Tippitt knew both the judge in the case and Alex Plank, the prosecutor. Tippitt—I suppose he'd be your grandfather—wanted Plank to go for first-degree murder. Lots of pressure to put Nash away or have him executed. He was from the wrong side of the tracks, a poor kid, and had known Melanie since seventh or eighth grade. On top of that—as I was to find out—he'd gotten her pregnant when she was only sixteen. I imagine that didn't stick well with Judge Tippitt. I guess the baby was you."

Beth nodded. "I've since learned I was given away in a closed adoption."

"I see." Muir paused again, as if he were thinking carefully about his words. "Plank went for murder, hoping to at least convict on a lesser charge. Judge Tippitt put pressure on everyone. The atmosphere of the trial only added to the probability he'd be found guilty. It was the 'Trial of the Century' for little Sweet Iron and was covered by media from St. Louis to Chicago. The jury was all white males, mostly professional people. Hardly Brian Nash's peers. Even made the national news channels. Beautiful girl, only nineteen, important wealthy family, poor boy, baby out of wedlock. It had all the hallmarks of Greek drama."

Beth pursed her lips, her voice frustrated. "But why would he kill my mother? Didn't he love her?"

Muir drank the last of his water and looked over her shoulder. Then he focused on Beth and said, "That's what I mean when I say it was complicated. Nash didn't know what happened that day. After the murder, he had a car accident and hit his head on the steering wheel. He woke up from a twenty-four-hour coma, and he remembered nothing."

"How did anyone know he did it? Was there a witness? Did they see him do it?" asked Beth, in a sharper tone than she'd meant to use.

"A bunch of teenagers. They were drinking alcohol and smoking pot at Tippitt Pond. The alcohol was legal at eighteen back then, but the pot definitely wasn't. I'm not sure anyone will know what happened that day except Melanie Tippitt. No one saw the murder, only the aftermath. It changed all their lives: The Tippitt family— which had already seen enough tragedy—the teenagers who were there—your mother, of course, Nash's—even mine."

"Yours?" asked Beth.

"Yes. I almost quit the law. You know, I was young then, believed in justice, and thought the scales balanced evenly for rich and poor. Obviously, too naïve for my own good. I mounted the best defense I could, even without much help from Brian. We had a good chance to win it, since all the evidence was circumstantial. Halfway through the trial, Nash decided to plead guilty against my advice."

"Why would he do that if he didn't remember what happened?"

Muir shook his head. "I think he just gave up. Like I said, no one will ever know. The judge is dead now, and so is Alex Plank, the prosecutor. I have no idea what happened to Brian Nash. I know he did time for the crime, but I never saw him again. He would have done fifteen years, plus another four of probation. That would bring him to 1990. I haven't seen or heard from him in all that time. He might be dead." Muir looked down at his hands on the table. "Now the families are all gone, except you."

Beth felt some resolution churning in her head. "Mr. Muir, I am going to the library to look up the news stories. I'm becoming quite curious about this murder."

"I can see why you'd want to know what happened."

Now it was Beth's turn to pause and consider if she wanted to confide in this stranger. Finally, she said, "I'm staying in the Tippitt house, and I feel a presence that is making me wonder if it isn't over. Almost as if my mother would like me to find out what happened that day at Tippitt Pond. I know this may sound crazy to you, and I assure you I'm a balanced, just-the-facts kind of person. Since I've heard your description of the trial, maybe my mother is hanging around, hoping for someone to find out the truth." She looked down at her hands, then up again. "Perhaps I am my adopted father's daughter. He was an attorney, and he always believed the truth was important. If Brian Nash didn't do this terrible thing I want him to have his day in court, even if he's dead."

He laughed a quiet little laugh. "I can almost hear your father's voice in the way you say that. He was resolute about one idea: he and Melanie had plans. I don't know what they were. He never explained to me, but I thought at the time that a man with plans isn't going to murder the woman he loves." He heaved a sigh, pausing, and his voice became quieter. "Once she died, I think his own dreams and his future fell apart. He didn't have anything else to live for. He stopped the trial, took a plea deal, all against my advice. Maybe that's why this case stuck in my head for so many years. It was one of those cases I didn't win, and I should have, so I rethought it over and over for a long time." He shook his head. "What a tragedy. I must say I liked Brian Nash, screwed up as he was. I can't quite explain it, but something pure and sweet ran through his love for your mother. Now you show up, and I can see it again as if it were yesterday. Funny. That death at Tippitt Pond changed everything for a lot of people. Especially you."

Beth pursed her lips and was silent for a moment. "May I call you or come by to ask you follow-up questions if I find I need to?"

"Of course. I'll help you as much as I can, but, like I said, everyone's gone now, and I'm not sure you'll get very far in trying to resurrect all of this. If you think of anything I can do to help, let me know."

Beth gave him her business card and wrote her personal cell phone number on the back. "If you think of something else you decide I should know, you can reach me here."

"One other thing I do remember, Beth. When your father talked about Melanie Tippitt and the baby girl they gave up, I had the feeling he loved both of you very much."

She lowered her head momentarily, and then looked up. "Thanks, Mr. Muir."

She headed back to Tippitt House, thinking about checking Molly's library for the newspaper accounts of the murder and trial. Her cell phone vibrated in her pocket, and she saw it was Molly.

"You know it's New Year's Eve tomorrow?"

"I hadn't really thought about it," Beth said.

"I'm going to a party at the country club, and my husband, Charlie, is down with a bad cold. He isn't much for parties anyway. Why don't you go with me? It's New Year's Eve."

Beth thought for a moment. "That's right. I'd forgotten what day it is." The holidays were always unsettling to her since her family was all gone. "I don't have anything to wear."

"You can pick up a dress at Danielle's Dress Shop. It's on Main Street, and it's bound to be cheaper than New York City."

"Oh, I don't know, Molly."

"You can meet some people from town at the party."

"But I'm planning to leave in a few weeks. What's the purpose?"

"Look, I know you're shy, and I promise I will stick to you like glue. As for purpose, you haven't asked who is throwing the party."

"Okay, I'll bite. Who?"

"Just the local US senator from Illinois, Sam Conklin."

She searched her memory and realized he was the man in the picture with her mother. Beth began to wonder if the ghostly presence was making these coincidences happen. First, Muir mentions him, and now, here was a chance to see him in person.

"I think I'd like to meet him, Molly. You're on."

Chapter Twelve

A fter Beth picked up a new dress, she walked past several stores looking for a place that stocked small table lamps. A light on a table in the foyer might discourage unwelcome visitors. She passed another clothing store, a pet shop, and a bank. Then she spied a furniture store called Bonnie's Furniture Boutique.

As she walked in, a bell hanging from the door jangled. A saleswoman was talking to another customer, so Beth wandered around. In a few minutes, she found a lamp that would work, examined it, and carried it to the counter. A second salesman came out of a doorway in the back and helped her.

He was wrapping the lamp when Beth's eyes noticed a credenza that appeared to have the same workmanship as Melanie's hope chest, but it was more battered and worn. She leaned over the counter, focusing on the finish.

"Would you mind if I walked around the counter and examined your desk?"

"Sure—no problem," the clerk said.

Beth studied the perfect finish and noted the double hearts on a lower leg. This time, however, she didn't see initials or a date.

"Would you have any idea where the store bought that desk?" she asked.

"Not really." He finished wrapping the lamp, typed in the information on the computer, and produced a bill. Beth handed him her credit card.

"It's been here a long time," he said. "I started working here in '95, and it was really old then. I think the boss said she got it in a close-out sale. The business owner was leaving town."

Beth signed the bill and said, "Could the store owner look up the bill and let me know the furniture company?"

"I can leave her a note and your contact information."

"Perfect."

*****

Beth walked into the foyer of Tippitt House carrying a dress bag with a cute little black tea dress and a turquoise shrug to keep her arms warm. Under her other arm was a shoe box with black pumps and a small sack filled with turquoise jewelry, a black hair clip, and a black clutch purse with glittery beading. She might as well make a social splash—the ghost of Melanie Tippitt come to life. Maybe it will stir the pot, and she might learn more about her parents.

What is that? Beth thought, spying a thick envelope on the foyer table. She hung the dress up on a hinge of the dining room door, set the bag and her purse on the table, and picked up the envelope. Then she remembered—papers from Remington.

Taking the heavy envelope into the kitchen, Beth made some lunch and sat down to look at Remington's latest instructions. Multiple pages of information explaining decisions she would have to make about the inheritance fell out on the table. This seems like a full-time job for me, Beth thought. What's this? Another envelope, sealed, was folded within the legal papers. "For my Niece" was written in black ink on the outside. Beth's breath caught in her throat, and she touched the words, not sure whether to open it or what it might contain. She laid it on the table, ate several more spoonsful of soup and a bite of bread, and stared at the envelope.

First, the smell of perfume, and now a letter from the past. It's as if I'm being sucked into this family tragedy one discovery at a time, she thought. Janet Landry knew her investigator was searching for me, so maybe she wrote this hoping he would find me even after she was consumed by the cancer. She touched the words thoughtfully, and then used her table knife to slash open the envelope. Four pages unfolded, and Beth began reading.

Dear Niece,

Many times over the years I wondered what had happened to you after my sister—your mother—gave you up for adoption. I hope, despite the shock you must feel, you don't hold it against our family that you grew up in what we were assured was a good home.

Perhaps you are angry your mother gave you up for adoption. If so, I wish you could understand how life and social rules were back in the sixties. At the time, our parents simply wanted to put this pregnancy chapter behind them, save face in the community, and keep Melanie's reputation safe at all costs. Melanie told me about the terrible scene when she revealed her pregnancy to our parents. Our father was angered beyond belief, less so at Melanie and more at Brian Nash. If it had been the Old West, he would have "horse whipped" him. Mother, of course, just cried. It was a horrible night with accusations flying everywhere. The judge accused Nash of statutory rape and vowed he would see him in prison. However, Melanie pleaded it wasn't his fault, and the judge had to be satisfied with Plan B, since his initial idea would make her pregnancy news all over town. He hated gossip and drama.

An illegal abortion was a risky choice in those days because so many women died at the hands of unlicensed butchers. Your father had left us with terrible choices. Our parents sent Melanie away to me in New York City, and she stayed with me until she had you.

I loved your mother. She was clever, beautiful, mischievous, and happy—well, until this happened. Your mother was always the rebel, and while it made our parents angry at times, I think the judge was secretly proud of her ability to stand up for herself. But it didn't make life easy in his household. She kept the place stirred up with drama.

When our brother, Jeff, died, Melanie was devastated because they were very close. I was away at college. Melanie's rebellious behavior worsened. Our father had always had rules for us, and woe be to him or her who broke those rules. He was tough on us, but for good reasons.

I was the compliant one, Jeff could do no wrong, and Melanie was the rebel. This was the sixties, too, when rebellion was in vogue. Your mother was certainly born at the right time for that. After Jeff's death, Melanie spent more time with her friends, and especially with Brian Nash, a West Side boy our parents found totally unsuitable. That, of course, pleased Melanie-the-rebel. It was almost as if Jeff's death threw her into a tailspin, and she blamed our parents for her unhappiness. I think Brian Nash was a weapon in Melanie's hands.

After your mother became pregnant, our parents waited two months and withdrew her from school and sent her to me while spreading a story in Sweet Iron that Melanie was going to a special prep school where she'd pick up college credit. I'm sure no one was fooled. They didn't tell the Nash boy where she went, and Melanie struck a deal: she would agree to the adoption, and she wouldn't try to contact him if they didn't have him charged with statutory rape. Over those months, I began to understand and know my little sister better. I wish you could have known her. She loved you so much.

I was there the night Melanie had you. Just sixteen, scared, amazed, and then pleased. She was so brave, and I believe the Tippitt resolve ran in her blood. She got to hold you for a few minutes, and then they took you away. Melanie did not want to give you up, but she had no choice. Besides, how could a sixteen-year-old kid be a mother to you? It simply would not have been the best life for you or her. We did what was best at the time for everyone.

After Melanie returned home, she fell into a deep depression, and they sent her to a psychiatrist to try to help her cope with the trauma. She finished high school and left for college. By the time 1971 came around, Melanie was dating someone more appropriate, more suitable to her class. It seemed like she had settled down. The last time I talked with her on the phone, your mother said she had a plan to "fix things." She was like her old self again. I understood her to mean this new guy she was dating had a secure future and all was going well. It would rectify all the unhappiness with the past, and mend fences if Melanie pursued this new boy.

The next thing I knew, my father was calling to tell me she had been murdered by Brian Nash. It was unthinkable, unbelievable. I never forgot my shock at that phone call. My father was devastated, my mother terribly sad. Things like this didn't happen to people like us. They attended Brian Nash's trial every day and sat in the front row, as did I. My parents and I all agree Nash did this terrible thing. You should have seen him in court—a beard, long hair, sullen and nonresponsive. Here he was, a no-account person from a terrible home, with no future, high on drugs and alcohol that day, murdering our beautiful girl, your mother. Every time I think about those days, I wish to God she had never met Brian Nash. He should have been executed for what he did to our Melanie. I wish I could be kinder, but I can't bring myself to see anything good about her killer.

I know my attorney will take care of helping you on all the legal ends that need to be tied up. I left a box of Melanie's things in the attic and marked them "Melanie." It's not much, but I thought you might want to see them.

I wish you could have met your mother. She would have been such an astonishing woman had she been allowed to live longer. She never got over her love and loss of you. I'm afraid her death at Tippitt Pond changed everything.

I sent my lawyer's investigator to try to find you, to make amends—if you could see your way to do that—for having you adopted so long ago. If nothing else, I hope this legacy will help you live a long and happy life. Maybe you can wipe away the shadow of our family's past and remove the sadness this whole chapter caused. I wish I could have met you in this life. Perhaps we'll meet in the next, where all things are possible.

Your aunt, Janet Tippitt Landry

Beth dropped solidly into a chair in the living room. Breathe, Beth, breathe. Turning back to the first page, she quickly skimmed the letter again. Such hatred for Brian Nash. Beth could understand that since this was Janet's second sibling to meet death in an unnatural way, and Janet was sure Brian Nash had killed Melanie.

And what was she to make of her mother? Melanie was only sixteen at the time, and she ultimately sacrificed both Beth and her father to keep him out of prison for statutory rape. How was Beth to balance that love with the hatred of the Tippitt family toward this Nash boy?

After reading this letter, Beth was even more determined to find out about her parents and this Senator Sam Conklin.

She set the papers down on the foyer table and thought about Janet Tippitt's words. Since Melanie had a plan to marry the more suitable Sam Conklin, she was trying to make amends and do the right thing. Why, then, was she murdered? After speaking with Ken Muir, Beth wanted more than ever to get at the bottom of this family's bewildering past.

Chapter Thirteen

"That's just it, Beth. The Christmas candy is in the trunk of this car, because if I leave it at home Charlie will eat it all. He believes in feeding a cold, and he doesn't need any more holiday treats since his cold is very well fed," said Molly, as they drove to the New Year's Eve party at the Sweet Iron Country Club. "I can always run those calories off, but in the winter, I'm not quite as faithful with my daily runs as I am when it isn't cold."

"I knew you were a runner," said Beth. "I thought so the first time I saw you. You have that runner's 'lean and hungry look,' to quote the Bard." She checked to make sure she had put her phone in her purse—she had—and then said, "I talked with Ken Muir. I'm aware that Sam Conklin and my father were at Tippitt Pond the day my mother died. I realize Sam will be at this party. Who else was at the pond that day that might be here? I'm selecting targets ahead of time."

Molly turned onto the country club drive and said, "Shelly Andrews. She was a friend of your mother's. Right now, four-legged creatures are her friends. She owns a pet grooming business down town, she's a buddy of Sam Conklin's, and she was there that day. I'll be sure to introduce you. She's—an anxious person."

"So maybe a little New Year's cheer will loosen her tongue?" said Beth.

"Absolutely. Ah, let me see. Who else? Maybe Justin Kaspar. He'll probably be there with his wife. Another lawyer, like Sam. If I remember correctly from reading the trial coverage in the paper, he and Shelly went for the police and ambulance for Melanie. Everyone thinks of him as a shadow of Sam. Both went out East for school, and they always seem to be together when they're in Sweet Iron. I must say, I'll be interested in your assessment of him; I, frankly, don't care for him."

"I guess we'll see what I think. Since he's a lawyer, he's going to be careful what he says about the past. I may just be sociable and not ask him any pertinent questions. Saving him for later seems to be the best route."

They pulled up to a parking lot already almost full. As Molly drove around looking for a spot, she suddenly said, "Oh, yes. I forgot. Elisha. She was there that day, too."

"Elisha Davis? The real estate agent? I've talked to her several times, and I don't remember her saying anything about being at Tippitt Pond that day."

"Oh, but she was. She and Sam are like peas in a pod. Ah, here we are. A space. Finally."

They walked through the double doors and left their coats in the nearby cloak room. As Beth waited on Molly, she looked around at the impressive wall of photographs in the foyer. The only photo of Conklin that she'd seen was the teenage one with Melanie. She examined many photos of an older Sam with very important people, including the president and first lady. Beth didn't recognize all of the people in the photos, and as Molly came back she said, "You'll know some of the politicians. Others, I think, are lobbyists. That's Sam shaking their hands before he passes some legislation that will make them all even wealthier."

"Does Senator Conklin have these parties very often, or only on New Year's?" asked Beth.

"You know politicians. It's all about pressing the flesh, smiling for photos, and patting the backs of people who can do something for you. Senator Sam is no different than the rest," said Molly. "He was just reelected for his third term, so this party is also a way of saying thank you to his constituents. Sam is on some powerful committees in the Senate."

They wandered into the main banquet room, each of them lifting a glass of champagne from a tray held by one of the many waiters.

"That's Shelly, over at the bar," said Molly. "She's the one in the purplish-reddish dress with the hem hanging down below the dress in places."

Beth turned toward the bar and saw an older woman with brown hair—definitely dyed—that was frizzy and shoulder-length. She was hunched over a plate of food, mostly picking at it. "I am off to glean what I can from the usual suspects. I'll catch up with you in a bit," said Beth.

"Perfect," said Molly. "I will cruise over toward the food."

Beth walked to the bar, noticing the gray roots in Shelly Andrews's hair and the wrinkles in her dress as she came closer. Time had not been kind to Shelly. She sat with her leg crossed over her knee, dangling in a nervous, shaking motion. Approaching her from behind, Beth sat on the next stool, put her champagne flute on the bar, and turned toward Shelly. When the woman looked around and saw Beth's eyes, she knocked over her drink and it went spilling across the bar. The Andrews woman froze, her mouth open, her eyes shocked, one hand reaching up to her mouth.

"Hi," said Beth. "I'm Beth Russell, Melanie Tippitt's daughter."

Still the woman did not move. Then her head shook slightly, her face relaxed, and she breathed out a long breath. "Oh, I'm sorry for the shock on my face. Someone told me you were in town, but I wasn't prepared to see Melanie Tippitt in the flesh. That's amazing—how... how much you look like her. You could be twins."

The bartender came over and began cleaning up the spill. Shelly apologized and turned back to Beth.

"I didn't mean to frighten you," Beth said, hoping Shelly believed her. "And you are—?"

"Oh, uh, Shelly Andrews. I was a friend of your mother's, and I knew she had a baby years ago, but I guess I didn't expect you to look so much like Melanie." The waiter handed her another drink, and she picked it up, taking several swallows.

"Hello, Shelly. I've heard kind thoughts from people about my mother, but you could fill in the blanks for me on Brian Nash. It was a long time ago, but I'd love to listen to you do me the kindness of telling me what he was like."

Shelly looked at her face again, shaking her head slowly. "Your eyes. It's amazing. You have her eyes." She signaled the waiter for another drink, and Beth realized Shelly was slurring her words a little.

"I am told that quite a lot," said Beth, "but I'm not hearing much about my father. Were you his friend?"

"Brian's. Yes, Brian's friend. We came from the same neighborhood. His house—his family's house, that is—was behind mine. Or was mine behind his?" she slurred. "Well, doesn't matter now. Yes, we were friends. Met him in junior high when he was the cock of the walk." She smiled and added, "Cock-a-doodle-doo! That was my Brian. All the girls swooned over his handsome, dark looks... brooding. Think that's what they call it in those romance novels." She took a couple of swallows of the new scotch-and-water the bartender had set down. Setting the glass down and pointing into it, she said to Beth, "Just the way I like it... mostly scotch with a hint of water." Then she laughed.

"Where was I? Oh, yes. Brian. Awful what happened to him in Vietnam. Heartbreaking. I was so sad. Never the same. But," she added, "good ole Brian. Never forgot where he came from, always spoke to me. He didn't have that sense of en—en—entitlement that some people have." She looked across the room. Beth followed her stare and saw Sam Conklin talking with Elisha Davis. About that time, Elisha looked in her direction and said something to Sam. He nodded, and Beth saw her come toward them in her usual high-speed gait. She watched Elisha: cherry-red silk dress, black silk jacket with an expensive, quilted design, heavy gold chain necklace, eyebrows thin, earrings long, red lipstick, and impossibly high, high, black heels. Practically running.

"Hi, Shelly," Elisha said. "Mind if I borrow Elizabeth?"

"Sure," Shelly said, and went back to her drink. "Be kind to her. She's like Melanie."

Elisha pulled Beth up off her bar stool, gave her a look that said Shelly was not the best person to talk to, and walked her away several feet from the bar.

"Sorry about that. Shelly Andrews is such a needy person, Elizabeth. Sam Conklin has been so good to her. Helped her get her

83

business started and helped again when one of her husbands—I think the third one—died. Sam personally flew him to Springfield in his plane to get medical help. Didn't matter in the end, I'm afraid. She's never been very stable, and when she's drinking you can't believe much of what she says. I don't know why Sam invites her to these things. Usually her boyfriend, Jack Hanson, keeps her drinking under control when he's with her. Can't think where he might be tonight, however." She looked around the room. "Now, I'd like to take you over to meet the senator."

Beth saw a waiter glance at her with a look of curiosity on his face. She was sure she saw that look out of the corner of her eye. Then his face was composed again. "Elisha, I need to go use the powder room. Promise I'll be over in a jiffy." She walked over to the young waiter, who was holding a small tray of champagne glasses. Before she could select one, he handed her a glass, and she could feel a piece of paper on the bottom of the flute. "Thank you," she said, and walked off to the restroom, quickly stashing the note in her pocket.

Molly was in the restroom—Beth had seen her walk in a few minutes earlier—and they had a fast conference about the party.

"Doing okay?" asked Molly. "Need me to make any more introductions or point anyone out?"

Beth fixed her lipstick and said, "I'm on my way to meet Sam. Elisha pulled me away from Shelly Andrews. I take it Shelly is not quite in Sam Conklin's financial bracket? She probably doesn't have her own plane?"

"Correct," said Molly. "I feel sorry for her. She's had several husbands, but she never seems to be able to settle with one, and I rarely see her smile. Shelly's a bit rough around the edges, as you can probably surmise."

"Well, I'm off to see the wizard," said Beth. "Elisha has been singing his praises already. From across the room, he looks like a politician—tanned, a little gray at the temples, perfect white-toothed smile, six-foot and trim. I sneaked a look at him when I was talking to Elisha."

"Yes, that would be our senator. Before you're done, I'm sure you'll meet his wife, too. If she sees you talking to him, she'll be over like Diana, the Huntress."

"I'd put money on that, but I'm sure you're probably right, Molly."

She left the restroom and walked over to the far wall where Sam Conklin was standing, a drink in his hand, with Elisha Davis. Beth was not surprised to see the look on his face when she was close enough for him to see her eyes.

"Senator Conklin," she said, extending her hand for a firm handshake. Beth could tell that his suit cost several thousand dollars, the loosened tie looked stylish, and he must have expensive cufflinks with—perhaps—diamonds in them, because they flashed every so often when the lights hit them.

"I'm speechless. If you aren't the spittin' image of my Melanie." He turned to Elisha and said, "You didn't tell me, Elisha."

The real estate agent shrugged her shoulders and turned a smile on Beth. "Guess I've been too busy trying to get her to sell that house of hers. Didn't think to mention it to you."

He was still shaking her hand, and finally realized he needed to let it go. "My, my. You are amazing."

"Pardon me," said Elisha. "I'll leave you two to reminisce while I go say hi to Angela."

"Here, have a seat, Elizabeth Russell. Here's a table that seems to be unoccupied," said Conklin. He pulled a chair out for Beth and she sat down, setting her champagne on the table.

"I understand you knew my mother, Senator."

"I certainly did," he said, and more quietly he intoned, "I certainly did. You are as beautiful as she was, and, from what Elisha says, very smart."

"Thank you. I've seen photos of Melanie, and it seems like everyone mentions her looks when I ask about her."

Conklin took a sip of his drink. "Sounds about right. Elisha told me you had come to town because the lawyer, Hatcher, was trying to figure out the recipient of Janet's estate. I guess he's settled on you. Quite a windfall, I'd imagine."

"It was nothing I knew about until he found me."

"You know, I always heard rumors that Mellie—that's what I

called her—had a baby, but I never believed them. Guess now I'll have to," said the senator.

"I plan to do a little research into her death," said Beth. She noticed his face didn't change, and he continued to stare across the room. "From what I understand, you were at Tippitt Pond that day."

"I was, although I had gone into town with Justin when she was—killed."

"And you and my mother were quite an item."

"An item?" He chuckled. "We were, indeed. We had planned to get married soon as I finished law school. That summer we were both home. Best summer of my life. Lots of good memories, except for that one." He took another sip of his drink and added, "Are you a trusting kind of person, Elizabeth Russell?"

"In what way do you mean?"

"You have your mother's looks, and evidently her brain, but she was too trusting. That bastard—Nash—came back all screwed up from 'Nam, and she was amazingly naïve. Figured she could help him. If I had known he was going to be out at the pond that day, I'd never have left her alone. Too trusting, that's what she was." He shook his head and put his hand up in the air for a waiter. Pointing to his empty glass, he once again returned his focus to Beth. Before he could continue his thought, another man came over to the table.

"Justin," he said. "I'd like you to meet Elizabeth Russell—she's Melanie's daughter."

"Really?" He leaned over, invading her space, and she could smell the alcohol on his breath as he stared at her eyes.

Beth gave him a slight push, moving him back from her. "You're a little too close, Justin."

"Oh, my God," he slurred. "Just like that bitch."

Sam stood up so quickly Beth was surprised, and he moved around the table, grabbing Justin by the shoulders. "You are drunk. Apologize to the lady."

"'Pologize," he said, bowing in a mock salute. "It's Sam, my friend, Ms. Russell. He always gets what he wants. Always has. Always will."

"Go out to the kitchen, get some coffee, drink it until you're sober, and then get Shelly Andrews home. Sober, Justin." He literally turned the man around and waved for a waiter who walked him out of the room.

"Sorry about that," said Sam. "Justin Kaspar. He's an attorney. We both went to school together out East. Normally, he's as sober as a judge, but New Year's Eve is obviously an excuse for excess. I apologize for my friend."

"Accepted," said Beth, and before she could say another word, a woman with a tiny body in a short blue cocktail number with diamonds on her ears and at her throat came over to the table and stood next to Beth, waiting to be introduced.

"My wife, Elizabeth," he said. "Bitsy, this is Elizabeth Russell. She's visiting for a little while. Has a house to sell here in town. Elizabeth, anything you want to shop for, Bitsy can tell you the place to go. She is an expert and has credit cards to burn."

*****

They left before midnight, Molly reassuring Beth she'd had one drink and a cup of coffee. "So, what did you think of Sweet Iron's finest?" asked Molly.

"I met so many people. It was nice to see the Bingleys again, since they were the first people I met in town. I felt sorry for Shelly Andrews. She was slurring drunk and obviously unhappy. Kind of out of place with that fast crowd."

Molly nodded. "I never understood how she fit into that group when she was a teenager. But she was there that day. They all had so much money, you know, and came from wealthy homes. But Shelly was from the West End, just like Brian Nash."

"She thought I was my mother's ghost. I almost felt bad I'd surprised her."

"Elisha mention selling your house forty times?"

"No, actually she was pretty good tonight. It was obvious she wanted me away from Shelly Andrews. She and the senator seem to be best buds."

"Elisha hasn't had an easy life," said Molly. "She told me once, some time ago, that after Melanie died, her parents took her on a trip to California to settle her nerves. I know she went to a small college in Chicago and met her husband there. They built up the real estate business her father left her, but the husband died about ten years ago. She's been soldiering on ever since. No children."

Beth looked out the window for a few moments. Then she said, "Justin Kaspar is a piece of work. He was falling-down drunk. Sam got all over him."

"What did you think of him?"

"He has shifty eyes." She laughed, and so did Molly. "He's handsome, even more so than Sam Conklin, but Sam smiles and makes happy with everyone. Kaspar is sure of himself, always has an answer. Not sure all of them are true." She was silent for a moment. "He did say something interesting about Sam. His words came out with a bitter edge. 'Sam always gets what he wants. Always has. Always will.' Then a switch clicked on in his head, and he was Smiling Justin again."

"And our senator. He flies his own plane, has places in Tucson, D.C., and here. He's been a senator two terms, just starting his third. The law degree from Yale didn't hurt, as well as clerking for a Supreme Court judge. He's on wife number two, and this one's no fool."

"I think I share your thoughts," said Beth. "After his wife showed up, she turned to talk to someone and he whispered beyond her hearing that he'd like to give me some advice as my mother's old friend. He put his hand on my arm and looked genuinely concerned. 'Let the past go,' he said, 'and don't go stirring things up.' Not sure I really answered him on that one."

"Well, it's a full cast of villains from that day at Tippitt Pond," said Molly. "Take your pick."

Beth laughed as Molly pulled up in front of her house. She thanked Molly and walked up the steps, sighing with relief when it appeared the door was locked. It was late, and she was ready for bed. Putting on her PJs, she slipped her dress onto a hanger, checking the pockets for tissues. She pulled out a wadded paper, remembering the waiter at the party had slipped it into her hand with the champagne. Unfolding all the little creases, she read, "Please, Ms. Russell, meet me at the Third Street Tap on Tuesday evening at six. I knew your father. Dominick Hendrickson."

"This town holds lots of surprises," she said to no one.

Chapter Fourteen

Beth spent much of Tuesday dealing with mundane items on her computer, like checking to see if author Jameson Otter had requested research yet. She didn't expect to hear from him until February, but it wasn't too early to start watching for his email. Kyle Warner called her to say he was checking in on her. Were the locks holding? When she hung up, Beth realized she was smiling. His voice was deep and velvety soft. Really? Seriously, did detectives "check in" on people as a routine part of their jobs?

Gabby was next. Beth called her in New York City, and casually mentioned she'd be staying a little longer than she had planned, and, of course, she got a mountain of flak from Gabby since she was the one who had literally convinced Beth to go to Illinois.

She was standing in the living room, looking out the front window as a gentle shower of snowflakes drifted down and landed softly on the front lawn. Across the street in the woods, it looked even lovelier. She turned and wandered back through the living room toward the baby grand piano, phone in hand, listening to Gabby.

"I've made up my mind, Gabby. I'm researching the Tippitt family, Brian Nash, and the murder trial. Something doesn't add up. Can't put my finger on it, but my gut feeling is that people are pushing me to leave, conversations about my parents are contradictory, and the talk with Ken Muir makes me even more suspicious."

"Suspicious of what?" Gabby asked.

"You're going to say I'm crazy, but I keep thinking of that line from Shakespeare's *Macbeth*, 'by the pricking of my thumbs, something wicked this way comes.' I can't explain it. Simply a sense of foreboding."

Beth wandered back into the living room and, sitting down on the sofa, she saw that the snow was coming down faster.

"I suppose it would be good to wrap it all up before you leave," said Gabby. "This is the perfect time—between projects."

Beth leaned forward on the sofa, straining to see through the snowfall. She could swear someone was standing between the trees across the street, watching her house. This is crazy, she thought.

"Beth—" said Gabby.

"Uh, let me call you back later, Gabby. Something's come up," she said, walking across the room to the coat closet in the foyer.

"Sure. Talk to you later."

Beth pushed the end button on her phone, threw her coat on quickly, and dropped the phone into a deep coat pocket. Pulling up the hood and wrapping a scarf around her neck, she opened the door and started down the stairs and across the street, all the while watching the woods.

Whoever it was didn't see her right away because of the falling snow. She watched him watching the house. He looked tall and thin and had on dark clothing with a hood that obscured his face. There was something sinister in the way he had pulled down the hood so he could see her house, but she couldn't clearly see his face. This is scary, she thought, confronting someone I don't know, but I'll be damned if I'll let him watch my house like a stalker. Standing between two tall trees, he first took a step backward. He had seen her. Picking up speed, she glanced both ways and ran across the street, trying not to slide on the gathering snow.

He turned, one hand on a tree, and began backing away, then turned around and raced through the tall pine trees away from her. He had quite a head start, but she climbed up the bank, slipping twice, and ran into the woods after him. The snow was slippery, and she grabbed at tree branches, trying to stay on her feet. She had caught a glimpse of him when she first ran up the snowy bank, but now she saw no one ahead of her. It was easy to follow his prints in the snow, but eventually she came to an area where the pine needles and several branches obscured the path.

After that, she saw prints in several directions. As she moved forward into a clearing, she saw a group of teenagers throwing snowballs and building a snowman at the end of the block. She came to a standstill, looking around the houses across the next street. He could have gone into any of them or even gotten into a car parked on the street. He was gone.

Why would someone be watching my house? she wondered. She wandered back through the clusters of pine trees and followed her path. Then she examined the snow in the area where she had first seen the dark-hooded man. It was dusk and becoming harder to see, but she walked all around the trees on the edge of the woods. Lots of footprints. He had stayed there for some time. His earlier location was protected by the trees, and she saw a patch of yellow grass as if he had been standing there before the snowfall.

Beth examined the ground very carefully, walking around and around the trees. She retrieved her phone from her pocket, shining its light near the base of the trees and found something. Leaning over, she picked up an empty matchbook. It might have fallen out of his pocket, or it might not have anything to do with the watcher. She looked closely, shining her phone light on it. It was really wet from the snow, soggy at best. It looked like piano keys were on the cover. More than that, she couldn't see.

Well, she thought. Yet another mystery. Thank goodness I changed the locks on the doors. Dropping the wet matchbook into her pocket, she glanced at her watch. It was time to go meet the mysterious Dominick Hendrickson.

Chapter Fifteen

Beth walked through the impressive front door of the Third Street Tap at exactly six. Hanging up her coat, she was about to speak to the hostess when a gentleman tapped her lightly on the shoulder and said, "Ms. Russell?"

"Why, yes," she said, and looked at the face of a handsome biracial man, whose skin was a light shade of honey and whose hair was sparse and white.

"I'm Dominick Hendrickson. Please, forgive me all the intrigue. I can assure you it was necessary."

Beth returned his smile and said, "Hello. The intrigue was what brought me here. I'm waiting for you to hand me a rose or something."

He laughed, a deep rumble. Then he said, "Shall we go to our table, and I'll explain, I promise you, over dinner? Oh, and please call me Dom." He nodded to the hostess and offered Beth his arm. Such beautiful manners, Beth thought.

The lights in the restaurant and bar were turned down, with linen on the tables and small, dim lamps. Beth studied the table settings, boasting expensive wine and water stemware and multiple pieces of sterling silver flatware. It reminded Beth of a jazz club back home. As she walked past the opening to the bar, she saw lots of brass fittings and a small, elevated stage for a piano. Even in the dining area, one corner was reserved for a stage with a piano.

Beth couldn't help but notice Dominick Hendrickson was dressed in a well-tailored, black suit with an expensive tie pin through his silver tie and a light blue shirt with silver cufflinks. She was glad she had worn her black dress from the New Year's Eve party. He pulled out her chair and pushed it back in; then he sat down across from her, putting his hand up for a waiter.

After they'd ordered wine and their dinner from an enormous menu where the entrees had no prices, he looked across at her and said, "You are as beautiful as your mother, but a hint of your father resides in the flash of your eyes and the way you carry yourself."

"You knew my parents?"

"I certainly did, Ms. Russell."

"Should I assume this has something to do with the 'intrigue,' as you call it?"

"Very much so. This is a small town and even as we sit here speaking, people are watching us and wondering what we are discussing. The beautiful lady, who is a visitor in town and has green and gold eyes, is the subject of conversation in many corners of the city."

Beth looked around at the other diners. Then, she leaned in, whispering, "Why have you asked me to meet you here?"

"Let us just say our meeting will continue to stir speculation in the minds of people who are very nervous by your presence in town." His voice had a deep timbre and Beth found herself falling under its charming spell.

Before he could say more, Beth was immediately aware of someone behind her. Turning, she saw Sam Conklin and Justin Kaspar.

"Good evening, Beth."

"Hello, Senator, Justin."

"Mr. Hendrickson."

"Senator, Justin."

"Is this some kind of special occasion?" Sam asked.

"Dominick is showing me one of the delightful spots in town," said Beth.

"Interesting," said Justin Kaspar. "And it is—delightful. It's good that you see a few pleasant places here before you go home, Ms. Russell."

"I've decided to stick around for a while, Justin."

Sam moved over to the other corner of the table, closer to Dominick. "Estate matters still to settle?"

"Oh, yes," said Beth. "Enough to keep me busy for a long time.

However, I'm also investigating the historical databases at the college. The librarian assures me she has lots of information on Sweet Iron's history. I want to find out about my mother's murder and what happened to my father. So, I'll be sticking around a bit longer. I'm a researcher, you know."

Sam smiled at her and said, "You're like my own children—never take my advice."

Conklin looked at Dom, and Beth could immediately feel the tension between the two men. "Well, enjoy your dinner." He turned and walked away, Justin Kaspar following.

Beth could see Dom visibly relax.

"As I said, some people are nervous about your presence in town. They would like to see you back in New York City."

"They may have to wait a few weeks," said Beth.

Dom smiled and put his hand up for the waiter, who had been waiting for Sam and Justin to leave.

Beth unfolded her linen napkin, placed it on her lap, and waited as the sommelier poured a little wine in Dom's glass. Once he had swirled a sample of wine and tasted it, he nodded to the waiter, who poured their wine and left. Beth said, "You obviously want something from me, so perhaps we should begin with your request."

"Another of your father's traits—skipping the preliminaries. And you are correct. I am afraid my request must come after a story. After all, an elegant dinner with a new acquaintance is best eaten at a leisurely pace. Don't you agree?"

"This seems to be your program tonight, so I'll enjoy the pleasant company and listen to what you have to say."

At that, his face relaxed into a smile again, his white teeth perfectly aligned and his hand graceful as he took another sip of wine. "It all began," he said, "when I met your father at five years of age. We may as well have been brothers from the start. I was there when he met your mother the summer before our eighth-grade year. We had paddled over in a canoe to the beach at McClendan Lake, where she was tanning with two of her friends. Of course, we weren't allowed at the lake since it was private, and we didn't 'belong' there, but we were curious. He fell in love with her that very day."

Beth bit her lip instead of rolling her eyes, and she cautioned herself to think before she spoke. "I hope you understand, Mr. Hendrickson, I will hear you out with skeptical thoughts when I consider I might have a mother these days if Brian Nash hadn't murdered her."

He looked down at the tablecloth in front of him for a moment, and then his eyes slowly lifted to hers. "I understand your agitation about the past, but I can assure you that what you believe is not true. It is why I asked to speak with you."

"All right, Dom. I am willing to listen. Please, go on."

He nodded, waiting while the waiter placed salads in front of them. "From that day forward, he spent every waking hour trying to figure out how to see her. I can attest to that fact since Jimbo Mead, Brian, and I enjoyed many days fishing at the river in the summer. Melanie lived, you see, in a mansion, and he was the poor kid down in the village. Melanie Tippitt was the most beautiful girl he'd ever seen, and he found ways to see her both in school and in the hours outside of school."

"Did my mother reciprocate his feelings?"

"Very much so. Brian was young and charming, but his future was in doubt and he was not of her social class. Melanie loved to taunt her parents with his lack of pedigree, but she had fallen hard for him. The judge and his wife tried everything: they took away her car, her phone privileges, her allowance, and even threatened to send her away to a private school. Still, she found ways to escape the house and see him. I'm sure the source of rebellion sprang from her youthfulness. But let me assure you, she cared very much for your father. She had no power when it came to arguments with her parents. Then, of course, she became pregnant with you."

Beth nodded, her lips set in a tight line. "Ah, yes. I have heard my conception explained as quite a dilemma. Might you describe it any differently?"

"Certainly, a dilemma for some, but a gift as far as Brian was concerned. I suppose we might say he was living in a dream because it would be difficult, if not impossible, to raise a child in those circumstances. The Tippitts made arrangements that did not include Brian, and when your mother disappeared, he was beside himself.

This child—you—was also his child, but that mattered not. The judge had him arrested when he pounded on their door demanding to know what they had done with Melanie and you."

"Really? I didn't realize how he felt about this whole situation."

Dominick reached across the table with one hand, as if to implore her. "Rest assured, he wanted to keep you, and he would have loved you as he loved your mother. I know it may seem strange to believe a seventeen-year-old would be so certain he could handle this, but you didn't know your father. Melanie was not as strong, at least not then."

While they paused for the waiter to place their dinner plates on the table, Beth considered his words. Perhaps she would be wise to do some investigating into Brian Nash's side of the story. So far, except for Ken Muir's talk with her, she had only heard about Melanie Tippitt.

"When Melanie returned the summer before their senior year, she had changed. Brian used to say the light had gone out of her eyes, and she admitted defeat at the hands of her family. He saw her from a distance, but his dream had ended."

"At the risk of seeming ungrateful for your concern, I must say this is beginning to sound like Jay Gatsby and Daisy," Beth said. "That didn't end well either." She slowly shook her head.

Dom smiled at her remark. "Many love stories begin like *The Great Gatsby*. In this case, they did return to each other, but not before Vietnam happened."

"Ah, yes. That was the war that killed my uncle."

"Yes. It was a classic war of classes. Boys like Jeff Tippitt, pushed by his father to be patriotic and return a hero, went into the conflict to fly helicopters since he was already a pilot who'd been flying for several years. Others, brown boys like me or poor white boys like your father, died together in the rice paddies and in helicopters that came crashing to the earth under heavy fire. The war divided the town even more into socioeconomic classes. Brian and I went into the army together after high school graduation. We heard rumors of a draft coming, and neither of us had a deferment, so we figured we might as well join so we could at least stay together.

"For Brian, it was a chance to get away from Sweet Iron and think about his increasingly impossible situation with Melanie. For me, it was to be an adventure. Brian hatched all kinds of plans, most of which he eventually rejected. He became more and more depressed until, one day, he received a letter from Melanie. She had not forgotten him after all. Several months later, the letters from her stopped. He heard from Jimbo she was dating Sam Conklin, the Yale University wonder whose life was filled with great expectations."

"I've met Sam Conklin, but only briefly," Beth said. "I think I'm glad my mother never ended up with him."

Hendrickson nodded, saying, "On that we can agree."

"Somehow my father and mother must have eventually seen each other again, or did she stay with Sam Conklin until she died?"

"Actually, Melanie was seeing both at that time. But how it happened takes us back to Vietnam. Your father—I can attest—slipped into a deep depression when he heard about Conklin. He began smoking more weed and drinking more. Besides that, he volunteered for reckless duty, like walking point—where he went out ahead of a column to test the area for enemies. That person was the easiest target for the Viet Cong. But Brian survived. We were often hit by tracer rounds when on patrol, or mortar rounds at night. He was still smoking too much weed, drinking too much, and having nightmares almost nightly. Finally, he changed course again and began to think he had been saved for a special purpose, and that destiny was to come back to Sweet Iron, marry Melanie, and find you."

Beth looked at Dominick as he paused. She said, "They were going to find me? That's the first time I've heard such a plan. I keep hearing he was still doing those risky acts when he came back home. How is that the choice of someone who thinks he has a destiny?"

"That is not true," Dominick said. "I was with him the morning your mother died. He was doing well, as well as he could. Brian worked amazingly hard to get himself back into some semblance of order, so he could put a plan into effect. Yes, he still was trying to overcome drugs, alcohol, nightmares. He had an idea for a business he could start, and then he would be able to support your mother and you."

"How could he do that with no money to start up a business?"

"He didn't explain to me, but he was quite optimistic. He'd been seeing your mother again, despite her outward appearance of dating Sam Conklin. His whole bearing had become confident and excited once more. He was sure they had a future. Her parents approved of Sam, so as long as Melanie was seeing him, her parents were happy. Then she would sneak out after a date with Sam and see your father. I understand that this may seem devious—to see Conklin but love Brian. However, the two of them were desperate to be together. They even discussed breaking into the lawyer's office to determine your location."

"This still doesn't explain why you believe he was innocent in the death of my mother."

"Patience, my dear. Here is where we come to that point." He suddenly looked beyond Beth's shoulder and nodded to someone she couldn't see. "I believe we will have a brief intermission first."

Chapter Sixteen

A tall African-American man pulled out one of the empty chairs at Beth and Dom's table, but before he made a move to sit down, Dom introduced him. He was as dark as Dom was light, with a smooth face and eyes that seemed to twinkle. Dressed as fashionably as Dom, he stood with a casual bearing as if he were quite at home in the club.

"Beth, this is Jerod Enslow, owner of the Third Street Tap. Jerod, Beth Russell."

"Good evening, Ms. Russell. I welcome you to my establishment."

"It is quite an elegant place, and our food was delicious," she said. "What a gem your restaurant is in such a small town in the middle of the Midwest."

"I thank you and will convey your thoughts to my chef. We have a jazz pianist who is quite good, along with a bass player, trombone, and trumpet players on the weekends. I don't know if you like jazz, but I invite you to stop in and hear their talented work."

"Sounds wonderful, Mr. Enslow."

"Oh, please. Call me Jerod."

"I will. I do enjoy jazz, and I've listened to it in New York City at a number of clubs, but my favorites are the Blue Note and Dizzy's."

Enslow smiled. "You have excellent taste, Ms. Russell."

"Make it Beth. Thank you. I assume you and Dom are friends?"

"Yes, we go way back," said Dom. "Jerod didn't grow up here, but decided this area would be a prime location for good food and jazz, and his club is packed on the weekends."

"A little slower on weeknights like tonight," Jerod said. He put his hand up, and immediately a waiter was on the spot. "Please, bring my friends some—" He glanced at Beth.

"Coffee."

"Yes, make it three," he added, nodding at Dom.

"So why exactly are you double-teaming me tonight? I can feel the vibes of collusion hanging in the air," said Beth.

Both the men laughed, and Jerod said, "Yes, the lady is intuitive, as well as lovely." He poured some cream into his coffee and waited for the waiter to leave before speaking again. "I would like to tell you a brief story about how I came to start my club here, Beth. Would that be all right?"

"Sure," she said. "So far this has been quite an educational evening. Please do."

"Thirty years ago, when I was twenty, I was imprisoned for a crime I didn't commit. No one would listen. Everyone knew I was guilty. I had few resources, and, let's just say the balance in the hand of the blindfolded Lady Justice is not always level when it comes to an accused black person with few resources."

"How terrible!"

"You've heard of organizations like the Innocence Project?"

"Of course."

Jerod took a sip of coffee and continued. "I began my own innocence project. I kept up my strength and resolve and studied law every day in prison. Eventually, DNA exonerated me, and I left prison after twenty years with a hefty settlement from the state of Indiana. Before I decided how to use this settlement money, I traveled throughout the Midwest figuring I would open a restaurant or lounge, but I wasn't sure where. I ended up settling here because this property was available, and it seemed like a good possibility. Now people from Chicago, Peoria, the Quad Cities, and even St. Louis come here to hear jazz and eat at my table. I hire only the best, and I treat them well. Some of my employees have been in prison."

"It sounds like you made some sound financial decisions," Beth said. She glanced at Dom. "How did you two become friends?"

"Oh, that is a much longer story," said Dom, "best saved for another night."

Jerod said, "One of the people who brought us together was your father."

"How?"

"I met your father, Brian, in prison. We were both in an AA program there. Nowadays, I go to the Illinois prison at Hillsdale, about twenty-five minutes away, and help other inmates who want to turn over wrongful convictions. It is meaningful work, and this location allows me the luxury of doing this once a week. I have an intuitive sense of whether someone is lying to me, and over the years I have been able to use that to help many people who were innocent. My feeling is that your father was one of those, although he served his sentence.

"AA saved your father. While I knew him, he never took another drink. But more to the point, he found himself by helping other members, and he was especially understanding of those who had been in Vietnam and were ensnared in the tentacles of PTSD."

Dom took over the conversation at this point.

Tag teaming me, thought Beth.

"To finish my story, Beth, the day of your mother's death I was working. I didn't go to the pond even though I knew Conklin and his friends often went out there on the weekends. Word spread like wildfire about your mother, and I heard Brian was in the hospital. The moment I could leave work, I raced to the hospital, but he was in a coma. I talked to his parents, his mother crying, and his father stern and stoic."

"His coma was from the car accident?"

"Yes, the car accident coming back from the pond. Lost control of the car and hit a tree off the side of the pond road. I found his hospital room, but even then, a policeman was stationed outside his door. I figured no matter what had happened, he was doomed. Here you had Sam Conklin, his powerful family, and his buddies, and Judge Tippitt and his contacts, so your father had no chance."

"The problem is, Dom, I haven't heard anything about his innocence. Everything I've heard points straight to him. Who else?"

"Have you read the coverage of the trial?"

"Well, no, not yet."

"I think you should do that," said Jerod. "Then we can talk more if you'd like."

"When Brian went into that trial, he was depressed, had no future, and simply lost his will to go on. I was really worried about him," said Dom, "worried that he might kill himself. All he thought about or talked about 24/7 in Vietnam was your mother."

"That still doesn't make him innocent," said Beth.

"Here's something you might want to consider. He and Melanie picked out wedding rings. He had hers engraved on the inside of the band. I saw the rings, but they have never been found. A man with a plan like that—he isn't going to turn around and kill the woman he loves, the woman he's waited for during that whole tour of Vietnam."

"How could he afford those rings? Why didn't anyone find a receipt?"

"He had saved his money to buy them, but no receipt existed because he bought them from a friend, someone who had occasion to acquire such things."

"Where are those rings now? Do you suppose the family destroyed them? With Janet's anger, I could imagine that happening." Beth paused and said nothing for a moment. Then she looked at Jerod and said, "And where do you fit into this? Why are you so interested in all of this?"

"Your father told me about your mother and his love for her. You have those same exotic eyes he described to me in prison. Why am I interested? Because I believe your father was railroaded. I believe in his innocence, and I'd like to see justice done," said Jerod Enslow. "My feeling, from what I hear about your intelligence and determination, is that you, too, find justice important."

Again, Beth looked down at her coffee and considered carefully what she should say. "I have, as you say, decided to delve into the murder back in 1971. I want to know how it happened. How my father was convicted. Even more, I'd like to find out what happened to my biological father. Where is he now? Is he dead?"

Jerod glanced at Dom as if they were deciding which one should answer that question. Then Dom said, "He disappeared after he did his prison time and his parole."

Beth drew a deep breath and looked at each of them, noting the plea in their eyes. "What do you want of me? This all happened long ago, and I don't even know my parents."

Jerod looked at her and said, "We heard you are an amazing researcher. This means you ask probing questions. We want you to find out the truth. Would you at least think about it?"

"Beth, Brian was like a brother to me. I went to 'Nam with him, and I visited him in prison. I'm telling you the man I knew could never have killed your mother. He loved her too much," Dom said.

"This seems like a wild-goose chase. They must have had overwhelming evidence. He was found guilty."

Jerod paused before he added, "So was I."

Chapter Seventeen

As Beth drove home from the Third Street Tap, she thought about the law and the stories her lawyer-father had often told her about poor clients, outsiders. Brian Nash was an outsider. That theme kept coming up no matter who talked about him, well, other than Janet Landry, who hated him. She wondered, if my father didn't kill my mother, who did? Who else would have a motive?

One thing's for sure: Jerod was right that innocent people go to prison every day. Ken Muir seemed to think the judge tipped the scales of justice with the pressure he exerted to railroad my father. She could understand that her grandfather was grieving, but what if her father was innocent? That's a tough question to answer, since none of the people she had met had given the impression they would have harmed Melanie. Maybe researching the trial would help her figure that out.

She sighed, as she turned on to Broad Street, brightening at the porch light she had left on. She saw someone sitting on her porch steps. As she drove closer to the house, she could see it was Kyle. She pulled into the drive and opened her car window.

"Looking for someone?" she asked.

He stood up and walked over to her car. "Hi, Long Island girl. Looks like you've been out for a night on the town. Thought I'd stop in."

"Oh, fantastic. Just let me put the car away, and I'll open the door."

Once they were in the house, Kyle said, "Wow. You look very nice. All dressed up. Big night on the town?"

"I met Dominick Hendrickson at the Third Street Tap. Do you

know him?"

"Sure."

"He also introduced me to Jerod Enslow. I gather you might know him because of his work with people at the prison."

"Yes, our paths have crossed quite often. I admire the work he does. Sometimes the justice system does get it wrong." He smiled at her and added, "Don't quote me on that, please."

"Brrr. I have goose bumps. Old houses are drafty. Can you stay for a while? Have a glass of wine? Should I light a fire in the living room?"

"Sure."

"Would you like a glass of wine or would you like coffee?"

"Wine sounds fine."

"I have a nice pinot grigio."

Once they were settled on the sofa in the living room, she kicked off her black pumps, pulled her legs up under her, and took a deep breath as the fire warmed the room. Kyle handed her a photo.

"Now you must remember this is an arrest photo. It was taken after Brian Nash came out of a coma in the hospital, so he looks drugged up and awful."

Beth took the photo and examined the face of her father. Young, he was so young. His long hair hung loose, and his dark brown eyes looked vacant and lost. He had a scraggly beard, also dark, and his complexion was swarthy, quite a contrast to her blond mother. She looked more closely. "I have his nose, and the shape of his ears. How strange to see the face of a father I never knew. And he still has cuts and bandages, I suppose from the car accident."

"I'd imagine."

"I wonder what he'd look like today. How old would he be? Let's see. Around sixty-six, maybe? Probably his picture now would be radically different, without the wildness of that time."

"I doubt that his hair would look like that," Kyle said, "and maybe he doesn't have hair anymore, or maybe it would be gray."

"Dom and Jerod said he disappeared after he finished his prison term and parole. Could he still be alive?"

"It's possible. Would you like me to do some tracing on that?"

She picked up her wineglass and seemed to mull over his idea. "Yes, please do. I could try to find him, too. I decided, while I was talking to Dom and Jerod, to do some research of my own. I'm going to go over to Molly's college library and use her databases to read about my mother's death and about the trial."

"What about going back to New York City? I thought you couldn't wait to get away from Sweet Iron."

"That's a good question. Right now, I'm between jobs, and it hasn't dawned on me yet that with this inheritance I wouldn't even have to do my next job, although I love researching." She took another sip of her wine.

Kyle looked at her, his eyes intent, and said, "I was hoping you might stay a bit longer."

Beth hesitated, thinking about what she should say. She put her hand on his and said, "I'll be glad to stay a little longer. I hope if I need help or have questions, maybe you could be that go-to person." She leaned back on the sofa, taking her hand away, and lifted her voice happily. "I don't know anything about you, Kyle Warner, except that you grew up near Milwaukee. So, who are you?"

He smiled back at her and said, "So it's time to turn the interrogation tables on me, right?" Then he chuckled.

"Absolutely. Here I am in my house with a man I hardly know. But somehow, in Sweet Iron, it seems perfectly normal. After all, you are the police."

"Yes. Well. Hmmm." He hemmed and hawed, trying to think about where to start. "I was raised in Milwaukee. Have two siblings, a brother now in Denver, Greg, who is an IT guy, and a sister, Holly, who lives in Houston, Texas, married and has three kids. She's a teacher. Her husband owns a business."

"That sounds like a good start," Beth said, trying to coax more information out of him.

"I went to college at Illinois Wesleyan and graduated in 1991... police academy in '93 and answered an ad for the St. Louis Police Department. Married Sarah—I'd met her in college—and we settled down in St. Louis while I climbed up the ranks to detective."

"Oh, so you're married," Beth said, thinking it was a good thing she'd pulled her hand away.

"Was."

"Divorced?"

"No. We decided to start a family and had a great deal of trouble getting pregnant. So, while they were doing tests, they discovered she had cervical cancer. She passed away in 2008."

"Oh, I'm so sorry," she said.

He turned to her and shook his head slightly. "It's okay. At first, I just buried myself in work. Then I decided to leave the St. Louis area. Too many memories."

"I understand," she said quietly.

"And you? No husband? Boyfriend?" he asked.

"Oh, I've had a few close calls. I was engaged once."

"Really? Did you call it off or did he?" He paused. "That was a dumb thing to ask, judging from your face."

"No, no, it's all right. It was so long ago. I met Richard in college. He was two years ahead of me and from out East, like me. Grew up in a family where he was the youngest of six kids. He really struggled to pay for school. After he graduated, he joined the army, thinking he'd be able to get money for grad school once he got out. We figured we'd get married after I graduated... but another rabbit hole, another direction."

Kyle waited through the silence and then asked, "He didn't come back?"

"No. He died in the First Gulf War—December 15, 1990." She looked at the flames in the fireplace. "Funny, one hundred forty-six soldiers killed, and I don't know, even now, which number he was."

"I guess we've both struggled with the deaths of people we love. You never forget, but you try to get on with your life. So, you've had other—what you call—'close calls?'"

She laughed. "I suppose that's a funny way to put it. I never found someone like Richard again. I guess it's that adage about your first love—you compare every one after that to the first. No, no serious relationships. I've dated off-and-on, but it always seemed they didn't value the work I did or feel it was as important as theirs. Something about an intelligent woman threatened them."

"That settles it. I've been looking for an intelligent woman all my life, so I won't have to think so hard about all the difficult decisions!"

Beth looked at his face with shock. "You're kidding, right?"

"Yes." And they both laughed.

"How long have you lived in Sweet Iron?" she asked.

"I came here to work in 2009, and I've been here ever since. I like the town and the people. Not a lot of crime. Oh, break-ins, like the one you had. Murder, though, is highly unusual, and that's why I know about the Tippitt murder. And you? Where did you grow up?"

Beth considered the swirling wine in her glass, thinking about what to say. "Well, I grew up in a small town in upstate New York. My father's death when I was fourteen left me with a paranoid mother. Now I know why—she lived in fear I'd be reclaimed by the Tippitt family."

"And you never knew you were adopted." He said it like a statement of fact.

"Correct." She looked back at the flames in the fireplace. "Maybe that's why I've always been fascinated by the historical research I do."

"Because of your own family history?"

She laughed. "Actually, I had no family history until now." She took a small sip of wine. "I remember a horrible day in seventh grade when my history teacher assigned a project on the Depression. I was supposed to interview a grandparent or great aunt or uncle. My mother explained that we didn't have any relatives still living who had experienced that. But my friend Ally's mom offered Ally's grandmother. That should have solved the problem, of course," she said. "However, one of the class bullies made fun of me because I had to 'borrow' another family. I had been angry with my mother at the time." The tightness of guilt spread through her chest, guilt at being angry with her adopted parents who had brought her up and loved her. She was quiet for a moment. "I guess I gravitated toward history because it's the adventure of the road chosen."

He cocked his head to the side. "How so?"

"I've always been fascinated by one event, one decision, one unexpected element of a situation that sends history down a different road. The domino theory in the 1960s—its believers sending 58,000 American boys to their deaths in Vietnam, not to mention thousands of Vietnamese casualties. Think of all the lives that went in different directions because of the deaths of people they loved. Everyone has a story, you know."

Kyle took up her refrain. "Like Robert E. Lee's decision to leave Gettysburg after three days, a mistake that cost the South the war? If he'd stayed and mounted another battle, they would have won. Think about the changes that would have made."

"Now you see what I mean. Even today, we see reverberations on the news from that terrible time. Just think, if Lincoln hadn't been assassinated, moving Johnson into office, that bitter Reconstruction Period might never have happened. One event, one decision, and history goes down a different rabbit hole. I love researching facts. They're always the same. People, well, often they let you down. My friend Gabby, of course, is the exception," said Beth.

"I see. And speaking of events causing changes, I suppose the same could be said of the Tippitts' decision to have you adopted," said Kyle.

"So true." She looked at him and laughed. "So maudlin. Let's talk about something less dark." She paused. "What do you do when you're not working?"

Kyle laughed. "I have some things I do for fun, I guess you'd say." He turned back to her. "Some people would say my life is quiet or boring, but I like it in a small town. I go to a local gym to work out, I play a little piano, and I love country music. We have a couple of clubs that have live music, and I go to those quite often. I hang around with friends I work with, but most of them are married. I have a classic car, a Corvette L88, that I work on when I can afford to buy more parts. I'm afraid that's an expensive hobby." He stopped and thought about what else to say. "Oh, and I go to the shooting range. I like to keep my skills up."

"Really?" Beth said. "Me, too. I think I mentioned my father got me started years ago. He loved collecting guns, and it was a way for us to—to connect. He was an attorney, always busy, and often gone. But when we went target-shooting together, we shared a love of the sport. I have wonderful memories of those trips to our property out in the country. He relaxed then, and I felt as if he cared for me." She looked at the fire a moment. "Of course, I had to leave my own gun in New York because you guys don't have a reciprocal agreement. Shame on you," she said jokingly.

He laughed and said, "If you stay six months as a resident, you'll be able to shoot again."

"Six months. Not sure I'm going to be here that long. It isn't in my plans."

He sat there quietly, thinking about what she had said. "This job you have—the research for authors. Do you only need a good library?"

"Yes, and a way to travel if I have to check out settings for them."

"Seems to me you'll find that Molly has an excellent library. I've read that the college has great resources. I know they have a huge endowment. Some of it is probably Tippitt money. Maybe you'll find that you can do your research here. International airports are easily within driving distance. Less than an hour." He took a last sip of wine and set his glass down on the end table. "Well, it's time I'm off. As you said just minutes ago, you never know what's coming down the road." He walked out to the foyer, Beth following him, and grabbed his jacket. "I think you'll find intelligent women don't scare me one bit, Ms. Russell." Then he leaned over and kissed her, a brief kiss on the lips. Suddenly, she put her arms around him and kissed him back.

Finally, he pulled away. "Goodnight, Beth," he said, and he was out the door, leaving her speechless.

Well, she thought, this certainly complicates things.

Chapter Eighteen

The following morning found Beth tapping away on her computer, trying to find a death date for Brian Nash. Suddenly, she slammed a pile of papers on the desk, pushed her chair back and stood up. Walking around in a circle, she stopped and stared out the dining room window. He must be in here somewhere, she thought.

She had found his birth on September 23, 1950. Brian Jameson Nash, son of Brian Sr. and Cindy Riverton Nash in the hospital in Sweet Iron. This means if he were alive today, she mused, he would be sixty-six years old.

She sat down again and checked out social security to see if anything had been filed at the time of his death: nothing. Dead end. Newspaper sites with obituaries were often hit-and-miss as far as getting deaths consistently into databases. They must actually be submitted, and Beth had spent more than one frustrating job trying to find a death that was never listed.

A gravesite database had nothing. She did a general search of a genealogical database, the same one that had yielded information on the Tippitt family. She could use his year of birth since she knew he was born in Sweet Iron and try to trace his death that way. However, after a fruitless hour, she gave up on that, too.

Prison records. Maybe Kyle could help her there. He could find out when Brian Nash was released and see if he could follow up with his last known whereabouts or his death. Perhaps he had more information at his disposal since Brian Nash had a prison record.

That last thought left her staring at the computer screen. Her father had a prison record. He killed her mother. Hatcher had said to just let it go, but she couldn't.

Why? Why? Why? What happened that day at Tippitt Pond?

Chapter Nineteen

B eth walked in the doors of McClendan College Library early on
Wednesday morning. She gazed across the expansive room, filled
with wooden library tables on carved pedestal legs. It was like home
to her. She had spent so many years in libraries; their smell of books
and paper and wood had become part of her very breathing. It was an
elegant facility, with tall windows allowing the light to stream in, and
long wooden tables like the New York City Public Library. Shelves
of books filled half the first floor, and the rest were undoubtedly in
the basement and a floor above. The place was deserted because of
Christmas break. A wide staircase led up to the second floor from the
front desk, and Beth figured Molly's office was somewhere near that
desk. She poked around a little, picking up an issue of the college
newspaper. Then she walked around the desk and began checking
the names on office doors. The third one was Molly's. The door was
open.

"Oh, you found me. Fantastic. I have a spot all set up for you,
and the coffee shop has only one canister of coffee going since the
students aren't here. But that's enough for about ten cups apiece!"

"Thanks," said Beth. "Brought my notebook and I'm ready to find
out about my parents' pasts."

"We have numerous databases about history, so if you wanted to do
your own research for your job here, you could, you know. We have
America: History and Life, Historical Abstracts for world history, and
many historical newspaper databases like *New York Times* Historical,
Chicago Tribune Historical, or NewspaperArchive.com. In addition,
we have at least thirty other historical research databases. They're all

listed on our website. What you'll want now are the local newspapers, and I have those all set up for you at this station over here."

After she demonstrated logging into the college's system, Molly left her alone to look at the old newspapers. It didn't take long to find the story about the discovery of her mother's body. July 20, 1971, the *Sweet Iron Sentinel*. Nothing came up on that day, but the next day's paper had a story about the death and a photo of the pond with police standing around a hearse.

Front-page news, Beth said to herself. "The police were called to the scene just after 3 p.m., and found the body of Melanie Tippitt, age nineteen, lying on the shore where she had been pulled out of the pond. Police suspect foul play and are investigating a person of interest." That would be my father, thought Beth. More details would become available after the initial investigation. Not a lot of coverage, but most likely the judge made sure they published as little as possible. Two days later came the article reporting the arrest of Brian Nash, age twenty. He was taken into custody at the hospital and charged with murder.

In that same paper was Melanie Tippitt's obituary. Beth stared at the photo—her high school senior picture. What a beautiful woman my mother was, she thought. The obituary followed the usual format with her birth in 1952 to her mother, Joellen Dawes Tippitt and father, Judge Emerson Tippitt. Her younger brother, Jeff, was deceased in 1967, and her sister Janet (Neal) Landry survived in Fort Worth, Texas. Memorials were left to McClendan College. Ah, but there is one other survivor, Beth thought.

She stopped for a moment and took a sip of her coffee. Then she got up and walked around the space over by the main desk, just to stretch her legs and blink her eyes. She supposed the newspaper would report the trial, starting with the opening statements and discussing the various witnesses. It would be interesting to see what those now-adult witnesses said when they were in their late teens or early twenties. She sat back down, did a few exercises with the joints of her fingers, and got back to it.

The trial began in early September, six weeks after the murder. The Honorable Matthew Weston was presiding with Alexander Plank, the district attorney, and Kenneth Muir, the public defender. It took them a week to seat a jury, and the result was twelve men. Beth sighed. Evidently, women were still not serving on juries in small towns. It's amazing, thought Beth, that they could find a jury in the town without changing the venue. But, as Ken Muir said, that made it possible for Judge Tippitt to help run the show.

Once she came to the description of the beginning of the trial, Beth was easily able to follow its course over a week. That was it? Only one week? Alexander Plank explained in his opening statement that on the afternoon of July 20, Melanie Tippitt was murdered by a blow to the head at Tippitt Pond. Her body was dropped into the pond after death by one Brian Nash. The motive for this heinous crime was jealousy. Pure and simple. The victim and Mr. Nash had been friends and dated prior to that summer, but on that day, Melanie Tippitt told him she and Mr. Sam Conklin were going to announce their engagement. In a jealous rage, he maliciously hit her with a piece of wood found on the shore and tossed her body into the pond.

Beth heard the front door of the library open, disturbing her concentration. But she didn't see anyone come past the main desk, so she went back to her reading.

DA Plank finished his opening statement: "Brian Nash is a cold-hearted killer who saw no other way to keep Sam Conklin from having Melanie Tippitt. He came back from Vietnam with anger in his heart, and murder came easily to him after his wartime experience. No one else was with the victim during that window of opportunity. No one else had a motive. Because of this murderer, a young woman from a fine family with her whole life ahead of her was brutally slain. Brian Nash decided to end her life in an act of pure evil that day at Tippitt Pond. I implore the jury to find Brian Nash guilty of first-degree murder."

Well, thought Beth. That was a very straightforward, clear narrative of what he planned to prove. She wasn't sure any of the teenagers who were there that day had a motive to kill her mother. He sure paints Brian Nash in a malevolent light.

Ken Muir followed Plank with a shorter speech that explained that the defense didn't really have to prove a thing. It was up to the prosecution to find evidence that showed, beyond a reasonable doubt, that Brian Nash did this terrible act. Unfortunately for the prosecution, all the evidence was circumstantial. No one saw what happened at the lake that day. Brian Nash had a subsequent car accident and didn't even remember what had occurred. Unless the prosecution could put his client at the pond committing this murder, the jury would need to find Nash innocent, he argued.

"Yes, Brian Nash came back from Vietnam a changed man. So did many others who have gone on to live respectable lives. But Brian was struggling to rid himself of drugs, and he was winning the battle each day. Since he loved Melanie Tippitt, he would never ever have done anything to harm her. In fact, she had consented to be his wife. She had no intention of marrying Sam Conklin. Gentlemen of the jury, jealousy was not a motive here. Despite the testimony you will hear from Sam Conklin's friends, Brian Nash and Melanie Tippitt had plans to elope the following day. You will hear the testimony of Brian's friends, who were aware of their plans. The defendant did not go to Tippitt Pond that day to kill Melanie Tippitt. Instead, he loved her, and their future was torn apart by whoever killed her. That day at Tippitt Pond, he had only love in his heart for his longtime girlfriend, Melanie Tippitt."

That pretty much sums up each side, thought Beth.

About that time, Molly came across the room and sat down in the chair next to her.

"Found anything yet that surprises you?" she asked.

"So far, I don't know enough about what happened. I'm only at the opening statements. I find it strange that they believed Brian Nash guilty when no one knew what happened for sure. No one saw the murder."

"You aren't to the end yet. Your father brought an abrupt end to the trial when he decided to change his plea."

"I wonder why," said Beth. "It sounded like he would get off."

Molly shook her head. "It's hard to know when you're reading about it years later."

"Seems to me I should consider the old motive, means, and opportunity idea. Any of them had the means since the murder weapon was right there. But Brian Nash was the only one alone with her. I'm getting confusing testimony about his state of mind that day, and I have no idea why he might have had a motive to kill her, especially if he planned to marry her, as Dominick Hendrickson has indicated."

"From what I read," Molly said, "I'm not sure why any of those kids had a motive to kill Melanie Tippitt. S'pose it could have been an accident?"

Beth shook her head. "If it were, how did it happen, why didn't someone admit it, and why would Brian Nash say he killed her? The more I read about it, the more mixed up the whole thing seems."

Molly smiled and stood up. "I think I'm going back to the book orders. They are strictly black and white, with no areas of gray. I'll leave all of this to you."

Beth picked up her pen and began taking notes again. After forty-five minutes, she had read a summary of the testimony by Justin Kasper, Sam Conklin, Shelly Andrews, and Elisha Foster. They were the principal witnesses. She rubbed her eyes, stood up, and ventured over to the restroom. Then she went in search of more coffee.

"Hi, Beth," she heard as she walked into the coffee shop. It was Ken Muir, sitting at a table in his sweatpants and sweatshirt, with a steaming cup of coffee and the *Wall Street Journal*.

"Oh, hello. I didn't realize you were here."

"I stop in occasionally to read the newspapers. Call it a privilege of being retired."

She nodded and pushed the button on the coffee canister.

"Making any headway on the murder trial research?"

"Boy, I don't know how you ever did that public defender job, or any attorney job in a murder trial for that matter. Mind if I sit down?"

"Not at all. Please do. I make a good listener."

Beth stirred her coffee and thought about where to start. "I wish I understood better the relationships within that group. It seems to me that Shelly Andrews was not really like the others."

"In what way?"

"She was closer to Brian Nash in the past, I think, because she talks about how he'd talk with her whenever he left one dating relationship for another. He and Shelly came from the same side of town. She wasn't affluent like the others, but she was more like Brian Nash. Melanie was kind to her and included her in what they did, but I had the feeling Shelly knew they were keeping her around on sufferance. I can see where the group split up that day. The guys went into town, leaving Elisha, Shelly, and Melanie at the pond. So, whatever happened occurred when the guys were gone."

"That is true. Justin and Sam said they went back to town for more food and Justin's guitar. More likely more beer and weed, I'd guess. As they reached town, they saw Brian driving toward the pond. It's about twelve miles from town to the pond. Later, when Sam and Justin returned to the pond, they found out Melanie had been murdered. Brian's car had rolled down an embankment, and Sam and Justin didn't see it. Shelly and Justin reported the murder at the police station. No cell phones back then. I remember Shelly Andrews was very emotional at the trial. We had to stop several times so she could get herself back together."

Beth sorted through her ideas, trying to untangle this story she hadn't experienced herself. "I get the feeling she was one of the chief witnesses who said Brian showed up at the pond both drunk and high."

"Yes. Erratic behavior. And yet, when they checked his blood levels after his car accident, he had nothing in his system. What might that indicate?"

"She lied?"

Muir nodded his head. "I had to be careful on cross not to sound like I was bullying her. She was very fragile. To hear her story, you would believe she was Brian's confidant. He poured his heart out to her, but she believed that Melanie was not worth his pain. Shelly thought Melanie's future was with Sam Conklin. This moves you into the jealousy thing. Motive."

"Another thing I don't understand. Sam Conklin had some abrasions and bruises on his face, hands, and arms. He said they were the result of helping Justin Kaspar lift a canoe down from the top of his car. They evidently almost dropped it. But Justin seemed fine. No bruises."

"He and Sam Conklin were good friends," said Ken, "both headed to Ivy League schools. He, like Sam, became a lawyer, married, and has two kids. He corroborated Sam's account of going into town to get something. He also mentioned the canoe, but I guess it mostly fell on Sam. Kaspar was dating Elisha Foster at the time. Unlike Conklin, Kaspar was middle-class, without the advantages Sam had."

"Hmm. I'll have to think about this a lot more. I have the general lay of the land as far as what happened that day."

Ken Muir smiled at her. "I wouldn't be so sure."

She smiled. "Well, do you have any advice for me?"

He chuckled. "My lawyering days are over, but a couple of things stand out to me. You may do what you want with them. First, as a lawyer, I'd start with the weakest link."

"And that would be Shelly Andrews, right?"

"Yes. Call it intuition or instinct, but every time I questioned her, I thought she seemed to act guilty about something. If she was jealous of Melanie and wanted Brian Nash for herself, she could have had a motive to kill Melanie Tippitt. Getting married was all teenage girls thought about back then. Despite the tumultuous times of the sixties, the revolution for women was just getting underway, especially in small towns. You have a wonderful job you love; it's unlikely you might have gone in that direction in the early seventies. Call me cynical, but I think Melanie might have mentioned her plans with Brian Nash to one or both of those women. If so, what might the result have been?"

Beth considered his advice. "That's an interesting theory. Starting with Shelly sounds like a good plan."

"Absolutely. Then I'd ask myself: Why did each of those kids have the exact same story about events that day? Letter-perfect, right down to the minute."

Beth sat in silence for a moment. "You think they might have concocted some story they all agreed to?"

Muir cocked his head sideways and one eyebrow went up. "I can't prove that. But, since they did, you should ask, 'Why?'"

*****

The library steps and sidewalk had been cleared of the earlier snow, and Beth figured the students still had at least another week before returning. For a moment, she stood on the top step of the library's porch looking out over the campus. It truly was a beautiful sight— red brick colonial buildings with huge, white pillars, and off to her right, the football field lying empty under its silent blanket of snow. In the distance, she could see the main building with its bell tower, and the crisscrossed paths of sidewalks connecting it all. What a well-designed campus, she thought. The pristine layer of snow on the grass made it seem like the buildings were waiting for the return of student voices, impromptu snowball fights, and midnight studying. I wonder what I might have been like, Beth thought, if I had gone to a small college like this instead of a huge university? Would I have felt less… anonymous?

She grabbed the metal handrail and was about to head to the parking lot when she saw a woman in a red coat walking two small dogs down the sidewalk toward the library steps. The woman's head was down, eyes watching the sidewalk.

"Shelly?" Beth called out.

Startled, Shelly Andrews looked up at Beth, a frown retreating as she recognized the speaker. She stopped, the shih tzus puzzled by her decision.

"Oh, hi, Beth," she said, keeping a tight hold on the straining leashes. "I thought maybe you'd gone back home."

Beth walked down the three steps and set down her laptop case. "No, I was just using Molly Grayson's library. It's a wonderful facility."

"Oh," said Shelly, looking down at the dogs and avoiding Beth's glance. She seemed to pause and consider her next words. "This doesn't mean you're—you're staying, does it? Are you doing your research job?" Beth saw Shelly's lower lip tremble slightly.

Beth leaned over and petted each of the dogs. Then she stood up and faced Shelly. "No, I'm actually researching my father's trial."

Shelly's eyes seemed to get bigger. "Why would you do that? That's ancient history."

"Maybe for you. After all, you were there. You testified."

"I guess," she said, her shoulders sagging. "There's nothing more to tell."

"Are you sure?"

"Yeah. I try to forget all that. It was traumatic for everyone."

"I was hoping," said Beth, "we could sit down and talk about it once I'm up to speed on the details." She heard the woman's sharp intake of breath.

Shelly looked away into the distance, her body rigid, a struggle on her face. She seemed to be making a decision. She took in a deep breath, an angry look on her face. "I wish you'd never come back here. You look too much like her. Brings back nightmares. I'd put that day away—buried it. Now you're making me remember just by coming back. I won't talk about it."

"Not ever?"

"No—no, not ever," she stammered.

"I hope you'll change your mind. I'm always open to listening. You know where to find me—at Melanie's house."

For a moment, Shelly seemed frozen to the spot. Then she took several steps away. Beth watched her untangle the dogs' leashes and was intrigued to see a terrified look on the woman's face.

"I gotta go," Shelly said, avoiding Beth's stare and moving off down the walk with the two dogs at a rapid clip.

Beth suddenly felt guilty. What a terrible thing to do to her. On the other hand, she is one frightened woman with a buried secret, thought Beth. Ken Muir was right—she's the link to pursue.

Chapter Twenty

The Sweet Iron Inn was a small café that Kyle had described with a menu of soups, sandwiches, and salads for lunch. He had asked her to meet him after her morning at the library.

She walked in, spied him at a booth, and looked around. Definitely not New York City. Gingham curtains with ruffles, numerous wall signs with cute sayings, and well-worn booths along the walls. At least the food might be good, she thought.

Kyle saw her, stood up, and soon they were examining menus in a booth near the back.

"Everything I've had here has been good. They have a great veggie wrap if you're into that, passable chili, and a French dip sandwich that's very tender. I eat here often when I'm working."

"All right, a French dip it is."

"You mean you aren't like those New York City girls who must eat rabbit food for every meal?" Kyle said.

"Not I. I have a great appetite, but I'd better start looking for a gym if I stay here much longer. Besides, we New York City girls are not all alike, you know."

After they ordered, he asked about her research. Beth thought he was genuinely interested and, as always, he was such a great listener.

"Some things stand out to me," said Beth. "I imagine when I go home and think about it all for a while, I'll begin to see inconsistencies and patterns that make some sense. The relationships among the group are not easy to figure out. Loyalties are important, and I imagine loyalty is a subject that might have played a part in my mother's death. They all knew each other for a long time."

He nodded and waited. When she didn't continue he asked, "Did you notice specific inconsistencies that might make a difference? In any trial, we find discrepancies that are part of being human, often just people remembering things inaccurately."

She nodded. "Whether my father, Brian, was sober that day or high on alcohol, pot, or both. Elisha said he was highly disturbed, and she was worried about leaving Melanie with him. Sam Conklin testified that Brian was a crazy man, and he never would have left Melanie with Brian had he known my father was going out to the pond. He believed my mother was naïve, thinking she could help my father with his demons. Plank, the DA, said Brian killed her in a jealous rage because he came home from Vietnam totally out of control, addicted to drugs, and filled with violence. Shelly, who described herself as a friend of Brian's, also said he was angry when he came to the pond."

"It would seem all of their impressions were quite similar."

"Sam Conklin was surmising. He wasn't even at the pond when Melanie died."

Kyle leaned back while the waiter brought their plates with thick French dip sandwiches on sourdough bread. As he opened his napkin and arranged his silverware, he asked, "How do you read that?"

"Two thoughts occur to me. First, Dom Hendrickson saw Brian just before he drove to the pond. He said Brian was perfectly sober and hadn't been on drugs or alcohol for some time at that point."

"Of course," said Kyle, "he was a friend of Brian's, so he might have a reason to say that."

"I agree," said Beth. "However, according to the report from the hospital, Brian's blood tests were perfectly normal. No substances in his blood. To me, the medical evidence surely contradicts what the group was saying about Brian's condition when he showed up. I suppose he could have been angry but not high."

"And, Madame Researcher, what do you make of all that?"

"People are lying?" They both laughed, and Beth continued. "After I thought about it, I went back and reread their testimonies. I found something quite strange. Each of them used almost the exact same words to describe Brian's demeanor when he showed up at the pond."

"You think they were coached?" Kyle asked.

Beth waited until she was done chewing on a perfectly tender piece of roast beef. Then she said, "Could be. Or they were all lying. If so, the question is, why and what were they hiding?"

"Good question."

"Ken Muir suggested I put some pressure on Shelly Andrews. Just saw her at the college. She's upset or guilty or both about something. It has to do with the murder, I'm sure. Just looking at my face gave her heart palpitations. She isn't good at hiding her emotions, and she looks like she hasn't slept for a while."

"Funny you should mention Shelly. Yesterday, I saw her going into Holy Trinity Church during their confession hours. She glanced around before opening the door. I happened to be driving by."

"Only a matter of time before she cracks," said Beth. "Hope I'm still here. I think she has something dark to confess. It's been preying on her, and I feel guilty for taking advantage of her mental state. Maybe I need to go to confession. I'd put money on her knowing something important about that day at Tippitt Pond."

Kyle looked at her for a moment and said nothing. As the silence grew longer, Beth stopped eating, glanced at him and said, "What?"

"Ever think of training to be a detective?"

She sputtered, putting her napkin up to her mouth. "No."

"What else?" he asked.

She put her sandwich down and took a great gulp of water. "Motive. I find inconsistencies in who was jealous of whom. Also, who was planning to marry whom. Sam says he and Melanie, were going to get engaged and then married after law school. Elisha corroborated that idea. She said she was Melanie's best friend. However, she never heard about a ring from Brian, and she said she knew Melanie had made the choice to marry Sam Conklin. According to Elisha, Melanie had 'settled down,' and Sam was the man. She believed the jealousy was on Brian's part because Melanie had chosen Sam."

Kyle wiped off his mouth, put his napkin down, and asked, "Did the group agree with that, too?"

"Conklin believes the reason Brian killed her was because she told him she and Sam planned to get engaged. Shelly said she was worried about leaving Melanie with Brian that day. Justin Kaspar said he was aware of Sam's engagement plan. Again, it seems like a solid front."

"So, is it too great a leap to suggest that Brian was, indeed, jealous? They had an argument over Sam and he either killed her, or somehow it happened as an accident. He had the means, the motive, and the opportunity. The way I read it in the case files, no one else was there. Melanie had sent the other two girls off to that old Whistler mill, so she could talk to Brian."

"Kyle, I agree, absolutely. But then I look at Dom Hendrickson's face and hear his voice, a voice that is so convincing. He swears that he saw those wedding rings Brian said he had, and one was engraved. If so, where did they go?"

The detective sat for a few moments, staring off into space. "Does it connect to someone breaking into your house after you came to town? Granted, they only took a scrapbook that was sitting on the table within easy reach. What if they had had more time and were perhaps looking for those rings? You come to town, stir up trouble because you want some answers, and people start to get nervous. Seem possible?"

"Oh, I don't know, Kyle. I think it's a stretch. I suppose if those rings exist they might be in the house, but I haven't found them. On top of that, Brian Nash didn't have cartloads of money. How would he buy engraved wedding rings? The other idea that bothers me are the scrapes and bruises on Sam Conklin that day. He said they were from unloading the canoe he took out to the pond on top of his car. Justin helped him, but he didn't have any cuts or scrapes. What was that all about?"

Kyle signaled the waitress and asked for more coffee. "Coffee? Dessert?"

Beth laughed. "No, I am full to the top of my head."

Kyle looked at Beth, the two of them done eating, and his index finger moved across the table and touched her hand. "I think, Ms. Russell, you are tweaking my interest in this case. What are the questions we need to have answered?"

"I'd say these are the main ones: Who was my mother dating and planning to marry? Was my father high, drunk, or angry that day? What were the relationships among the group? Who owed loyalty to whom? What secret is Shelly Andrews hiding? Did Brian have wedding rings, and had he given them to my mother? Was my mother the flirtatious type, wanting men to fight over her? Finally, if my father didn't kill her, why did he say he did?" She folded her napkin, set it beside her plate, and turned to look at him. "I think, Mr. Detective, you are helping me sort it out in my mind. Thank you."

Chapter Twenty-One

As she left the restaurant and unlocked her car, Beth heard the text jingle on her phone. Climbing into the front seat, she started the car, turning up the heat. Then she retrieved her phone. The text was from Dominick Hendrickson. He asked if she could meet him at Methodist Nursing Home on Larkspur Lane because he wanted to introduce her to someone. "Sure," she texted back, putting the name of the nursing home in her GPS.

It's so easy, she thought, to change plans because she didn't have to figure out two or three connections to get wherever she was going. Five or ten minutes and she was there. In the city, she could never say "yes" and be there in five minutes. She'd have to make elaborate transportation plans.

The Methodist Nursing Home sat on the west edge of town and appeared to be a recently built structure. Dom met her at the front desk and walked back to a community room with her.

"I mentioned to my aunt that you were in town, and she wanted to meet you. She's having a good day today. Her name is Shirley Denny. She's ninety-three and has been a huge part of my life and was part of your parents' lives, too. She was the housekeeper at the Tippitt home from 1943 to 1975, when she left to take care of her husband's parents. Here, it's just up ahead. She doesn't see so well, but her brain is still sharp."

Beth walked into a common room where only three people were sitting in chairs, playing cards, or watching television. Dom steered her over to an elderly lady in a rocking chair with a blanket over her lap. Her short hair was a fuzzy halo of white, and her eyes peeked out of a field of wrinkles in a face darker than Dom's. She had a large nose, situated in a group of broad lines that connected to her mouth. Beth thought she had never seen so many wrinkles before. A small cross hung from her neck, framed by the cowl neckline of a deep lavender blouse.

"I've brought Beth Russell, Brian and Melanie's daughter, to meet you, Aunt Shirley."

Instantly, the elderly lady's mouth broke into a smile, but her eyes continued to stare straight ahead.

"Oh, please come over here, child," the lady said, putting both of her arms out.

Beth walked over, leaned forward, and gave Dom's aunt both of her hands. When she went to pull back, Shirley gently asked, "Could I touch your face? I don't see well anymore. Would that be okay? My fingers do that for me."

"Sure," said Beth. She leaned over the rocking chair while Dom's aunt put each hand on a check and then explored the shape of her lips, nose, and eyes. Then she sat back with a sigh.

"Oh, child," she said. "You have her lips, the bow just perfect. And I can remember Brian's nose shape, too. It's yours. I don't forget those things. And your eyes and hair? What color are they?"

Dom brought a chair over, and Beth pulled back and sat down. "My hair is blond like my mother's, and my eyes are green with gold flecks."

Suddenly, Mrs. Denny's face broke into a huge smile. "I knew it. I prayed someday that child would survive and find her way home, and here you are! I loved your mama and papa. They were just kids, and often so silly, especially Brian. Sometimes when the judge and his wife were out at a charity event, Brian would sneak in and have some of my peach cobbler. Your mama, she was the belle of the ball—but not with me. She was just little Melanie with me."

"He loved that cobbler, Aunt Shirley," Dom said.

She sat silently for a moment and finally said, "Please, Beth. Just call me 'Aunt Shirley.' I feel like we're family. And how about your life, child? How has that gone?"

"I can't complain Ms.—Aunt Shirley. My adoptive parents passed

129

away, and I've been on my own, but I've had a good life. I do research for writers, and I love what I do."

Again, Dom's aunt thought about her answer and said, "New York City? Is that where Dom told me you lived?"

"Yes, on Long Island."

She shook her head slowly and said, "What a huge place to live. How do you do that? Do you have friends who help you sometimes?"

Beth pressed her lips together, considering how to answer. "I do. Have friends, that is. But I'm used to being on my own."

The silence stretched out as the elderly woman looked straight ahead, still shaking her head a little. She appeared to be digesting "New York City."

Dom pulled up another chair, rearranged the blanket better over his aunt's legs, and sat down. Changing the subject, he said, "Perhaps you could tell Beth about your memories from Tippitt House. She'd probably like to hear about her parents."

"My, my. That was so long ago. Let's see. Where to begin? I loved your mother, and she was like my own baby. In fact, I was twenty-seven when the judge and Mrs. Tippitt brought her home. 1952. She was the light of my life, and if you have her green and gold eyes, you probably look just like her. Beautiful. When she got dressed up to go out, she was a vision. I can see her now in my memory. I loved all three of those children, but Miss Melanie, she was special. She had a lot of beaux as she got older, but she always had a special place in her heart for your father."

"I've been told by so many people about her beauty, but what was she like?"

The elderly lady sat back and pursed her lips. "'S'pose it's hard to explain what someone is like. Well, let's see. What I remember the most is that she was thoughtful. Oh, you know teenagers. They live in a world of their own. But Melanie was always asking me about my family. I got sick one time… I was never sick. But I had some, some—we'd call them 'female problems' back then—and had to have surgery. It was a real worry. That would have been back in— oh—sixty-five. I couldn't go to work, and my husband and I worried about how we'd be able to afford the bills. Miss Melanie came over and brought me chicken noodle soup she'd made herself. When she saw how worried I was, she marched right back over to her father and told him he would have to help because I'd practically raised his children! Imagine that! He was a fierce old man, and she never blinked about standing up to him. She told me later about what she'd done. We hated to take charity, but we didn't know what else to do. Miss Melanie was just like that.

"That was a—a different time—the early nineteen sixties. Even finding a doctor or hospital to do the surgery was hard for us, you know, since we were black. But the judge found us a hospital and doctor in Chicago. He even took care of the transportation. We were forever grateful. Miss Melanie made that happen." She slumped back in her chair, shaking her head slowly back and forth. "She had a fierce loyalty."

"Thank you, Aunt Shirley. That helps me understand her. I find loyalty and kindness virtues that are important."

Dom leaned over and patted his aunt's hand. Turning to Beth, he said, "Of course, my aunt knew your father, too. Aunt Shirley was worried when Brian and I went into the service and off to Vietnam. But we had each other, and she knew it. Right, Aunt Shirley?"

"Oh, that was a terrible worrisome time, Dominick. I prayed every day you two were gone until you got back home. Changed. You were no longer little boys.

"Poor Mrs. Tippitt. She took both of those children's deaths so hard. The judge did, too, but he tried not to show it. You could see it in the lines of his face and around his eyes. After they died, he aged considerably. He was angry. Someone was going to pay for Melanie's death. I couldn't blame him for feeling vengeful. The house just wasn't the same after Mr. Jeff and Miss Melanie passed."

She stared in the direction of her nephew. "Dom, go to my room and get that photo with the children and me. I'd like to have Beth see it."

"Sure, Aunt Shirley."

While he was gone, Shirley Denny asked, "Did the Tippitts ever clear out those rooms? I know Mrs. Tippitt left them just as they were by the time I left in the mid-seventies. I thought at the time she shouldn't do that—leave them, that is. What was done was done. But that house was never the same."

"I'm afraid not," Beth said. "Everything is just the same as it was."

"Lordy, Lordy. I thought for sure Janet would take care of all that." She paused, as if she were thinking back to the past again. "Your mother, Miss Melanie, regretted arguing with her mama. When she was a teenager, especially after she had you, it seemed like Mrs. Tippitt could never do or say anything right. It was always her papa she was close to, even when they were arguing. But, despite those teenage tantrums, she loved your grandparents. She'd often talk to me about why they couldn't always get along. She and the judge were always butting heads because they were so much alike. Miss Melanie usually regretted whatever it was she said that started the fireworks."

"Sounds like a typical teenager to me," said Beth.

Dom returned with a framed photo, handing it to Beth. She looked at a much younger Shirley Denny with the Tippitt children. Someone had written "1965" at the bottom of the black-and-white picture. She did the math quickly in her head. The children would have been thirteen, seventeen, and nineteen. They were sitting on the front steps of Tippitt House. Everyone was smiling. Better times, Beth thought. Jeff only had four more years to live, and Melanie, six. But their smiles and their love for their housekeeper shone through their faces, and she looked so proudly at the camera with their arms around her shoulders. Her presence in their lives must have been an anchor, thought Beth.

She handed the photo to Shirley Denny. "I can see how much they loved you, Aunt Shirley. What a lovely photo."

The elderly lady laid the photo on her lap. Then she seemed to remember their prior conversation. "Brian was so good to your mother. He made her a wooden box to put precious keepsakes in. Gave her a set of pearl earrings to go in it. Melanie was such a little, bitty thing. Did you see a dress in her closet that had daisies on it?"

"I think I remember that," said Beth.

"She wore that one night when they had a date. He took her

across the river into Iowa to go to a club where they had live music. Some band was playing that she liked. I think maybe that was when he gave her the pearl earrings."

"They must have loved each other very much," Beth said.

Dom's aunt leaned forward and put her hand on Beth's. "I know they did. They had plans. Melanie told me, but it had to be a secret. Brian was going to marry her. Somehow, they'd make it work. But, of course, the good Lord must have had other plans." She closed her eyes momentarily and looked down, clutching the picture frame a little tighter.

Dom leaned over and took her hand. "I think we're tiring you out, Aunt Shirley. Maybe we should let you rest and come back another time."

Mrs. Denny looked at Beth. "Will you do that, please? Come back and see me?"

"If I'm back in town, Ms. Denny. I will probably go home to Long Island before too long. I like Sweet Iron, but my life is back in the city."

Dom's aunt asked him to help her up. When she did, Aunt Shirley gave Beth a hug for a long moment and whispered in her ear, "You might find more here that would make you happier than you'll ever know."

Chapter Twenty-Two

What a lovely lady, Beth thought as she walked up the sidewalk to her kitchen door. A little mixed up, but mostly still vibrant at ninety-three. Amazing. I should be so lucky to live that long, that well. She unlocked the door, put her purse on the kitchen table, and started to take off her coat. Wait. Something didn't seem right. Then she smelled the sweet scent of Chantilly.

Taking off her coat, she threw it over a chair and followed the scent up the front stairway to Melanie Tippitt's room. What she saw shocked her. Melanie's belongings were everywhere, strewn on the floor, hanging out of open drawers, thrown in a heap on the bed. Beth looked at the totally empty closet. Why would someone empty out the closet? What were they looking for? What happened to the locks on my doors?

Racing down the stairs, she checked the other two doors she hadn't come through. They were both securely locked. How did someone get in? Then she climbed the stairs more slowly, thinking about what they might have been after. Walking back into Melanie's room, she noticed all the jewelry was thrown in a heap on the dresser, and the hope chest's contents were strewn on the floor. This is insane. She pulled her phone out of her pocket and dialed Kyle's number. It rang once, twice, three times—"

"Come on, Kyle, answer the phone," she said, her voice shaky, her chin trembling. Then the click of an answer. Hopeful, she started to talk when she heard, "Kyle Warner, Sweet Iron Police Department. Please leave your message after the beep."

Oh, why can't you be there when I need you? she thought. Beth left him a short message, telling him about the break-in, and hung up. I guess it wasn't a break-in since people got in without disturbing the locks or doors. Jewelry, hope chest. Could they have been looking for the rings that keep coming up in the narrative of the murder? Did they find what they were looking for, and she just didn't know it?

Sitting on the bed, on top of Melanie's clothing, she thought about the break-ins. Someone is looking for something, and it's only happened since I showed up in Sweet Iron. This means, more than ever, that the story of Melanie's death and who murdered her is making someone very anxious. Two can play at this. She would need to cover every square inch of the house trying to figure out what they were looking for and how they got in. She kept forgetting that she needed to go up to the attic and start with the box that said "Melanie" on it. Maybe the wedding rings were there.

The attic was undisturbed as far as she could tell. She took the "Melanie" box downstairs to the office, setting it on a table. She wondered what Janet Landry felt was so important that she needed to leave it for Beth, putting it in a place where other people wouldn't see it immediately. Her fingers shook as she opened the flaps on the box. She lifted out tissue paper, plunging her hand in to feel what lay below.

A baby bracelet, made with tiny square beads of pink and blue strung on a piece of elastic string, came out of the box first. The middle beads, which were white, said "Tippitt," and the bracelet's elastic string was tiny, indicating that Beth must have worn this on her wrist in the hospital. Beth smiled at its miniscule size. She wore this forty-seven years ago. Strangely, tears welled up in her eyes, a reaction she hadn't expected. Tears for the mother who'd had her at age sixteen. Tears for the mother she would never meet.

She held it up, admiring the little beads and thought that today's plastic wristbands didn't compare. Her mother had held her in her arms for a brief time, and Beth had this bracelet on. Again, she felt the warmth throughout her body, a sense of being loved, and the fragrance of her mother seemed to envelop her. She closed her eyes and allowed the love to enfold her, feeling the warmth.

Then she went back to examining the contents of the box. What else is in here? she wondered. A book lay against the side of the box. Beth pulled it out and discovered it was a baby book with a faded cover that said, "Our Baby." She opened it, but the pages were blank. Maybe Melanie had planned to use this if her parents relented and let her keep me. She thumbed through the pages but found nothing.

A puffy ball of tissue surrounded something else. Unwrapping it, Beth found a tiny pink knit sweater, booties, and cap. Someone had obviously knit these by hand. Who? Janet? Melanie? Joellen Tippitt? Aunt Shirley? She felt the tiny stitches and marveled at how perfectly they marched across row after row. Whoever knit these must have been planning on a girl, Beth thought. And she must have loved Melanie. But who?

She felt around the bottom of the box but found no other objects. Pulling the tissue out just to make sure, she discovered a couple of pieces of paper in the bottom with writing on them. Turning them around so she could read them, Beth drew in her breath. She saw more of her mother's script, like the writing in the notebooks.

She moved over to the desk and sat down in the leather desk chair. The papers appeared to be pages torn from a diary. Beth stood up and looked in the box again, thinking she might find more pages. No, only these. Then she remembered Janet's letter saying she'd found only two pages of a diary.

The first page was from June 2, 1970. Melanie wrote about going out to the lake to "lay out" with Elisha and Shelly. Baby oil and iodine were the best way to get really tan. She wrote about fights with her mother, ending with her father intervening and grounding her for two days. She got a new, yellow miniskirt she was going to wear to a dance that weekend. Brian was in Vietnam. Melanie was seeing Sam Conklin. One passage caught Beth's eye: "Brian was always so moody. At least with Sam I know what to expect. We play tennis, go out to the lake, drive around town and get a burger… He's heard talk of a lottery replacing the draft. Maybe Sam's lottery number will be high, and he won't have to go. In any case, I'm sure his father would find him a deferment. Favorite songs: 'Love Me Tonight' (Tom Jones), 'My Cherie Amour' (Stevie Wonder), and 'Bad Moon Rising' (CCR)."

Well, thought Beth. This must have been the period when Brian Nash wasn't around. He's hardly mentioned. It corroborates what Dom said about the war being a have/have not situation for those who had to go or those who got deferments. She sounds like most teenagers, thought Beth, getting tan, loving rock and roll, talking about boys, and spending time with Shelly and Elisha.

The second page, with several creased lines, was harder to read. It was from early summer, 1971. She was dating Sam to keep her parents happy. Brian was back home and kept pushing her to run away and get married, but she wanted to finish college first. Justin Kaspar. Unbeknownst to Sam or Brian, Justin—who was Elisha's boyfriend—kept making suggestive remarks to Melanie. He wouldn't leave her alone. She couldn't tell Sam because he and Justin were best friends. Brian would be angry and might do something stupid. Well, she'd just have to figure out how to handle Justin. Sam was pushing her to talk engagement, and she wasn't sure how she'd keep him at arm's length. She didn't want to get engaged to anyone before she finished college. Why were they all pressuring her?

Beth sat back in her chair and thought about her mother's complicated life with men. All of this was going on late spring before that fatal summer. Justin Kaspar was there that day at the pond. Supposedly, he and Sam went into town to get supplies while the girls were left at the lake. Brian showed up during that interval. How does Justin Kaspar fit into all of this? Did Sam or Brian find out he was flirting with Melanie? Beth wondered. Did they really go into town or were they at the lake when Brian showed up?

She sat there and thought about the significance of it. Suddenly, an idea popped into her head. If Janet had found two diary pages, Melanie must have had a diary. But where could she have hidden it?

The second idea stemmed from thinking about the attic. She thought about the "Underground Railroad" box. This house was here during the Civil War, thought Beth. It was right on track to help slaves coming north after crossing the Ohio River, following the Mississippi, and moving on north to Canada. Could Tippitt House have been on that circuit? Might it have been a safe house on the Underground Railroad? The box from the attic suggested the possibility. And if it had been a safe house, might there be a hidden room or tunnel to hide in and use to enter and exit the house? If so, who might have known about that? If Melanie were sneaking out to see Brian, was a tunnel the way she left and returned? And whoever just came in and tried to find something in Tippitt House could have known about this if they were friends of Melanie's so long ago.

Beth crossed her arms and looked at the diary pages, her mind formulating a plan.

Chapter Twenty-Three

Thursday morning, Beth woke up with the sun streaming in the bedroom windows. The night before, she had barricaded her bedroom door with a chair up against the door handle. How many times am I going to have to do this? she wondered.

Kyle had finally called, listened to her information about the break-in, said words of concern, asked if she wanted them to check for fingerprints again, was confused about how someone got in, and gave her Jimbo Mead's number in California. Jim Mead, called Jimbo, was a close friend of Brian Nash's, and he might know something about that day. Kyle had talked to Jimbo's sister, who was still in town, and got his phone number. Beth looked at her watch and figured she'd call him later. Two-hour time difference or three? By the time she'd heard from Kyle, she had cleaned up Melanie's room and brooded on the question of how people were still getting into her house.

As she crossed the living room with her coffee and looked out the front window, she saw an elderly lady in a plum-colored coat walking a white toy terrier down the sidewalk. Beth had observed her on other days and believed the woman lived in the next house to the north. She finished her coffee, studying the neighborhood. She knew a family with small children lived across the street to the east, and the house just south of it was empty and had a For Sale sign in the yard.

The elderly lady, Mrs. Plum in the Conservatory with the Dog Leash, Beth thought, was turning and coming back past the house. Beth threw on her coat and walked out the front door, thinking she might introduce herself and ask about the neighborhood. She reached the end of the sidewalk just as the woman crossed into her yard. The elderly woman seemed startled.

"Good morning," Beth said. "I'm your temporary neighbor, Beth Russell." She put out her hand, shaking the woman's hand gently, and then let the terrier sniff her fingers.

"I'm Virginia Atley. Everyone just calls me 'Ginny.' I wondered if you were staying permanently."

"Right now, I'm visiting. Have you lived in the neighborhood very long, Ginny?

"Been here since the mid-1960s. My husband and I bought our house here when we moved from Ohio. He had a job at the power company, but he's been gone now for the last fifteen years." She reached down and petted her terrier. "Anastasia here wondered who was living in Tippitt House these days. She helps me keep an eye on the neighborhood. Ever since the house has been empty, Anastasia has been feeling bereft. She liked Janet."

"Oh, my. You've been here a long time, and yes, quite a few people miss Janet. Any chance you remember the other Tippitt children?"

Ginny pulled Anastasia back from some weeds she was exploring. "Of course. Jeff was a regular daredevil. He was always climbing out his bedroom window and up onto the roof to smoke cigarettes, although I never told the judge that. Melanie, I mostly remember because cars with loud music would come up to the front door at all hours. I could hear the drums even when I had my windows closed. She was very popular when she was a teenager."

"Somehow I imagine you know a lot about what happens in this block."

Ginny looked down at her feet for a moment. Then she said, "Walking Anastasia does that. Whenever I take her out for a walk, we see what's happening, who's about. Often I talk with the neighbors."

Beth thought as much. Ginny Atley might be a real asset as well as a pleasant neighbor. "Since I'm new and I don't know anyone on the block, what can you tell me about the neighborhood?"

"I can tell you who lives in each house. If they have a regular schedule because they're taking children to school or going to work, I know what it is."

"That's amazing. Would you mind if I asked some questions?"

"Sure. Ask away."

"Who lives over in the light blue house on the corner with white trim?"

"Easy. That's the Bigelows. Mister works for an insurance company downtown, but if you ask me he spends way too much time on the golf course. Missus works in one of the offices over at the college. They have a little boy and girl, Jeffrey and Jessica, who both go to the elementary school two blocks over. They walk back and forth—I think they're called latchkey kids these days—and seem to do just fine with getting each other out the door. One day they got locked out, and I let them use my phone to call their mother. Both nice kids. Very polite. Raised by two parents who teach them good manners. I approve."

"You pass the quiz with flying colors."

"If Anastasia could talk, you'd probably hear a lot more."

Beth looked around at the other houses on the block. Then she turned to Ms. Atley and asked, "Do you ever notice people coming in and out of my house?"

"Sometimes."

"Might you have seen anyone here yesterday in the afternoon?"

"Some woman came to the front door. I don't know who she was because she had her coat up around her neck, dark glasses on, and a scarf over her head. Almost like she didn't want to be seen. I saw her go down the driveway to the back. The bushes are in the way between our houses, so I'm not sure what she did next."

"Did she have a car?"

"Maybe, but if she did it was parked away from this block."

"Did you ever see her come back out to the front again?"

"No, and I thought that was kind of strange," said Ginny Atley.

Beth looked across the street at the vacant lot. Filled with trees and undeveloped, she knew it to be the haunt of the man she had seen watching the house. She turned to Ginny. "You know, I swear I've seen a man lately watching my house. Maybe I'm imagining it, but I occasionally look out the curtains at night, and I'm sure I see a man across the street in that lot, looking in this direction. It makes me really nervous. Have you seen him or am I just crazy?"

Ginny tightened her hold on Anastasia's leash. "Now that I'm not sure about. I don't see as well at night as I used to."

"Thanks, Ginny. I bow to your amazing powers of observation. I don't know how much longer I'll be around, but I feel a lot safer with you keeping an eye on my house and me."

She smiled. "You're so welcome. I know I'm just an old woman who doesn't have a lot to do, and nobody notices me, but it interests me to walk Anastasia and see what's going on. I'll keep an eye on your house for you."

"Thanks. Oh"—Beth looked at her watch—"I need to make a phone call. Thanks again." Beth went back up the stairs and into her house. Who had the visitor to her house been? Elisha? Shelly? Someone else? How had she gotten in? She looked at her watch again. I could probably call Jimbo Mead now, she thought.

Twenty minutes later, Beth hit the end button on her cell phone. Jimbo Mead had been interested, but not all that helpful. He had moved to California shortly after the trial, married, and had three kids. When Beth told him who she was, he was surprised. Brian had told him he had a daughter, but Jimbo hadn't believed it. He was retired now from the railroad, but he did remember the day Melanie died. Jimbo had been at the hospital sitting in Brian's room when Brian finally awoke from his coma.

"The first word Brian said was 'Melanie,' and then he closed his eyes again. I called the nurse and she came in and talked to Brian. He opened his eyes and asked where he was. I told him he'd been in an accident in his car, but he was going to be fine. All he could talk about was Melanie. I looked at the nurse, and she said she'd call his parents so they could come now that he was awake."

"Did he say anything else?" Beth asked.

"He closed his eyes again like he was resting them. He asked what day it was. When I said it was two days since they'd brought him in, he wanted to know the date. I explained it was July 23, and he became really agitated."

"Why?"

"He and Melanie had plans. Now he'd screwed it all up."

"Did he explain what he meant by that?"

"No. But I have to tell you, Ms. Russell, he did *not* mean that he had killed her. He talked like she was alive. I know—knew—Brian Nash and he could never have laid a finger on Melanie Tippitt. I don't know what happened that day at the pond, but I'd stake my life on the fact that he was not in any way involved in her death." He let out a deep breath and added, "That was such a travesty of justice."

"You said you 'knew' Brian Tippitt. What did you mean by that?"

"I heard some time ago that he'd died down South somewhere."

"Do you remember when or where?"

"Not exactly. I just thought at the time that his death closed the door on that whole sad story."

They had spoken for a few more minutes about Jimbo's life and how things were going for him in retirement, and then Beth had ended the call.

Her shoulders slumped as she realized that if Jimbo were right, she would never get to meet either of her parents in this life.

Chapter Twenty-Four

Beth had finished dealing with some errands—the post office, Remington's office, the grocery store, and the bank—on Friday afternoon when she decided to drop in and have a glass of wine at the wine shop. She needed to check it out.

It was quite a clever store with merchandise all related to wine and drinking—corkscrews, coasters, wineglass identifiers, party supplies, and pretty much any kind of wine or spirits a person might want to buy. Beth noticed the store stocked nothing but the best in labels and vintners. The owner, Cliff Beldon, had introduced himself and given her a glass of wine on the house since he already knew who she was. As always, Beth thought. It's the eyes again.

She was finishing the last swallow of an Italian moscato at the bar when someone came up behind her and said, "Refill the little lady's glass, and give me a double scotch on the rocks, Cliff."

Sam Conklin sat down next to her at the bar, and she caught a whiff of exquisite aftershave. What was it about men and scents in this town?

"Hello, Senator."

"Oh, please. Just call me Sam. It isn't every day I get to buy my almost-daughter a glass of wine."

Beldon brought her another glass of wine. Beth thanked him and asked Sam about his wife.

"Bitsy is probably out putting a few thousand dollars in charges on my credit card, shopping in Peoria with some of her friends. It keeps her happy," he said, but Beth noticed the edge to his voice. "We have a dinner this evening for the local pet shelter. It's one of those charities I do to make Shelly Andrews happy. Dogs and cats are her life."

"You've known each other a long time, haven't you?" Beth asked.

"Shelly and me? Longer than mud, little girl. We go back a long way. And you? Elisha tells me you haven't put the house on the market yet." He chuckled. "You know how to drive her crazy."

Beth smiled. "It's not really my intention to drive her crazy. I just need to find out some things before I decide to leave town again." Suddenly, her phone chimed, and she said, "Pardon me, Senator. Quick call."

"Hello."

"Elizabeth, this is Shelly. I need to talk to you."

"Oh, I was just sitting here having a glass of wine with Sam."

Silence. "Is—is he there with you now?"

"Yes."

"I'll call you in a few days. I need to talk to you. Don't tell Sam I called. Please." She hung up.

Sam flipped several large-denomination bills on the counter and said, "Hit me again, Cliff." Then he turned to her and said, "Maybe I can help you with the answers you seem to need."

"You too? Why does it seem like everyone wants me out of town as quickly as possible? I was just starting to feel like Sweet Iron was home."

Now it was Sam's turn to laugh. "Big City Girl finds her roots, huh? I'm not concerned with you leaving. Fact is, I'm not concerned with you, if you want to know the truth. I try to be kind because you are Melanie's daughter. I feel I owe her that much. All that was such a long time ago when we were just kids. Seems like a lifetime. Hell, I guess it was." He took a swallow of the new scotch and added, "I'm at your service. What can I help you with?"

"I'm a bit confused about the relationships within your group of chums. How did Shelly Andrews fit into that whole group, and what part did Justin Kaspar play in your lives?"

"Well, let me see now." He shifted his weight a bit on the bar stool and considered how to answer her question. "Shelly. She is a piece of work. Melanie let her hang around because she was kind of a forlorn, sad sack. Didn't have friends other than Melanie. But they weren't anything alike. If I could have read Shelly's mind, I'd have bet my money that she was interested in Brian Nash. He was more her type. Truth to tell, our crowd was a bit too fast and expensive for Shelly. But Shelly managed to make herself indispensable to Mellie, and that's why she was at the pond that day."

"You think she was jealous of my mother?"

He almost choked. Once he got his breath back, he said, "Sorry. When you put it like that—my mother—it jolts me. But, yeah, Shelly was definitely in the chase for Brian Nash. If only she'd been able to land him, this whole story might not have happened. Jealous? You'd better believe it."

"I suppose a detective might say that would be a motive for murder."

Conklin turned to her with a skeptical look on his face. "Motive? They caught the guy who did it. No one else's motives were in question."

"Well, Sam, I'm not convinced that's the case."

He chuckled and smiled, shaking his head. "All that's over, Elizabeth. I don't know where you were raised with your cockamamie sense of fair play. Justice isn't what the courts are about. Whether he did it or not didn't really matter. Justice is for the guy who can afford the top lawyer." He snorted. "A public defender was hardly that."

Beth thought about a reply. "I tend to believe that amazing man who said that over time the arc bends toward justice."

"That's just a sound bite for suckers, my dear."

Beth drained the last of her wine, set her glass on the counter, and turned toward Conklin. "To answer your question about my 'cockamamie sense of fair play,' Sam, I was raised by a father who was damn close to Atticus Finch in my eyes. He had his own law practice with a partner in upstate New York. My dad did much more than his share of pro bono work, and he believed that adage that a society is judged by how it cares for its weakest, most vulnerable members."

"Okay, okay. Don't get all into an uproar here," Sam said, patting her hand. "Actually, sounds like something Mellie would say."

Beth took a long breath, removed her hand, and counted to five. "You know," she said, "to go back to Tippitt Pond decades ago, as I understand the story, you weren't there when Melanie was killed."

"No, Ma'am. Justin and I had gone into town. The girls headed off to the old mill once Brian showed up. That's what they both said."

"And where does Justin Kaspar fit into all of this? Wasn't he your friend?"

"Justin. He was dating Elisha that summer. Course, that didn't last. I think he also had a sweet spot for Mellie, but he'd never have acted on it since I was his best friend. Your mama was really something." He smiled and shook his head. "All the guys were after her."

"But you caught her, right?"

"Damn right. We had plans, Mellie and me."

Beth saw a remote look in his eyes.

"Yes…" he said softly, as if he were continuing a story in his head. "We had plans that were… disrupted. And so, here I am with Bitsy and all the things that don't matter, like the houses and the cars and the plane and the accolades." He paused, and Beth heard him sigh deeply. "I'd trade them all for your mother if I could have made that day not happen."

"You and me both, Senator." She stood up from the stool at the counter and picked up her coat. "Thank you for the wine."

"You're so welcome, my dear. One thing I might mention, but maybe I said it before. The past is over and done. Neither of us can change it. Wishing won't make it go away. It simply is what it is. I hope you get things settled with your estate, and safe travels back to New York." He took a deep drink of his scotch and turned to her. "Believe me, I understand, but it might not be wise to ask so many questions."

"Thanks, Sam. You've helped me with some of my questions. The others can wait."

He stood up, made a stately bow, and helped her on with her coat. Then he turned her around to face him and said, "Goodbye, Melanie's daughter. Just had to have one more look at those eyes."

On her way out of the store, Beth thought about Sam. He's either an amazing actor with great charm, or he really did feel sad about my mother's death. But what part did he play in it?

Chapter Twenty-Five

On Sunday, after taking care of some mundane projects around the house, Beth looked at her phone and noticed it was 1:15. Where had the time gone? She had spent much of the morning looking for a high-end furniture business that might have made the credenza she saw at the furniture store. No luck. Now, she was expecting people at 1:30 with a special mission. Beth, the problem-solver, has done it again. If I'm right, she thought, we'll get at the root of these break-ins.

Walking out to the kitchen, she double-checked the refrigerator. She had bought three different craft-brewed beers and a couple of bottles of wine for the non-beer drinkers. The doorbell rang at 1:25, and Molly showed up at the kitchen door at the same time. She let Molly in with a "Hi, come in. Wine in the fridge. I have to answer the front door," and scurried out of the kitchen.

Dom and Kyle had shown up at the exact same time.

"I assume you know each other?" she asked.

The guys looked at each other, smiled, and said, "Sure." She noticed they had followed her directions and were dressed for dirty work—jeans, tennies, and sweatshirts. Each had a flashlight in his hands.

"Perfect!" she said, taking their coats. "Beer in the kitchen in the fridge!"

"Let's go check out the beer before we get down to the dirty business. Or—hey, maybe there's a good football game on," said Dom.

They met Molly in the kitchen as she was pouring a couple of glasses of wine for herself and Beth. She said hi to the guys and handed Beth her glass.

149

Once Dom and Kyle had opened beers, Beth said, "Have a seat at the table. I need help, and I figure you are the three people in town I can trust. And you're smart. Molly said she knew both of you—at least this once I'm thankful for small towns—so I figure we can keep this among ourselves."

Everyone nodded.

Kyle said, "Is this volunteer work? Minimum wage? I figure you can at least afford minimum wage, right?"

"Oh dear," Beth said, mopping her brow. "I was hoping you'd work for beer."

"I can't speak for them," Dom began, "but your message was so intriguing I had to come simply to find out what's up. Beer works for me."

"Perfect," said Beth. "Here is the problem we need to solve. As you know, I've experienced break-ins, and the most recent was after I had all the locks changed. I checked all the doors and windows, as well as the door that leads out of the basement to the back yard. Everything is locked. Somehow people are getting into my house, and, short of materializing as spirits, they aren't coming in through the doors or windows."

"Are you sure you're the only one with keys?" asked Molly.

"Caleca did the work," said Kyle. "He's known for his honesty." Dom nodded at that.

"A couple of other thoughts come to mind," said Beth. "I'm aware that my mother used to sneak out of this house somehow. Maybe she had a key, but my guess is that she knew a way to get out, one that didn't go past her parents' bedroom. Add to that the idea that some man has been watching my house. We haven't caught him since he seems to disappear into the darkness. I don't know who he is, but he makes me nervous, and maybe he's the lookout for the woman who came into my house."

"Beats me," Kyle said. "Each time you've phoned he's been gone before I could nab him. I can't figure out why anyone might want to come in and destroy your mother's room, however. Doesn't make sense."

"Here's my thought," said Beth, "and Molly backs me up since it's a research angle. This house was built in 1845, shortly after the town began. I know for a fact that one of the biggest years for the Underground Railroad in Illinois was 1856. Slaves came over the Ohio River and made their way up the Mississippi from southern Illinois. They were headed toward Sweet Iron and then on up to Princeton, and finally to Canada. From what Molly and I found in the attic, this house was a station on the Underground Railroad. Often that meant a secret room or a trapdoor to hide slaves. It could also mean a tunnel to come in, hide, or go out. If that's the case, we might have a tunnel connected somehow to the basement. Where it goes is another question, but I figured with four of us, maybe we could check out the basement and see if we can find a tunnel opening. Make sense?"

Molly said, "This is exciting!"

"So, what do you think? Is it worth a try?" asked Beth.

"I'm in," said Dom.

"Me too," echoed Kyle.

The basement stairs were hidden at the back of the butler's pantry, a narrow room with lots of shelves on either side for storing food. Beth led the way, turning on the light at the top of the stairs. They followed her down to a cavernous basement with several rooms and overhead bulbs that turned on with small chains. The initial room was huge and lay under most of the main structure of the house. Beyond that, however, were rooms used to store canned goods back in the day, a furnace, a utility room for a washer and dryer, and at least five rooms that could be used for storage. It wasn't a basement with finished living space, but the floor was covered with linoleum.

"First," said Molly, "I'd guess it is likely that the tunnel—if it exists—went out from the back of the house. The lots in the 1800s were huge, and houses sat on either side of this one, but the yard extended quite a way back before any building was behind it. Right now, Beth owns the lot to the back of this one, probably because the family wanted to control the property and who might settle on it. I checked those records yesterday at the courthouse when Beth mentioned this project. I wonder if we should start with the back walls. What do you think?"

They all agreed it made sense. They split up into two groups, starting at the west side of the basement and going to the north and south corners. Kyle and Beth took the north end of the back wall, looking for cracks or openings or anything that might look like the edge of a door. They tapped on the walls, plaster occasionally falling in small pieces, but everything sounded the same. After fifteen minutes, they agreed to move on. About that time, Molly showed up and said they'd found nothing and were moving to the next room.

Beth told Kyle, "I hadn't considered the idea that if we have a tunnel it's somehow hidden. I just expected to see a boarded-up door, I guess. That would be too easy. This is not getting us anywhere."

"You never know," he said. "We may strike pay dirt yet. Let's keep going."

After another half hour, they all met together in the large room.

"We've been over every inch," said Molly. "Nothing. Maybe there is a way in and could be it's on a different wall."

They studied the main room.

"Okay, so let's think about this," said Beth. "You own this house back in the 1850s, and you have to be sneaky so no one will find you out, but you also need a place where you can hide people. If this is the main room, what other alternatives do we have besides a door in the wall?"

They each looked around, and Dom and Beth both noticed the stairs at the same time.

"These stairs are really wide. What if they enclosed the stairs in the 1850s after the house was built? Maybe, to begin with, the stairs were open all around. Then, when they decided to hide slaves, they constructed these walls on either side of the steps. Each side has a door that goes in, under the stairs, and it looked like a storage area. Let's investigate behind those doors," said Beth.

They opened the doors on either side of the stairs, expecting a space, but instead they found shelves.

"Dead end again," said Dom, from the other side of the stairs.

"Just wait a minute. Let's think about this," said Kyle. "Back then, they might have filled these shelves with food they had canned for the winter, kind of like a root cellar. Maybe the stored jars on the shelves were camouflage. But the shelf space we can see isn't deep. What's behind the shelves? Let's see if these shelves move. Come over here, Dom, and help me."

Both men moved over to the right side of the door opening. Kyle put his hands on the doorframe near the floor, and Dom reached up above.

"Alright," said Kyle. "See if you can feel a spring or lever that might trigger the shelves to move."

They both felt every inch of the sides of the doorframe on the right, but nothing happened.

"How about checking on the left side, same way?" Dom said.

They moved over and began feeling their way up the left side of the doorframe, and, to their astonishment, the shelves moved smoothly toward the right as if they'd recently been oiled.

"Got it," said Kyle. "Here, Beth. Put your finger right here and you can feel the indentation for the spring."

"Oh, my gosh," shouted Beth, and she grabbed her flashlight from a table a few feet away. She shone it into the darkness, and they saw an empty space with a dirt floor leading off to the right under the stairway.

Chapter Twenty-Six

"Who's going first?" Beth asked, a dare in her voice to her three companions.

"I will," said Dom, folding his tall body into the doorway, his shoulder disappearing last as he wormed his way into the darkness.

"Shouldn't we do something to keep the shelves from closing? I've seen too many television shows where people go through a hidden door and then get locked in," said Beth.

"I'll grab that cinder block and put it in the doorway," Kyle said. "My assumption is, however, that the other end of this space has a door, too."

Molly walked over and looked in the space where Dom had disappeared. "If you guys don't mind, I think I'm going to wait for you."

"Really?" Beth asked.

"I get kind of claustrophobic, and the thought of being underground in the dark is one of my worst nightmares. It's okay. I'll stay here and guard the entrance in case any ghosts show up."

"Are you guys coming?" Dom called out, sticking his head back through the doorway. "Or am I the only volunteer who's going to be stuck in here? Come to think of it, my dad always told me never to volunteer."

"Coming," Kyle said, and he pulled Beth's arm and took her with him through the doorway.

Once inside, Beth immediately noticed the smell of mildew, probably from the dampness in the tunnel. It was pitch black, but it didn't take long for her eyes to adjust. Everything smelled earthy and the silence was complete.

After she turned on her flashlight she said, "Hey, I see footprints in the dirt. Look, Kyle," she pointed her flashlight at the prints. "Looks like tennis shoes, and either a small man's foot or a woman's. Do you suppose those belong to the person who tore up Melanie's room?"

"Could very well be," he said. "Those prints head in both directions—into the house and back out."

Beth trained her flashlight on the walls and ceiling. Bricks and large stones had been used to shore up the sides. Touching either wall, she felt the dampness. I wonder who put in all these stones and bricks, she thought. I'd guess the town had a brick yard since many of these small towns did. How did the builder get these many bricks without someone wondering what was going on? she wondered. Occasionally, a stabilizing piece of lumber held up the ceiling on either side of the tunnel. Dirt was solidly packed in between the stones.

"Look," said Dom. He pointed his flashlight at the sconces on either side of the tunnel in the walls. "Probably for torches way back when."

Beth eyed them with wonder. Who carried those torches and walked these tunnel floors? I'd give anything to be able to see back into those journeys, she thought.

All three of them had to bend over as they walked. The ceiling was only about five feet high, and in some places the tunnel narrowed so they had to walk single file. The smell of dampness got worse as the ground went downhill for several yards. Then the walkway leveled off. Beth trained her flashlight all around and examined the walls. In some places, stones had fallen from the ceiling and were kicked aside to the walls. They had to be careful where they walked. Kyle had Molly's flashlight too, so he trained it mostly on the floor in front of them.

"You know," said Beth, "this tunnel could go clear back to 1850. When they expanded the Fugitive Slave Law that year, Underground Railroad activity picked up considerably. Oh, I'd love to research this property, find out who built this tunnel, and see how this house changed hands."

"Well," said Dom, "all that might be kind of tough if you plan to do it from New York."

Before Beth could reply, Kyle said, "Look over here."

They walked a few yards to where his flashlight was aimed at the floor.

"Lots of old glass and bottles. I'll bet some of these are from the 1920s. I wouldn't put it past the judge's ancestors to bring illegal alcohol in through this tunnel, too. It certainly has the smell of lawbreaking, no matter what century you're talking about," said Kyle.

Beth leaned down and picked up one of the bottles. The label could no longer be read, and it was covered with dry mud that had probably been caked on it multiple times. "I think I'll take this back up to the house with me and see what's under the mud," she said.

Kyle and Beth heard Dom's voice come out of the darkness. "Your tour guide feels that we are reaching the end of the road in a few yards. Time to find out where this secret hideaway ends." He trained his light on a set of wooden stairs that had been placed in a corner against what appeared to be the side and end of the tunnel. Kyle moved his beam up to the ceiling and they all saw a trapdoor that sat on a wooden frame. The stairs led up to the ceiling and a handle could be seen on the underside of the door. The question was, where would they be when they opened the door?

"Can you get it, Dom?" Beth called out.

"Think so. If someone has been down here recently, it's probably not in bad shape. Watch the stairs. Rickety." He climbed as high as he could, leaned over, and pushed on the handle of the door. It creaked several times, screeching its complaint in being opened. Dom's body went up through the door and out of sight.

Beth stepped up next. She climbed the stairs tentatively, held on to the handles on either side of the doorframe, and lifted herself out through the door.

"Where are we, Dom?"

"Looks to be about seventy yards from the house. Copse of trees. Who knows what used to be here? Maybe a shed or outbuilding covered this up." He pointed at the ground. "More recently, someone has placed some branches over the door."

Kyle stuck his head out of the underground passage and breathed in cold, fresh air. "Ah, that's better." He pulled himself out and looked around the area. "You know, this is probably about three blocks from where the old railroad station used to be."

"That would make sense," Beth said. "Lots of times fugitive slaves were transported by train. Wish I could see those ghosts."

"Well, wishing and hoping isn't going to get us back to the house, and I'd guess Molly is about to call 9-1-1. Want to go back this way or go back down to the tunnel? Do you have your keys, Beth?" asked Kyle.

"I do. Right here in my pocket. I vote we walk back to the house and tell Molly. I'm not real excited about bending over again for seventy yards. However, let's put the brush back over the door so it doesn't look disturbed."

Once they got back to the house, they rescued Molly from the basement, closing the door to the tunnel, and reported on the underground passage.

"I am going to go down there again and check it out when I have more time and a better light source," said Beth.

"Let's go upstairs for another beer and hash this out," Dom said, and Kyle seconded the motion.

Once back in the kitchen, beers and wine in hand, they continued their meeting.

Kyle began by saying, "I think we need to close down that tunnel. Anyone who knows about it can get into your house, and already has. We have no clue as to how many people might know about it."

"I think Kyle's right," said Dom.

Beth and Molly said, "No," at the same time, and then they laughed.

Beth took the lead. "Historical researchers would be upset if we messed with the door to that tunnel. I find it amazing that someone created that gizmo so the shelves could move. This seems to me like a great research project, finding out who built it and who the genius was behind the hidden door."

"I agree," said Molly. "It needs to be videotaped and documented."

Kyle put his hand up. "But we're forgetting that Beth lives here alone for the moment, and why would she want people gaining access to her house? We don't even know who broke in before."

Beth thought for a moment. "Kyle, why don't we have Antonio Caleca with his bag of tricks come back over and put a dead bolt on the pantry side of the basement door? If someone got into the basement through the tunnel, they couldn't go any farther than the basement. I can't imagine we have anything in the basement they'd want."

"I think that sounds like a good idea," said Dom, and he took a swig of his beer.

"I still don't like the idea of unknown people prowling around your house at night with you in the house alone," said Kyle.

"What if we put motion lights in the basement?" said Molly. "If someone came out of the tunnel, they'd set them all off, not to mention being momentarily blinded. If anyone were monitoring the house—like a 'random' police car that was assigned the task of watching the house since Beth has had two break-ins—they would see the lights go on through the basement windows and be at the other end of the tunnel before the person could get out."

"Brilliant, Molly!" said Beth.

"I approve. It's worth a try. I have time off tomorrow. I'll pick up the motion lights and call Caleca," said Kyle.

"I can help," added Dom.

"Hey, wait a minute. Don't I have a vote?" asked Beth. "It's my house."

All three of them said "No!"

"I guess that settles that," said Beth.

Kyle moved his chair back and put his beer bottle in the recycling bin. Then he turned and said, "Now we know *how* they got into the house. The next question is who?"

"Any of Melanie's friends would probably know about the tunnel," said Beth.

Molly asked, "So that means—"

"Sam Conklin, Shelly Andrews, Justin Kaspar, Brian Nash, Elisha Davis, or Jimbo Mead," said Beth.

"Well, Jimbo Mead isn't in the area. Perhaps Brian Nash is dead," said Kyle.

"Is Brian Nash dead?" asked Beth.

"Nobody knows. I heard that rumor some time back, but from whom or what the details were, I can't remember," said Dom.

"I heard it too from Jimbo Mead," said Beth.

"So that leaves Sam Conklin, Justin Kaspar, Shelly Andrews, and Elisha Davis," said Kyle. "But we also have the possibility they told other people. That's something we have no control over."

"At least that limits the number of people we do know," said Beth in a quiet voice. She glanced out the kitchen window at the gray winter sky and admitted to herself the bitter disappointment of never meeting Brian Nash in this life.

Chapter Twenty-Seven

When the young clerk at the McClendan County Courthouse brought Beth one of the first plat books for Sweet Iron, she plopped it on the counter and dust flew in billowing clouds. Coughing, she stepped back, rubbed her eyes, and coughed again.

"That's—it," she stuttered, through her wheezing. "Sorry it took so long. Had to go up to the attic... pretty dusty in the old stuff."

"Thank you so much," said Beth. "I really appreciate your help."

"No problem. Hope you find what you need." She backed off, shaking dust from her blouse, removing herself from the fog, and retreating to a desk.

Beth opened the heavy tome. She had determined that Tippitt House was in Lot 5, Block 7, in the Winters Addition to Sweet Iron. Turning the pages and standing back from the dust, she finally found the right page. Amazing.

Tippitt House was simply a lot in the late 1830s. It appeared that building developers split up a subdivision into lots, and Beth's house was in Lot 5. The date of surveying the subdivision was January 17, 1842, and it was recorded the following February 2 in Book 28, Page 23. Beth put her finger on the columns, reading across the narrow lines, written by hand. A smaller building sat on the lot for several years.

Then in 1850, the first Tippitt name appeared. He was W.W. Tippitt, and he must have commissioned James McBroom to build the house a few years earlier. Beth couldn't tell how long the construction had taken, but W.W. Tippitt took possession of the house, which sat on a double plot of land, on April 28, 1850. After that, another twenty-five lines followed, but each time the house stayed in the hands of the Tippitt family. 1850 to 2016.

"Nicole," Beth said. The clerk looked up, a forlorn sag to her features. Beth figured she was afraid she was going to send her back to the attic. "Could you make a copy of this page for me, and look up this document?" She pointed to a line on the page.

The girl sighed with relief. "Sure. I have that on microfilm. Just a few minutes."

As Beth waited, she thought about the phone call from Antonio Caleca earlier this morning. He was coming over to work on her house at 11. She glanced at her cell phone. Still enough time.

"Here you are," said Nicole the clerk, handing her the plat sheet and a document on legal-sized paper. It was a legal agreement by W.W. Tippitt to borrow money from a homestead and loan association to buy the house. Beth touched her fingers to the intricate, loopy handwriting. Just to think that W.W. Tippitt had signed the original of this page, his signature inked with a flourish. And the old-fashioned language like "whereas" and "witnesseth" always humbled her. Amazing.

More handwriting went sideways up the margin on the left side. "Filed for Record on this 28th day of April, A.D. 1850, at 2:05 o'clock P.M." The signature of the recorder was also penned with curlicues and impossibly long, angled crosses on the t's.

Maybe, when she had time, she could find out about this W.W. Tippitt. Boy, she thought. I love to look at these old papers with handwriting that resembles a work of art. One hundred and sixty-six years ago—through the Civil War, the Gilded Age, World Wars I and II, and the Vietnam War when my mother was still alive. She closed her eyes, overcome by her emotions. How impossible that this house, which had seen so much history, was now—hers.

Chapter Twenty-Eight

By late Monday afternoon, Mr. Caleca had installed a dead bolt on the pantry door leading down to the basement. Charming as ever, he was curious about the order, so Beth told him she was worried about so many windows in the basement being available to anyone who wanted to break in. He shook his head slightly, mumbling something about paranoia from living in the big city. Meanwhile, Kyle had stayed true to his word, and he and Dom brought the motion lights over late in the morning, installing them at every angle outside the tunnel door. Kyle was courteous and kind as ever, but slightly distant. She didn't think she was imagining it. Must be New York. He was unlikely to date some woman fourteen hours away.

She sat in the office staring out the window and thinking about the tunnel in her basement. Who might have built this underground access to the house? She knew that many houses in the Midwest claimed to have been stations on that historic route, but often researchers found no evidence to corroborate their assertions.

She had skimmed through the materials in the Underground Railroad box and was convinced that the documents there would create an authentic claim for the house. But she'd need to do some more research. Then she heaved a sigh. This would open a can of worms before she went back to New York to start her next project. Besides, every time she found something else out about the house or family, it was another tentacle slowly tightening around her, tying her to this place.

She thought about her apartment on Long Island. She'd lived there since 2000 when she turned thirty-one and was able to make a good living from her research. Following grad school, her early jobs gave her enough credibility that she found herself in demand. Eventually, she could choose which jobs interested her. The apartment on Long Island was her first big move away from living in the homes of authors or doing part-time jobs to keep her going. She had found safety and refuge in the Sea Cliff apartment, closing the door on the world and tackling her issues with the help of her friends. Yes, she was still single, and that was why her mother had worried about her, until her mother had ended up with dementia and fretted about imaginary things.

This whole house thing, as well as Kyle, was making her life much more complicated. Simple was so much easier. She would have to decide what to do before too long, but she would worry about that when she absolutely had to figure it out. In the meantime, she wondered where her mother's diary went. Maybe it didn't exist. Maybe it had been tossed. Could Janet have destroyed it, thinking it revealed too many family secrets? This house already has a secret in the basement. What other secrets might it hold? Secret rooms? Compartments? She looked at her watch. I think I'll go up and search for that diary one more time, she thought.

She had put all the clothes and objects strewn over the room back in their proper places. She was as bad as the rest of the family, trying to keep everything the way it was. Now she opened the hope chest and placed its contents on the bed: blankets, towels, a few records, more notebooks, and other items. Getting down on her knees on the floor, she began to feel around all the edges of the hope chest. The bottom felt solid. Sometimes, she knew, hidden compartments were put in the lid, but she couldn't find anything that opened. The lid was heavy enough, but it contained no buttons or springs or anything that moved. Replacing everything, she closed the lid and once again marveled at the perfect smoothness of the finish, the lovingly polished wood, and the obvious craftsmanship that went into matching the grains. It seemed like more than a piece of furniture. She ran her hand over the lid. It was a partnership between craftsman and nature, a work of art. She'd never seen anything like this in high-end furniture stores in New York City.

She thought about what it represented: her mother's dream of finding someone who would love her forever. Those dreams were stitched into the embroidery on the dishtowels and pillow slips. Hours and hours of painstaking work. Too bad, Beth thought. Too bad.

She looked out one of the windows in Melanie's room and saw that the afternoon was almost over, and if she wanted to get a walk in she'd better do it soon. She slid her phone into her jeans pocket, but it rang as soon as she got up from the floor. It was Gabby.

"Hi, Gabby. What's up?"

"Hi. I was just wondering what is going on there in the middle of the country. I haven't talked with you lately. Come to think of it, you've been gone two weeks now on a situation that was only going to take a few days. Any thoughts about coming home?"

Beth sat down on the bed and moved her cell phone from one ear to the other.

"Oh, Gabby, I'm not sure what I'm doing."

"Is it the guy? The police detective?" She lowered her voice. "Is he coming on to you?"

Beth laughed out loud. "One kiss. That's it. Frankly, this whole situation is more complicated than I originally thought." She went on to tell Gabby of the Underground Railroad tunnel, the various people who surrounded her mother and father, the hope chest and her email, and, finally, the inspiration she'd had about researching the house and family.

"You're right. For a woman who loves New York City, you are in new territory. Nothing, of course, going on here. The kids have an open house at school tomorrow night, but otherwise, business as usual. You know, you're lucky you have so many intriguing surprises. Underground tunnels, kissing detectives, historic house, people breaking in. How exciting. Can't blame you for staying there."

"Oh, and I didn't mention that every so often I see some dark figure watching my house. Tonight, if I turn off the lights, I'll probably see him across the street in the woods. It is eerie. I don't know what that's about, but so far he hasn't come to the house, and now that Kyle has motion lights in the basement and a lock on the pantry door, I feel so much safer."

"Who knew small towns could be so scary."

"Certainly not I," said Beth. "Well, it is turning to dusk, and I need to get a quick walk in. I'll talk to you later in the week. Maybe I'll have some decisions made by then."

Beth went downstairs, grabbed a jacket, scarf and hat, took her cell phone out of her pocket, and added her house keys instead. Fifteen minutes, she thought. She would go on a walk before it got dark and clear her head. She peeked out the front window first. No man was watching the house. It probably wasn't dark enough yet. Maybe she could go over again and confront him one of these nights. Then she recalculated. He could have a gun. That might not be such a good idea after all, or Antonio might be right. Big city paranoia.

Walking through the quiet neighborhoods, she turned east this time. She had explored Sweet Iron in several directions from her house. She glanced at the picture window of a house three doors down and saw two children sitting at a table, probably doing their homework. Walking along at a brisk pace, Beth heard a woman's voice calling, "Okay, kids. Time to come in!" A school bus passed her, empty of its cargo, heading back to the garage. She smiled thinking of the times she and her friend, Ally, had taken the school bus home from their elementary school in Spring Harbor. It dropped them two blocks from home, and they walked in different directions to their houses. Her mother was always at home when she walked in the door and shouted, "Mom, I'm home!" For a moment, tears filled her eyes, thinking of her "other" mother and all she'd sacrificed to raise Beth alone for most of her life. "You'll always be my mom," she whispered under her breath, and caught herself before she choked up.

After Beth had walked a mile, she turned back and headed to the house, thinking about what she should make for dinner. Discarding several ideas, she decided maybe she would go out. Dom could be at the Third Street Tap, and on a week night it wouldn't be as busy or formal. Beth had gone there a few times since she'd met Jerod and Dom, and she was beginning to feel like a regular. She glanced at her watch and thought she could still stop at home, change clothes into something less casual, and drive over to the jazz club. Either Dom or Jerod would be there, and they were always good company.

She reached her house, bounding up the stairs to her bedroom to change clothes. Humming a tune she'd heard recently on a radio station on her computer, she brushed her teeth, checked her makeup, and went back down to the foyer. She grabbed her coat and scarf, feeling in the pocket for her phone. Not there. Beth looked over at the foyer table and there it was. She picked it up and checked the display. She had a voice message.

She hit the arrow to listen to the message. "Beth, this is Molly. My scanner said a hit-and-run accident happened in front of Shelly Andrew's business on Ferris Street. 261. I knew you were concerned about her and told me she'd been depressed lately. You might want to check it out. It's… oh… it's about 6:30 p.m. Thought you'd want to know."

Beth looked at her watch. It was 6:45. She put her coat and scarf back on, felt for the car keys, dropped her phone in her purse with her driver's license, and left through the kitchen door. It wouldn't take too long to drive to Shelly's because this was Sweet Iron. Putting the address in her GPS, she left. Dinner will have to wait, she told her stomach.

She was right. It didn't take her long to find Ferris Street, but her progress was impeded because the darkness on Shelly's block was broken by firetruck lights blinking, police car red and blue emergency lights splitting the darkness, and an ambulance. A crowd had already gathered.

Chapter Twenty-Nine

Beth looked for a place to park. Cars were stopped in the street, moving only a few inches at a time. People were walking toward the police lights, curious about the accident, Beth thought. It's like high school when a fight starts. She turned around a block and finally found a space about two and a half blocks away. She locked her car and walked toward Shelly's business address.

A good-sized crowd had gathered, and the police had a block cordoned off with police scene tape. With all the fire engine lights on and police cars, it was practically bright as day. The first thing Beth saw were medics helping someone lying on the street. One had a portable IV in his hand, holding it up while the other one worked over what must have been a body. Then Beth saw something that made her heart drop… peeking out from behind the medic was a splash of red. Shelly had a red coat. Beth remembered seeing it at the college when she went over to research with the newspapers.

Beyond the medics, Beth saw Kyle talking to another man whose body was visibly shaking and whose hands were over his face. Maybe that's Shelly's boyfriend, Jack Hanson, she thought. Beth had never met him, but she had heard him mentioned at the New Year's party. She stood there watching for a good ten minutes in a hushed crowd. Occasionally, she heard quiet voices, but otherwise people were respectful, even if they did have a salacious interest.

Now the medics were lifting the stretcher into an ambulance for what seemed like forever. Almost like slow motion, Beth thought. She watched as the ambulance slowly moved out of the scene. People began dispersing, a few at a time. Others stood in clumps, talking about what happened and glancing back at the scene.

Beth felt a hand on her shoulder and, turning around, she saw Sam Conklin.

"I had a talk with the medics. It's not looking good." He shook his head slowly, and his face looked grim.

"What happened?" asked Beth. "Were you here?"

"No, not here, but I was having coffee with the police chief when the call came in, and I came down to see what was going on. I talked to one of the policemen. Shelly Andrews. Hit-and-run around 6:25. Dark car, tinted windows, no plates."

"How horrible. Is she going to make it?"

"Don't know, but it does not look good. I figure I'll go over to the hospital and see if I can find out any more," said Sam.

"I'm so sorry. I know she was a friend of yours."

Sam looked down at the street. Then, in a hoarse voice, he said, "Yes, yes, she was. We go way back. That's her boyfriend, Jack. Jack Hanson." Beth turned to him and saw him, from a distance, shake his head. Then Sam said, "People are so irresponsible. How can you hit someone with a car and not stop?"

"Good question, Sam. These days people seem to mostly look out for themselves."

Sam had taken his hat off out of respect. Now he said quietly, "She always had the worst luck. But no one was more loyal and dependable than Shelly."

"She's not dead yet," said Beth. "Maybe they'll be able to save her."

About that time, Kyle saw her and walked over to the edge of the slowly thinning crowd.

"Hi, Beth, Sam. What a bad day. She couldn't have seen it coming. Whoever it was plowed right into her. Not sure she's going to make it. Looks pretty bad."

Suddenly, they were practically broadsided by Elisha Davis, hysterical, running into them on her spindly shoes and shouting, "What happened? What happened?"

Sam put his arm on her shoulder, trying to quiet her down. "It's Shelly. Hit-and-run. Don't know if she'll make it. They just took her to the hospital."

"Oh my God, oh my God!" shouted Elisha. "This is horrible! Horrible! How could this happen?"

Kyle talked with her very quietly and calmly. "We don't know yet, Elisha, but we're working on it. She might pull through."

Sam and Elisha looked at each other, and then Elisha started bawling loudly.

"I'll take her home and find her a drink," said Sam, his voice heavy, "and then I'll stop out at the hospital." He literally turned Elisha around and held her waist while they walked back to his car.

Beth looked at Kyle and said, "He seems genuinely sad about this."

"How did you know about the hit-and-run?"

"Molly called me."

"How did she know?"

"She has a scanner."

Kyle looked at her, disbelief spread across his face. "The head librarian at the college has a police scanner?"

Beth shrugged her shoulders. "We researchers deal in facts. Information."

Kyle shook his head, trying not to smile. "I hate to tell you, Beth the Researcher, but you're implicated in this accident."

Her eyes opened wide and she said, "What? How?"

He pulled an evidence bag from his pocket and Beth saw a small piece of paper, wrinkled but smoothed out inside the plastic.

"What is my phone number doing in that bag?" she said.

"Shelly was clutching this in her hand. She must have been planning to call you, and she left her office, I suppose, to do so in privacy. Maybe outside where no one could hear her. Perhaps this was not an accident at all. If someone knew she had something to tell you, they might have wanted to ensure her silence. She must have told the wrong person. The timing could be coincidental."

"We don't have too many people that might pertain to. Two of them were right here a few minutes ago," said Beth.

"It's obvious Shelly knew something, especially since she was talking to a priest. That's a dead end, of course, since a priest won't tell me." He shook his head. "How many crimes might be prevented if priests weren't sealed by the confessional?"

"That would hardly work," said Beth, smiling. "No one would confess anything."

Kyle smiled. "Of course, practical Beth Russell. It's obvious she was going to talk to you about that day at Tippitt Pond. She knows something. If she pulls through, we'll find out what it is. Or, an alternative theory might be that Brian Nash isn't dead at all. Maybe your arrival has started stirring up memories of long ago. Could be your father has decided to take revenge on those people he blames for your mother's death."

"What? I can't believe that."

"It makes about as much sense as Sam or Elisha," said Kyle. "To change the subject, are you going back to New York in the next few days?"

"Probably not."

"If you're not busy, we might go out for dinner Wednesday, if you'd like, that is. Dom told me they're having a jazz pianist in at Third Street Tap to play one set around eight. Sounds like fun. Want to try it?"

"Sure."

"Perfect. Well, I need to go over to the hospital once we're done here. Could be a long night."

"I will see you Wednesday then."

She turned and walked back to her car, trying not to think about the smile on her face as she blushed. Wednesday night. An actual date.

*****

Later that evening, around nine o'clock, Beth got a text from Kyle. "Shelly didn't make it. Never regained consciousness. Sorry."

She slowly shook her head and said out loud, "Poor Shelly. Just when she had figured things out and was going to solve a huge mystery and clear her conscience." She closed her book and sent a short text thanking Kyle for letting her know.

Beth sat back in her chair and looked around at the Tippitt living room. If only I hadn't come here, she thought, Shelly would still be alive. Why did I do this? Why didn't I simply go back to New York and leave all this alone?

She stood up and walked over to the window, looking out at the night, noticing the streetlamps with haloes lighting up the cold air. Hardly a car moved on the street. Why did I think I could figure this all out? Me? The person who deals with books, not people. Molly tried to warn me. She said this history would stir things up. So did Sam.

She remembered talking with Shelly at the New Year's Eve party at the country club. Even though Shelly was way too drunk, she was probably the most straight-talking person in the group of friends involved in the murder at Tippitt Pond. If she kept secrets, she must have been protecting other people. She was always on the outside, looking in at people who had so much more than she did. Now, the secret-keeper was dead, and all because Beth wanted to find out about her mother's death. Why couldn't she have left it alone? Never listened to her stupid curiosity to try to figure it out.

She collapsed onto the sofa and thought, I should go back to New York. Leave this all behind. Go back to Gabby and my little apartment and go on with the life I've always known. It was life enough. Now Shelly Andrews's death is on my conscience. Oh, why did I ever come back here in the first place?

Molly warned me, Molly warned me. Why didn't I listen?

Then she was crying, her hands over her face. Eventually, her tears began to lessen, and she reached for a tissue, wiping her eyes. Too late, she thought. Too late to save Shelly Andrews.

She would have to stay long enough to clear up the legal matters that still had to be dealt with, and then she'd go home. Back to New York City, back to her apartment on Long Island, back to who she used to be. She sniffled a few times, trying to staunch the flow of guilt.

Beth jumped when her phone rang. It was Kyle. She used a tissue to blow her nose and try to get her voice back into talking mode.

"Hi, Kyle. Didn't you just text me?"

"Yeah, and it was very thoughtless of me. I should have called or come over and told you. I'm sorry."

"It's fine. I was just upset over Shelly."

"I can hear that in your voice," he said. A long pause, quiet, and then they both talked at once.

"You go first," Kyle said.

"I can't help feeling this was my fault," she said.

"It's not, Beth," said Kyle. "We don't know the accident was intentional. Maybe it was. Even so, you didn't cause it. If it was intentional, the driver's motive goes back to 1971. You had nothing to do with that."

Beth sniffled again and moved the phone so she could blow her nose. "I came back."

"You sure did, and I'm really glad you did. Good things can come of your decision to come back. If you leave now, you'll always regret you never found out the truth... and I'll always regret you didn't stay."

Beth didn't know what to say.

"Beth?"

"Yes, sorry. I had temporary speechlessness. I feel the same way... happy that I met you. And you're right. I want to know what happened to my mother and father. My biological ones. I can't help wondering if my father is involved in this—some revenge plot. But my coming wouldn't have instigated that. All right. I'm in. Until we get this mess resolved, I am with you. I think I need to keep looking for Melanie's diary."

They hung up, and Beth once again pondered how she could resolve the problem of spending time with Kyle and having her life in New York City. *I don't suppose I could convince him to move to Long Island,* she thought.

Chapter Thirty

Beth spent much of Wednesday morning working on legal matters with Remington Hatcher. She had so much to learn about timberland and farms. Two weeks ago, she didn't know about any of this. She was even getting used to her germaphobe, OCD lawyer.

She picked up the newspaper and continued reading the obituary for Shelly Andrews. The funeral would be on Thursday at the Catholic church. *What did she want to tell me? Did she know who killed my mother or was she in on it? Maybe it was like an Agatha Christie mystery where they all did it together. But why?*

If Beth could find Melanie's diary, perhaps she could figure it all out. She looked around the room, thinking about her mother, and said out loud, "At least you could use your perfume to tell me if I'm hot or cold, Mother." Nothing.

She stared at a stunning Shaker cabinet sitting on the east wall of the room. *The Tippitts had such good taste,* she thought. She got up and walked over to the cabinet, admiring its beautiful finish. Suddenly, she knew who she'd call about the hope chest. Walking over to the foyer where her purse sat on a table, she pulled out Elisha's business card. She'd have to phrase the questions carefully. Elisha would probably think Beth was calling to put the house on the market. Beth didn't want to give her a heart attack.

To her surprise, Elisha answered her phone. No voicemail.

"Hello, Elizabeth."

"Hi, Elisha. First, I'm so sorry to hear about Shelly's passing. I know you were friends."

"Thank you, Elizabeth. I'm not really myself today. This has hit me very hard. What can I do for you?"

"Say, I just called because I've been looking around at the furniture in the Tippitt living room. I think we could auction the less expensive pieces and save the high-end ones for a special sale, that is, once I put the house on the market."

She could practically sense Elisha Davis salivating, despite her grief.

"You are so right, Elizabeth. That was part of my plan. Some of those pieces are gorgeous and should go for high prices. I could easily choose which ones to auction and which ones to hold back for a special sale. Just say the word. I think you are doing the right thing, thinking about how to go about this, that is."

Beth considered how to turn the conversation around to her mother's hope chest. "I have been checking the furniture in the living room. It appears to be quite expensive to me. But one piece of furniture that's upstairs interests me because of its sheer beauty: Melanie's hope chest. What do you know about it? Do you remember when she ordered it? Or maybe her parents did."

"You have such an eye for quality, Elizabeth. That is a beautiful piece. I agree. Melanie always said she was putting things in it for her eventual wedding to Sam. Sam Conklin."

"Oh," said Beth. She added innocently, "Had they set a date way back then?"

"Sam always told me once he finished law school."

"That would have made sense. I was looking at the items that are still in her hope chest. Blankets, towels, that kind of thing."

Elisha paused for a moment. "That sounds about right. The last time I saw those things—it was years ago—that's what I remember."

Now Beth began to head in for the kill. "I was looking at it the other day, and the finish is so perfect. Every care was taken to match the grains. I think it's cherry. Not sure I've ever seen a piece of furniture so carefully made."

"Yes. That would be right. Melanie loved that hope chest. She would have moved it to wherever she and Sam ended up once they married." Elisha paused a moment, and silence hung in the air.

174

"Seems ironic, doesn't it?"

"Ironic?"

Elisha chuckled. "Well, yes, that she loved it so much she would keep it for her wedding day when she became Mrs. Sam Conklin."

"Why ironic?" asked Beth.

"Brian Nash made it for her."

Beth moved backward to a chair and felt for the arm before she fell into it. She couldn't breathe, couldn't move. She had to count to ten before she could get back to Elisha.

"What?"

"Sure. He was talented at carpentry, for a kid. I think he did that in eighth or ninth grade."

Afterward, Beth didn't remember the rest of their conversation. She was on autopilot while Elisha jabbered on about furniture, her house, money, auctions. Did she even say goodbye to Elisha?

If Brian made that hope chest, he made the other pieces she had seen around town, too. Were any of them more recent than Melanie's death in 1971? If so, what would that mean?

She glanced at her watch. I think I'll keep this to myself while I think about it. I need to shower and get ready to go out with Kyle.

*****

"So," Beth said, after they were seated at Jerod Enslow's place, "how did your day go, honey?"

Kyle laughed at her question. He took a sip of wine, thought over his answer, and said, "Pretty routine. Checking all the chop shops and places a car might have been fixed illegally. Since that car hit Shelly so violently, it should have some damage. So far, we've found nothing locally. We'll enlarge our net over the next few days. By the way, I've done a search for your father in death databases. Found nothing."

"Does this mean he's alive?"

"Could be."

Beth considered that possibility. She recalled her anger when she had first heard of his part in Melanie Tippitt's death. Now that he might be alive, she found herself longing for an opportunity to at least meet him.

The jazz pianist, Brewster something, was just starting another set, and a saxophonist joined him, even though, according to Jerod, that hadn't been scheduled. "Sometimes guys just show up to play with Brewster. Word gets around that he's going to be here."

They began on salads and Kyle asked, "And how about your day? No one breaking in? No motion lights going off? No bombs in the mail? No strange people watching your house?"

"It was a very quiet day. Remington worked with me organizing my kingdom. I must say, I never knew the difference between a cultivator and a harrow, but I'm learning a little more each day. Not sure they're going to do me any good on Long Island, of course."

Kyle paused a moment. "I don't suppose, in those moments between thinking about back hoes and cultivators and harrows, you ever stop and think about whether you might be able to have a life here."

"Here? As in Sweet Iron?" she asked, looking up in surprise.

He sat back, his shoulders slumping. "Yes. Here."

Beth cocked her head to one side and improvised a speculative look. "That would depend."

Kyle sat up in his chair and leaned forward. "Depend? On what?"

"On whether I could see my way to living in a small town where everyone knows your business, and people make assumptions about you that usually aren't true."

Kyle looked at her, his eyes wide open, and both palms of his hands out. He exaggerated his voice as he said, "Oh, Ms. Russell. I think you protest too much. Look at all of the friends you've made here: Molly, Dom, Jerod, Crazy Elisha and, of course, me."

Beth put her hand over her mouth and blew out through her fingers. "All right. I'll give you that. If I could just move my best friend Gabby here."

"Give me her address and phone number, and I'll do my best."

Beth started laughing. "I'm just kidding. They wouldn't move here. She has a husband and two kids. They are dug in in New York City."

The music had stopped, the pianist taking a break between sets.

They had finished their salads, poured more wine, and were smiling at each other with the pleasant ambiance that wine can induce.

Jerod Enslow stopped at their table. "Hope you two are having a good time."

"Definitely, Jerod," said Beth. "Feeling very relaxed after two glasses of wine, bread, olive oil, parmesan. Just waiting for the main course. Your food is such a pleasure. I look forward to coming here."

Jerod smiled broadly and looked at Kyle. "Want to sit in for a song or two with the saxophonist?"

Beth stared at Kyle and wondered what this was all about.

Kyle looked at her for a moment and then at Jerod. "Sure, but just one or two."

"Perfect," said Jerod.

Then, to Beth's amazement, Kyle excused himself, took the stage, sat down at the piano, and began a jazz rendition of "Stella by Starlight," a Miles Davis arrangement. Beth looked at him in amazement. What else don't I know about him? she wondered. This was followed by a Coltrane song, "In a Sentimental Mood." As she watched him, she marveled at how relaxed he was, the music coming from his fingertips as if they knew the keys intimately. When he finished, everyone clapped politely, and he came back over and sat down.

"What did you do with the guy I came with?" she asked.

He looked up at the ceiling and said, "I took lots of piano lessons while I was growing up. I did mention I play a little. Don't have much time to practice anything these days."

"That was beautiful," said Beth. "It's as if you were born to play jazz."

"I do enjoy it," he added, as the waiter brought their entrees.

They were almost finished with their meals when Kyle's phone buzzed. He checked it, got up, and said to Beth, "I need to take this." Then he left to look for some privacy.

What an amazing guy, she thought. So humble. She had no idea he could play the piano like that. Who would have thought? She took a few more bites of her penne with brown butter, arugula, and pine nuts, and he came back in. Jerod was with him.

"Beth," Kyle said. "So sorry, but I have to go. A break-in downtown."

Jerod said, "Don't worry. I'll get Beth home, well, if that's okay with you, Beth."

"No problem," said Beth. "Talk with you later, Kyle? Or tomorrow?"

"Yes," Kyle said, and he was gone.

"Go ahead and finish. Stay as long as you'd like and listen to Brewster Nedley. He and Kyle are both amazing on the piano. When you're ready, just come past the coatroom and you'll see my office door. I'll be in there and can take you home whenever you're ready."

"Thanks so much, Jerod. I'll stay a bit and listen to the music. Maybe have a nightcap."

Beth was feeling no pain after two or three—she'd lost count—glasses of wine. Eventually, she checked her phone. It was almost closing time. She called the waiter for the check, but he assured her it had already been paid.

She stood up and walked past the hostess's area at the front, glancing at the counter. She stopped in her tracks and walked back. Besides the usual toothpicks and mints, a small tray of matchbooks sat near the corner of the counter.

She picked up a matchbook and stared at the piano keys on the front cover. It was a duplicate to the one she had found in the woods. I'm sure that person wasn't Dom or Jerod, she thought. Wrong shape and size. That watcher was tall and slender. Besides, anyone could grab a matchbook from here after eating dinner. Whoever was watching her had good taste.

After stopping at the ladies' room, she found her coat and walked over to the door that said "office." Knocking, she heard Jerod's voice, and went on into his inner sanctum. She'd never been here before.

"Just checking one more figure here," he said, a laptop sitting in front of him on the desk.

Beth said nothing. She was stunned. Rooted to the floor. Couldn't move. Jerod looked up when she didn't say anything.

"Beth?"

She felt like she couldn't breathe, but she could hear her heart pounding, so she must still be breathing. Practically falling into a chair, she put her hand on the beautiful polished surface of the massive walnut desk. Every bit of grain matched, and every decorative flourish fit smoothly into a magnificent piece of furniture. She looked down at the lower corner, checking for the double hearts. There they were. On the one in front she saw the initials "M" and "T" and the date: 2010.

Just as she looked up, she realized Jerod had seen her searching for the double hearts. She detected terror behind what was usually a smooth veneer.

"Beth, I can explain—"

She felt herself go cold sober with a focus she didn't know she had.

"Only one thing you need to explain, Jerod. Where is my father?"

Chapter Thirty-One

Friday, Dom picked her up around noon in a dark car with tinted windows. Just like some spy thriller, she thought.

"I take it this means he's agreed to talk to me?" Beth asked.

"Yes. But I must say we have some ground rules."

"Seriously?" She looked out the window, then back to Dom. "And why do we seem to be driving around in circles?"

"I need to make sure we're the only ones headed to your father's workshop. He lives in an isolated spot, and he'd rather keep it that way," said Dom.

Beth looked down at her hands and noticed they were trembling slightly. They didn't begin to match the more serious waves in her stomach. She hadn't considered what she would say to her biological father, a man she had never met and didn't know existed until two weeks ago. A man who could be a murderer. She settled in and listened to the jazz pouring from Dom's radio, trying to think about anything that had nothing to do with her father.

She had attended Shelly's funeral the day before. It was a somber event with many of her customers in attendance. Justin and Sam were two of the six pallbearers. Elisha was dressed in black and sobbed through it all. Sam and Justin looked stoic and somber. It had lasted about an hour, and then they went to the cemetery for a graveside prayer and benediction. While Shelly's death might be considered accidental, Beth had no doubt that someone had killed her to silence her. She gazed at the faces of the mourners but didn't see any sidelong glances among the three friends who had been at Tippitt Pond that day with Melanie and Shelly.

Five minutes into the ride, Dom broke the silence. "The privacy is partly because after prison Brian was a changed man. He doesn't trust most people and lives alone."

"So," Beth asked, "why are you allowed to see him?"

"He trusts Jerod and me. He's known me forever, and he met Jerod in prison in AA. We help him with his business. Sometimes he needs people on the outside."

"His business is making this expensive, high-end furniture?"

"Yes. It sells to people who don't worry about what the price tag says, and much of it goes to Europe or the Middle East." Dom fiddled with the satellite radio, changing the station.

Beth looked out the window and noticed they were coming to a dirt road off the two-lane highway. Dom turned onto the heavily tree-lined road.

"No signs, Dom. How does anyone know where he's going?"

"That's the idea," Dom said. "You can get really lost in these woods, but I know them like the back of my hand. In a few more minutes I must put a blindfold on you," he said nonchalantly.

"What?" Beth raised her voice and stared at him.

"Boss's orders. It's for your own protection. If you know how to get here, he worries that someone might want to harm you to find out the location."

Beth decided to simply be quiet for a moment.

"What? No more questions, Ms. Researcher?"

"One for sure. How does he deliver this furniture to these people who want to pay so much money for it when he lives in an enchanted forest?"

"He works with a trucking firm," Dom said, "that can deliver to either coast. We've arranged a pickup station about five miles from his workshop. I get the pieces there—it's a small building where I can wait until the truck arrives on a schedule. Then they're shipped off to the coast and flown to wherever the buyer lives."

"It seems well thought-out," Beth said.

Silence again with the quiet notes of "Mood Indigo" in the background.

"What is he like, Dom? My biological father."

He chuckled as if this were a funny question. "These days he's quiet. Peaceful. The opposite of how he was after Nam. He's been sober for thirty-five years. Occasionally, usually at night, if he wants to see people, he has an old beat-up pickup truck he drives into town. He was the one watching you from a distance at your house. Obviously, he's curious, but he's kept his distance not knowing what you might think."

Beth was quiet. Then she asked, "Does anyone else in town know he's alive?"

"Just Jerod and me. It's probably wise to keep this among ourselves. He'd rather people didn't know. We spread a rumor—you heard it— that he had died in a car accident down South somewhere. Best way to leave it so no one comes snooping around."

"All these people who buy furniture never meet him or know anything about him?"

"Correct. He is an artisan of the highest rank in the world of furniture design, and many of his pieces go for fifty thousand or more. They sell especially well overseas. A little mystery never hurts. Quality is the entire story. People who truly want quality and will pay for it pass his name around."

"So why couldn't I find out this story online?"

"He does have a website. His business is called 'With the Grain.' And, his slogan is that every masterpiece he makes is 'Dedicated to the One I Love.' It was their song. And he kept the double heart logo he put on her hope chest so long ago. It's a testimony to her love, he says."

She was silent, thinking about Dominick's words. No one spoke for several minutes.

Finally, Beth felt the car slowing down and eventually it came to a standstill just before a fork in the road. Dom handed her a black scarf.

"Really? You weren't kidding?"

"Nope. For your own protection. Have to do it, or I have to turn around."

Beth considered and let out a deep sigh. "Oh, all right." She put on the blindfold and sat back in the seat. It was disconcerting not being in charge and not having her eyesight.

Once the car began to move again, she said, "Does he want to meet me?"

He paused before answering her question. "You want an honest answer?"

"I think so," said Beth.

"He's been told you were in town. Watched you from a distance, never up close. I think your presence disturbs him because he still thinks he murdered Melanie. Because of that, he figures he has no right to see you. Since you found out he was still alive, you pushed the issue. He's agreed. Let's put it that way."

"Oh. But the rage he felt years ago is gone?"

"He's a warm puppy now. I don't know how he is going to react to seeing you. Your eyes might be hard for him."

"Does that mean you want me to keep this blindfold on?" Beth asked, laughing.

"Of course not. You can take it off now. We're here."

Dom got out of the car and came around to open Beth's door. Once beyond the tinted windows, she saw a modern house sitting in a veritable forest. A pond lay off to the left side of the house with a small dock and a canoe lying on the grass. On the other side of the house was a battered old Ford truck parked under a huge oak tree.

"Stay right there a minute," Dom said. He walked over to a box attached to a long pole. Reaching inside, he punched in some numbers. "Have to turn off the security system," he said.

Beth watched as a man opened the door to the house. At first, she thought it was her father, but he turned out to be a security person checking on the code change. This place has quite a security setup, she thought. Barbed wire, electricity, guards, and nestled in a forest. She looked up at the trees and saw security cameras. I could never find my way back here. I guess that was the point.

Once the security man saw Dom wave, he went back in the house. Dom walked back to Beth and said, "Follow me. He said to come to his workshop." She walked with him to another building beyond the house. It was also an oversized building with a metal roof and a single front door.

Beth followed Dom in the door, but no one was in the huge main room.

Dom said, "Brian will be with you in a minute or two."

Beth began looking around as soon as Dom left. She saw various worktables constructed of wood pieces that were perfectly matched. Hanging from every wall were tools, organized carefully. A lead pipe hung down from the ceiling, about seven feet up on each wall. It was used to hang electrical cords, curly rubber wires, and handsaws of various sizes. Below them, on the tables, sat small drawers with different sizes of screws or nails, and slightly larger plastic bins that probably held pieces and parts. Glue bottles of every shape and size presided over one corner of the table.

Beth turned and looked behind her. More tables—handmade, she thought—held brushes, screwdrivers, tool sharpeners, an electrical strip with plugs in every outlet, a mallet, wire brushes, an angle finder, wrenches, and some tools she'd never seen before. Many, like the screwdrivers and tool sharpeners, stood at attention in specially made pieces of wood with holes to contain their handles. Next to those, on the far wall, were table saws.

This is what an artisan's shop looks like, Beth thought. Everything in its place. Kept clean—not a speck of dust or sawdust. She walked over to one table and picked up a hand tool she couldn't name. "1870" was etched on its handle. Feeling guilty, she hastily put it back in its place.

I see what Dom meant when he called Brian Nash a master craftsman. If he is as meticulous as this workshop, quality is a top priority. She saw an open door into another room and walked over to peer in. Pieces of furniture in various stages of completion sat in each corner. Not a lot, she thought. He works on a few at a time. Here the smell of oil and varnish was stronger. She walked back to the tool room.

In the quiet she heard voices and feet plunging into the gravel driveway. Then nothing. She waited in the center of the room, literally holding her breath. Her muscles tightened, even her hands at her sides became fists, and she watched for the doorknob to move.

The door opened and in walked a slightly built man, about five feet, eleven inches tall. He closed the door behind him, stopping in front of it. His black hair, largely turned white, was tied in a ponytail at the nape of his neck. White eyebrows topped blue eyes that squinted now as he got used to the lights. A broad nose rose above a moustache that was white, and beneath his mouth was an equally white, small goatee. She had noticed he walked with a stoop to his shoulders, and right now his whole aspect was turned to her. She stood in the center of the room, not quite sure what to say. Beth had envisioned this moment ever since she had found out he was alive. Now she was frozen.

His eyes scanned her face and appeared troubled, then fearful. He spoke first.

"Melanie?"

She knew why her mother had fallen in love. His voice had a deep timbre, with velvety, melodious tones. It was like a song.

"No, Mr. Nash. I'm Elizabeth, your daughter."

Chapter Thirty-Two

A silence followed her comment.

Then, Beth saw his facial expression change and he said, "Yes, yes. I knew that. Forgive an old man for talking gibberish. Of course you are." He stopped on the edge of another sentence. An awkward silence followed. "So many days I hoped you would find your way back here. And now here you are, and I—I'm an old man."

Beth's eyes narrowed, and she carefully controlled her voice. Why was she so angry? She suddenly went blank, having no idea what to say.

Brian Nash stood perfectly still. "I wish things had been different. Did you have kind parents? Did they love you?" His eyes rested on her, his voice quiet and slow.

She considered what she should say about the past forty-seven years of her life. "Yes. My adoptive parents were fine. I only had my father for fourteen years, but my mother did as well as she could. She died, and I knew nothing about my adoption, my history, about you or my biological mother, Melanie. I don't even know what to call you."

He moved a couple of steps in her direction.

He chuckled quietly; it was a nervous sound. "'Brian' would work. I'm sorry, so sorry that you never knew. The circumstances around your birth and adoption were horrifying to me and affected Melanie for a long time. I heard that her sister, Janet, finally came to her senses and tried to find you."

"She did. It turned my world upside down, but I'll be going back

186

to New York City soon." She crossed her arms and made no move to close the distance between them.

Again, silence descended, and Beth thought, I know why I'm so angry. He's the only one I can take it out on. The only one left.

Brian Nash, his shoulders hunched, walked haltingly over to a window and pulled a table and two chairs out from the wall. "Here. Would you like to sit, and we'll talk? I'll tell you anything you want to know." His eyes never left her, as if he had been transported back in time.

"I have so many questions. They'd probably take a lifetime," she said, standing her own ground.

He shook his head slowly and smiled. "Not sure I have a whole lifetime, but you have my entire attention and whatever time I have left." He gestured toward a chair. "Come, sit."

Annoyed because he was so reasonable, she looked away at the door she'd come in, and then turned and wandered over to the chair he'd pulled out for her. Now they would have a table between them. Lowering herself into the chair, she crossed her arms and watched him move to the other side of the table and sit down. She found herself staring at his eyes. They held a world of sadness.

"Where would you like to start?" he asked, his quiet voice welcoming her response. She noticed his eyes, a light blue, centered on her, concerned, focused only on her.

"Well," she said, her voice quivering, "I'd like to know how long you were in prison."

"Fifteen years. A plea back then capped at fifteen years. I'm sure Judge Tippitt would have liked more, but the law was the law."

She swallowed and went on. "Did you ever try to find me?"

"Of course, once I had the resources. But the records were sealed. By the time I had the money to hire someone, you would have been in your early thirties. I didn't even know if you knew about your mother or me." He looked down at the floor, pausing. "Or if you would want to."

Beth considered his hesitation. "I guess I understand that. I didn't know about you until recently." She didn't quite know how to phrase the next question, so she decided she'd just jump right in.

"I'd—I'd like to know about my mother."

"That question could take several months."

"Just a capsule description. That's a good start," she said, frowning.

"Your mother. Melanie. She was beautiful, just like you." He smiled. "You have her eyes, her mouth, her blond hair, and some simple mannerisms of hers. The way you turn away when you're annoyed—just like her. I remember that look. Your voice. It's almost as if she were speaking through you. The way you walked up the driveway. You have her walk, too."

"What was she like?"

Nash looked out the window for a minute. "How to describe her to you when you never got to meet her. She was the love of my life... the only woman I ever loved or ever wanted. Melanie was funny, playful, and never concerned about breaking a rule. Her laughter was like bubbles floating on the air. She was much smarter than I, and would have finished college, if she'd been allowed to." He paused for a moment, swallowing hard.

"Her best friend was Elisha Foster—Davis, I guess, now. They did everything together. Even the day Melanie died, Elisha was there—at least, so I'm told. Melanie loved the newest dance craze, the latest rock-and-roll music, and she ate enormous amounts of food—I don't know how—and still stayed tiny. She loved romantic stories, whether they were in books or on the movie screen. Of course, this is what she was like at nineteen. I don't know what she would have been like in her sixties. I would prefer to believe we would still be together, and she would still be in love. I know I would."

Beth sat back, a little more relaxed, but the nails in her hand were biting into the palm of her other hand splayed across her lap. She didn't want to look at Brian Nash, didn't want to like him. In a sharp tone she said, "So were you planning to get married like I heard?"

His eyes went down to the table for a moment. Then he nodded.

"What happened?"

He stood up and walked a few feet away from the table. He didn't say anything for a moment. Then he turned to her. "I had asked her a month earlier. Her only condition was that she finish college, even married. I agreed absolutely. Whatever she wanted. Somehow, we would make it work, even if I had to take carpentry jobs or flip burgers at a restaurant. Somehow, some way, we would make it work. The biggest obstacle, of course, was her family. Her father and mother would never have me as a son-in-law. Never. She told me not to worry. She'd take care of her old man, and her mother would do whatever he said." He paused and came closer to the table. Beth could see his eyes glistened.

She looked away, unwilling to see his emotions.

"You believed my mother was determined," said Beth, staring out the window.

He nodded and relaxed his clenched hands. "I wasn't as positive she could handle the judge. We made a plan. July 21, before she had to go back to school, we would elope... simply disappear and have a justice of the peace marry us two counties away. She didn't care about a big wedding if we could be together. Once we had done the deed, no one could stop us."

"Do you have evidence of this? Dom told me he saw rings."

"Yes, two rings. Hers was engraved."

"Why didn't you have a receipt? It would have been proof at the trial."

He was silent. Then he said, "I bought them through a friend, one who would sell them to me cheaply, no questions asked. I didn't have a lot of money back then. Had a jeweler engrave them."

"What happened to them? I would think, if we could find them, that Kyle Warner could reopen the case, show that you didn't have a motive to kill her."

"Why? Past history. What's done is done. The door's closed, and I did my time. The dirt was shoveled on her coffin, and the rings no longer mattered."

Beth was thoughtful for a moment. Then she said, "It matters to me."

He put his hand on the table and studied the veins and brown spots. Then he said, still in that quiet, hypnotic voice, "Why? Because you'd rather not have a murderer for a father? Because you're angry that I killed her?"

Beth looked away and then focused on Brian Nash. She could hear her voice, angry and sullen, say, "Because you don't even know if that's what happened. Because maybe you did that time in prison for someone else. You don't know. And why would you plead guilty and go to prison anyway? That makes no sense. If you didn't do it, people should know that."

She was disturbed, angry. Brian Nash nodded sympathetically, sensing why she would be so upset. "Elizabeth, don't you see? It didn't matter. My life was over. Without your mother, I had no life. They took you away, and I never even got to see you. That, alone, made me hate the Tippitts." He pursed his lips and blew out a stream of air. It seemed to settle him, help him think about what he would say next. His tone became quieter again. "When I came back from 'Nam, I wasn't me. I spent months trying to get myself right again. The drinking, smoking weed—they were from a time when I thought I'd lost her, and I'd never get her back. Life wasn't worth living. I didn't care. I did a lot of stupid things that made folks in Sweet Iron think I was crazy. I'm not proud of that man. Of course they could imagine I might kill someone."

"What made you change?"

"Melanie Tippitt. She gave me hope. All those days when I was off the rails crazy about losing her, well, they were gone. I worked so hard to make myself right so we could have a future. I had to be right for her, for you."

Beth swallowed and raised her head. "For me?"

"Of course. Once we were married, we were going to find out where they had sent you, no matter what it took. We planned to find you and have the family we were meant to have."

She concentrated on his face to see if he were lying. "You did?"

"Of course. But when she died, everything else did, too. I thought about—about ending it many times, but in prison I got into AA, met Jerod Enslow, began to have some ideas for how I could have a life again, even if it was without Melanie or you."

"Is that when you came back and started this business of making furniture?"

"Yes. Jerod staked me to begin with, and once my business took off, I paid him back, and he and Dom helped me with security, setting up this place so I could be alone. I'm fine with myself for company. I disappeared to here because I didn't want to remember those people, that time. People generally let you down, so I keep to myself and no one knows where I am. Well, only Dom, Jerod, and now, you."

Beth looked down at her quiet hands in her lap, no longer clenching and opening. Something about Brian Nash made her feel calm. Perhaps she was reacting to his sense of quietness.

"How did you find this peace of mind?"

He smiled. "That took a long time. I had to swallow all the anger that was in me and realize I'm not in charge. Like they say in AA, some things I can't change. And now that I'm no longer angry, I have the wisdom to know the difference."

"Do you remember anything about that horrible day?" asked Beth.

"Doctor said it might come back, but it never did. I've tried and tried to bring it back, but it's useless."

"Did you give those wedding rings to Melanie?"

He chuckled quietly. "Oh, so it's back to the rings again. Yes, she had them."

"Do you have any idea where she might have put them?"

"You know, you are a lot like your mother. You have her dogged persistence. Of course, you look exactly like her—well, except maybe for your nose. But you aren't like her in some ways. You have a kind of quiet dignity, a reserve she never had. Maybe in time she would have been more... cautious. You never give up. I have an idea where those rings might be, but what would you do if you knew?"

"I'd take them right down to the police department and give them to Kyle Warner, demanding that he reopen the case."

"And then you'd go back to New York City, right?"

"Right." She bit her lip a moment and then added, "Well, I would stay long enough to see what happens."

He shook his head, giving in. "You are so like your mother."

This time, she smiled.

Chapter Thirty-Three

"Would you like me to show you around my shop with some of the projects I'm working on?" Brian Nash asked.

"I—I guess," Beth said.

He pointed at all the walls and tables. "All of these tools I've accumulated over time, and some are my favorites. Some I've made myself. Many are from the 1800s. See, this one is called a coffin plane because of its shape." He picked up a coffin-shaped tool with a handle. "It will take a tear out of a piece of wood when you push it against the grain." He held it up so she could see its unique shape. "I love working with this particular tool. It fits my hand perfectly."

"This whole huge area is filled with so many tools. Do you use them all?"

"Not on every project, obviously. Some I've had for years. Look at this one," he said, handing her another plane. Notice the numbers '1870' on the side? That is how old it is. It was made the year John D. Rockefeller began Standard Oil..."

"And the Fifteenth Amendment was passed, allowing African-American men to vote..." said Beth.

"And the team that would become the Chicago Cubs played their first game..."

She was laughing now, noting the enthusiasm in his voice. "And postcards were first used in this country..."

"Ah, I love history," Nash said. "To think this tool was made a hundred and forty-seven years ago, and it passed through so many hands of artisans who worked with wood, too. When I use it, I can almost feel other hands who used it before me. It gives me a sense of peace, a feeling that I'm part of a long line of craftsmen who made beautiful things and respected and cherished the wood and its nature long before I did." He paused and added, "I love history and the flow of it."

"Me, too," said Beth. "Maybe I got that from you."

"What's your favorite period of time to research?"

Beth thought he was asking her that just to keep a conversation going, but she decided she'd play along. "I love the late 1800s. The Gilded Age. I recently did a project where I discovered the Dow Jones Industrial Average published only twelve initial stocks, averaging around forty dollars apiece, in 1896. From those twelve stocks, the only current company with its original name is General Electric. The author was going to use characters who invested in those early days of the stock market."

"That would be a fascinating period with the robber barons and all," he said. Then he pointed to some geometric shapes hanging on the wall. "These are jigs. I guess you'd call them patterns. I've made most of these myself. Details on furniture are most important. They're the small touches that draw your eyes and delight your senses. Jigs help you use variations on themes so you see repetition."

"I didn't realize furniture-making involved so much thinking about design or geometry."

"Oh, yes. Most of the pieces I make are variations on Shaker furniture from centuries ago. I love their honest, simple, restrained elegance. They take all the messiness and complexity of the world and reduce them to straight lines and perfect balance and proportion."

"Was Melanie's hope chest a Shaker piece?"

He sighed and was quiet. "No. I made that way back in early high school. I didn't know much about creativity back then."

"But it's beautiful. The attention to the grain in the wood and the smooth, perfect finish make it a work of art."

Nash laughed. "That was the work of a young kid in love, a totally unformed, lovelorn idiot. I've learned so much since then. For example, wood expands across the grain. I was just learning about that in high school, and over the years I've added so much more understanding of how wood expands. The bottom of that chest can

193

move. It floats on grooves on each side. So seasonal movement, especially with humidity, keeps it fitting perfectly. Here, come into this other room and you can see what I mean."

Beth followed him into the outer room. Now she saw a large door, like a garage door, that must have been used to take the furniture out the back of the workshop and load it on a truck.

"These are the orders I'm working on now. As you can see, they are in varying stages of completion." He put his hand on top of a table, slowly moving it over the finish.

"Why do you love this furniture-making so much?" asked Beth.

Nash paused for a moment. "I believe it's because the work represents a world where everything is consistent. I can depend on it. Perfect degrees always work. The laws of nature and mathematics are always the same. They don't change, unlike people. Every angle, every measurement is perfectly proportioned. It all balances. The universe was constructed with underlying laws of nature, and furniture-making is the same. A forty-five-degree angle is always the same. The pieces fit together perfectly because I've measured them precisely. No surprises."

Beth walked over to a cabinet Brian Nash was still working on. She studied the joint work and the perfect angles. Then she put her hand on a chest, much like Melanie's, that was finished. The grain of the wood was perfectly matched, the finish silky smooth. "I find it amazing that you can construct these pieces with the pattern of the grain so perfectly matched."

"I feel like they're my children. Give them love and affection and they seem to talk to me. Each piece of wood I've chosen carefully, and each piece is different. Wood, you know, is a living thing, and if you treat it with respect, listen to what it has to say to you, and work on it thoughtfully, you create not just a piece of furniture, but an object you can love and cherish, one with which you emotionally connect."

Beth paused, thinking about what he had said. "I know you have security here, but I remember reading that rural areas often have a lot of crime. These tools and pieces of furniture are terribly expensive. That 1870 tool, for example—it's value couldn't even be calculated."

"I know," Brian said. "See this cabinet over here? It has dovetail joints so the drawers fit perfectly flush. But over on the side is a spring that will open this secret drawer. No one would know that. Just me. Here's what's inside." He pushed on the hidden spring and pulled out a handgun. Beth could tell it was a Smith &Wesson. "I'm showing you this because I trust you. I'm a felon, you know. I'm not supposed to have weapons. But living out here, it's necessary."

"Your secret is safe with me, Brian. I have a Glock back home in New York, and I love taking it to a shooting range. That Smith & Wesson is expensive, partly because it's so perfectly balanced."

"Like my tools. Must have no surprises. Craftsmanship, quality, good materials make so much difference."

They walked back into the main shop area, Beth deep in thought.

"I thought you were dead," she said. "Now that I find out you're alive, I also realize you aren't at all what I thought you'd be."

"I've kept watch on your house most nights. I didn't mean to scare you. I hope I didn't. Dom told me about the motion lights he put in with the detective. Once, I saw them go on."

"Really?"

"Yes. But I also knew about the dead bolt at the top of the stairs. I knew about that tunnel years ago. I can't imagine it's a safe place to explore these days. It hasn't been used in years. Melanie always said it had something to do with the Underground Railroad."

"I gather she used it to sneak out and see you."

"Yes," he said. "I have no idea who else might know about it. Probably Elisha since she and Melanie were like glue."

"And Sam Conklin. What did you think about him?"

"I suppose, now that I'm older, I feel sorry for him. He was under such pressure to be what his parents wanted him to be. Melanie was part of that plan, although she didn't love him. It was easier to let her parents—and Sam—think she was seriously dating him. It provided a cover for us. I guess now I realize that wasn't fair to him. Melanie felt guilty about it, even back then, but she couldn't figure out any other way for us to be together. Sam hasn't had a particularly happy life. Airplanes, big houses, and all that."

"Do you think he could have killed Melanie? Maybe he found out you were planning to run away."

"Doubtful. Melanie and I kept that secret. I suppose if he somehow found out about us, he might have been able to kill her. Melanie's leaving with me would have proved embarrassing. Sam smoking weed and drinking at the pond before he was accepted at his East Coast college might have been a problem. I, on the other hand, had nothing to lose."

"That's a lot to think about. May I come again?"

"If you'd like."

"Would *you* like that?"

"Of course," Brian said.

"Then I will. Can we forego the blindfold?"

"No. I don't want you put in a compromising position."

"Fair enough," said Beth, but she rolled her eyes.

*****

Driving back to Sweet Iron with Dom, Beth smiled to herself. I think I know where those rings are, she thought.

"Something funny?" asked Dom.

"Mmm, not really. I'm just formulating a plan."

"A plan? For what?"

"For justice. I am going to call a meeting with people I can trust. You are included in that group. We need to design a plan. I think I can flush out the person who really killed Melanie. A gentle man like Brian Nash should not have the label 'murderer' around his neck for the rest of his life."

"Did you discuss this with Brian?" asked Dom.

"Of course not. I know what he'd say. So, you keep quiet, Dom." Dom shook his head and laughed. "He's right, you know."

"Right about what?" she asked in an innocent tone.

"You are just like your mother."

Chapter Thirty-Four

B eth thought back to her meeting with Brian Nash last Friday. She'd been thinking about him all weekend. She had to do something to change the injustice of the past. No way could she see Brian Nash killing her mother, despite everyone's talk about how awful he was after Vietnam. Beth considered herself a pretty good judge of character, and she could believe Sam Conklin killing Melanie, especially if he found out she was running off with Brian Nash. As Justin had mentioned to Beth several weeks ago, Sam always got what he wanted. Maybe he didn't like to share.

After Dom dropped Beth at the house, she went straight up to Melanie's room. Dragging the hope chest out into the middle of the bedroom, she got down on her hands and knees and explored every inch of the bottom of the chest. She knew it had no hidden secrets in the lid; she had checked there already. But she hadn't checked the bottom carefully. It sat a good four inches off the floor. Placing her hand under the bottom's edge, which was surrounded by a trim piece, she felt all along the wood, hoping to find a place where a spring opened a secret drawer. Brian Nash was very keen on secrets and hiding things. He had said he'd taken a page from Melanie's book with his secret gun drawer. Did that mean he had such a drawer in Melanie's hope chest?

All around the outside edge she moved, her fingers checking every inch of wood. When she came back around to the front of the chest, she moved her fingers farther underneath the front edge to make a second search. Immediately, she felt a round indentation, so small and hidden that a person would have to know exactly where it was.

Beth pushed on it and was almost knocked backward by a drawer that sprang forward into her. Well, she thought, let's hope he got better at making secret compartments smoother, less lethal as time went by. She studied the drawer, discovering that it sat below the chest, the front covered by a piece of trim. It had been designed so cleverly that part of the trim was on the front of the drawer. But it fit so carefully with the other trim that it was impossible to see it was a separate piece.

Inside the drawer was a small book. Beth opened it, recognized the handwriting, and immediately realized it was Melanie's diary, matching the two pages Janet had found. Perhaps Melanie had torn them out for some reason. She laid the book on the floor next to her and felt around farther back in the drawer. Her fingers touched a piece of tissue that stuck out of a small leather bag with a drawstring.

Pulling out the edges of the bag, she drew out the tissue and unfolded it very carefully. Inside were two gold rings, both simple wide bands. She remembered that Brian had said Melanie's was engraved. The larger one she inspected—no engraving. The second band had tiny letters on the inside. She got up from the floor and walked over to the window for better light. Turning it over so the letters were right side up, she read the inscription: "Love You Forever B."

Beth sat down on the bed and looked at the bands again. He hadn't lied. Her father. They were going to get married. Tears filled her eyes, realizing how that day at Tippitt Pond had changed everything: their hopes, their dreams, and their future. The scent of Chantilly enveloped her, and she felt the love and warmth it always brought. "Small use you were in this little search," said Beth out loud, laughing despite her tears. "And yes, I met Brian, and I see why you loved him. What a gentle man he is now. Is that why you hung around? To encourage me to find him?" Silence. It doesn't help when no one answers you, she thought.

She put the rings in the tissue and back into the bag. What should she do with the diary to keep it safe? She opened it, seeing the familiar handwriting of Melanie Tippitt. Turning to the last page, she discovered, with dismay, that the last date was March,1971, long before the murder. She'd put it back in the compartment for safekeeping. She wanted to read it, but it was more important to put a plan in motion. She would read it later since right now it wouldn't help her. Pushing the hope chest back in front of the bed, she took the drawstring bag downstairs with her.

*****

Sunday morning, Beth greeted what she decided to call The Committee to Clear Brian Nash. Kyle, Molly, Dom, Jerod, and Ken Muir came to her house around eleven and sat around her dining room table. She had called each one of them and explained. Elizabeth Russell: Demon Problem-Solver. Each person would have an assignment and a place to be. For the next hour, they combined their ideas to come up with a plan. The purpose was to put pressure on Elisha, so she'd tell Sam Conklin or Justin Kaspar about the rings. Molly would contact the newspaper and have them put in a story about reopening the Melanie Tippitt case. Kyle would be quoted. Dom would obtain a necklace with a chip in it that would send out a signal so he could keep track of Beth's location. This was a layer of security he insisted on. Kyle's contribution was to suggest they lie about Brian Nash's shirt, and say a DNA test confirmed the blood was only Brian's, not Melanie Tippitt's.

"So," Beth said, "everyone knows where they must be and what their assignment is, right?"

They all nodded their heads.

"I'll call and get Elisha here tomorrow morning. As Ken said a few weeks ago, Shelly was the weak link. Now they've shut her up, so Elisha is the next weak link. She's such an anxious wreck. One word about reopening this case, and she'll go running to Sam Conklin."

Kyle added, "The story will go in tomorrow morning, so we're expecting some action by tomorrow night. Someone like Sam would work in cover of darkness. If anything goes wrong, Beth's necklace should tell us where she is. I don't mind saying, Beth, that I'm not real excited about making you the bait for all this."

"My father, my plan. What can go wrong? We have the basement covered with motion lights, and Sam will show up eventually, maybe with Justin. I still believe the blood and cuts on their hands and arms had nothing to do with trying to get a canoe down from his car. I am betting they got into an altercation with Brian. It's possible they're both in this together. We'll see. And thank you, everyone, for your help. Before I go back to New York, I want to see Brian Nash cleared of this terrible crime."

They left by both front and back doors, and Kyle hung around.

"Still going back to New York?" he asked.

"I think that's the plan. I would feel better, however, if we could clear Brian Nash first. I'll hang around to get that done. It's possible, too, that I'll come back for short visits. I must do some thinking about the house."

Kyle turned to her, putting his hands on her shoulders. "You could keep both a house here and one in New York, you know. You have the resources to do that."

She nodded, looking into his eyes. "I understand. I think, however, my life is in New York. I have my friend Gabby there, and I have meaningful work to do. You understand, don't you? I've only been here two weeks, and I must admit this place is growing on me, but I'm a big city person. I'd hate this small town very quickly if I pulled up roots and moved here."

He checked her eyes, searching for any degree of hesitation. Seeing none, he said, "All right. Stay safe." And he turned and followed the others from the house.

Chapter Thirty-Five

Beth had barely drunk her first cup of coffee the next morning when she heard the rapid-fire knocking on the front door. She smiled to herself, thinking about Elisha's panic when she read the newspaper story Abigail Sandstrom had carefully planted in the *Sweet Iron Sentinel*. Beth had dressed very early this morning, expecting company and not wanting to be in a bathrobe.

"And what is the meaning of this?" Elisha shouted through the window glass, holding up the newspaper and following Beth into the house with her usual clickety-clack. In fact, she was holding up the paper, wide-eyed and hair disheveled, before Beth even opened the two front doors. Without fanfare, she went charging into Beth's living room, totally oblivious to the slight smile on Beth's face, a smile she wiped off before Elisha turned around, dropping her coat on a corner of the sofa and her typically huge purse on the floor.

"Come on in, Elisha. Have a chair," Beth said calmly to the woman who had already sprinted past her.

"A chair? How can I sit down when the newspaper is printing such drivel about my friend, your mother?" True to her words, the real estate agent paced up and down the living room. "I was barely into my first cup of coffee when I picked this up from my porch, opened it, and was shocked. Overcome. I had to come over here immediately. Why are you letting them do this?"

Her voice calm and her manner steady, Beth said the lines she'd rehearsed when she'd envisioned this scene. "It's out of my hands, Elisha. The police department made the decision to reopen the case."

"But Brian Nash isn't even alive anymore."

Beth plastered an incredulous look on her face. "And you know this because—"

Elisha turned, pausing before she spoke. "Of course he isn't alive. If he were, don't you think someone here would know it? I heard he had died in a car accident somewhere down South."

"I don't know, Elisha. I have yet to see a death certificate, and I'm a 'leave no stones unturned' researcher. I keep digging up every detail until I find the answer. So far, no Brian Nash in any cemeteries in the country."

Was it Beth's imagination, or did Elisha's face turn pale?

"But—but," she sputtered, "that's impossible. He can't be alive. And since he's dead, why dig this garbage up again? The past is over and done. Sam always says what's done is done, and it does no one any good to go back and plow this field again."

Once Elisha had stopped moving and was staring out the window, Beth examined her state of collapse. Elisha's hair with its usual perfect lines was marred this morning by bits and pieces sticking out everywhere. Her typically expensive look had been replaced by sweatpants and a shirt that wasn't buttoned correctly, the hem hanging lopsidedly. Incongruously, below the hem of the sweatpants were the usual stiletto heels. Without makeup, Elisha looked much older than her sixty-some years. Her eyes were slits, and normally tucked-away wrinkles were defying their regularly scheduled shots she probably endured to keep her face smooth. Her lips, without their usual color, were pale relatives of their red cousins, turned downward in an uncomfortable frown.

"Why don't you sit down a minute," Beth said, "and maybe we can talk. You look like you could use a few minutes of peace and calm."

Elisha looked closely at Beth's face for signs of concern. She didn't sit down, however. She resumed her pacing.

"How can you sit there so calmly? Whatever this new evidence is will probably only add to the perception that Brian did this... this horrible crime."

Beth noticed that Elisha always avoided saying Melanie was murdered. It was as if she didn't want to think about what that might have looked like. Or perhaps she didn't want to remember what it did look like.

"Part of that evidence is the shirt Brian Nash was wearing that day," Beth said. "Everyone assumed it had Melanie's blood on it. Instead, they did a DNA test—a test unavailable back then—and the blood was Brian's. This means one of the pieces of evidence that might have convicted him if he hadn't pled guilty should be thrown out of the equation. What else do you suppose might also go out the window once they start digging?"

"This is absurd, ridiculous," Elisha retorted. "He did it. Everyone knows he did it. I was there that day. No one else could have done it. They were alone the whole time Shelly and I were walking to the old mill. He confessed. He did it."

"Funny you should bring up Shelly. Her death makes me wonder what she knew. What did she know, Elisha? Why would someone purposely run her down? Did she have secrets? Did she see who really killed Melanie Tippitt?"

Now Elisha turned around and walked over to Beth. She leaned over and moved into her space. "Shelly was hit accidently. Everyone knows she walks those dogs and doesn't pay any attention to what's going on around her. It was an accident."

"It seemed awfully coincidental since I came back to town and started asking questions."

And now Elisha walked to the center of the room. She was motionless for several moments. Then she made up her mind, and her shoulders lost their hunched look, matching a change in her face. She smiled and seemed to regain her composure. "Elizabeth, don't you see? Even if Brian Nash had lost a lot of blood from that car accident, the evidence was still overwhelming that he did it. No one else had a motive. No one else was there. He was acting crazy and was horribly angry. He'd have killed Shelly and me if we hadn't left so he could talk to Melanie. Maybe he'd heard that she and Sam were getting engaged. He was a madman, someone not to be toyed with."

"So, you left your best friend with him? Alone?"

"What else could we do? Brian was not one to reason with when he was like that. So different than he'd been before he went away to Vietnam. Everyone knew that."

"I suppose he made up the story about buying rings for his own wedding to Melanie. Maybe he'd fabricated the idea that they were getting engaged and running away together. I think that is what the newspaper said back then," said Beth.

"Of course he did. Brian Nash would lie to stay out of jail. He'd say anything to make people believe he—he hadn't done this thing."

"What if he had bought those rings, Elisha? What if they existed?"

Elisha sat down and crossed her legs, one of them moving rapidly up and down. "He didn't, Beth. You didn't know Brian Nash like I did. He was a liar and a murderer. He'd say anything about Melanie, do anything to make sure no one else could have her."

"No one else. You mean like Sam Conklin?"

"That's right."

Beth leaned over, looking straight into Elisha's face. "And what might Sam Conklin have done for the same reason?"

"Sam?" Her eyes looked away. "Sam didn't have anything to do with this. He was in town with Justin."

"I see," said Beth. She rose from the sofa and walked out to the foyer. Opening the drawer in a small table, she retrieved the bag with Brian's rings. Then she walked back to Elisha and handed her the bag. "Check out what I found in Melanie's room."

Elisha looked down at the bag and started to say something. Then she thought better of it and silently opened the leather pouch. Out slipped the two wedding bands. Momentarily, she was stunned. She looked at them, lying in the palm of her hand, and then her face resolved itself into a new story. "These could be anyone's rings."

"Check out the inscription in the impossibly small one that would have been on Melanie's finger."

Elisha held up the ring, peering at it. "Just a minute," she said, pulling her reading glasses out of her purse on the floor. She scrunched up her eyes and then stood, walking over to the window. Beth could see her lips moving as she read the words. "Oh, my God. Where did you find these?"

"In a secret compartment of the hope chest Brian Nash made for

Melanie Tippitt."

"I've never seen these before. Your mother told me everything. She would have shown me these if they'd existed," said Elisha.

"They *did* exist," Beth said, holding out her hand to take them back. Elisha dropped them into her hand and once again collapsed onto the chair. Beth watched her face contort into a picture of uncertainty. "And, when I found those rings, I also found my mother's diary. Very interesting reading, and now in the hands of Detective Warner."

Elisha stood perfectly still, no words coming out of her mouth. Just when Beth wondered if her mother's best friend was catatonic, Elisha said, "Do you have an extra cup of coffee?"

"Sure. Come out to the kitchen with me."

Beth poured Elisha's coffee just as her phone rang out in the foyer. "Cream in the fridge and sugar on the counter over there. I'll be back in a second."

Walking out to the foyer, she picked up her phone. It was Gabrielle.

"Hi, Gabby." She listened to her friend asking about when she was going to be back in New York City. She had tickets to go to a concert Beth had been hoping to see. Vaguely, as she spoke, Beth could hear Elisha moving around, but the woman was so jittery and nervous she couldn't sit still. Finally, Beth ended the conversation, telling Gabby she'd call her back soon.

Elisha was standing up, looking out the glass doors, holding a coffee cup, and much more composed, Beth noted, when she returned to the kitchen.

"Coffee always helps in a moment of… concern," Elisha said. "I think no matter what old stuff they dig up from the past, Brian Nash will still be guilty. He even pleaded guilty. Reopening this case isn't going to make any difference, Elizabeth. Besides, those rings could have been manufactured anytime."

"Are you saying I lied about the rings?" Beth asked.

"Uh, well, not exactly. Maybe it's the police."

"What reason would they have to manufacture rings, Elisha? I did find these in Melanie's hope chest, the one Brian Nash made for her." And, thought Beth, Elisha probably doesn't believe that because she went through that chest, throwing things in every direction.

Suddenly, Elisha did a three-sixty and asked about the necklace Beth had on.

"Oh, it was my mother's, Melanie's," Beth said, using that unusual word—"mother"—and fingering the necklace with the chip in it.

"Funny, I don't remember it, and I thought I knew all of Melanie's jewelry."

"To get back to the subject," Beth said, "I guess we'll let the police reopen the case and, as they say, 'let the chips fall where they may.'"

Now Elisha tried a new line of thinking. "Why is this so important to you? Brian Nash is undoubtedly dead. He pleaded guilty. Case closed. Why go back to that time and try to change everything?"

Beth considered that briefly. "I still have to acknowledge that he was my biological father. If his reputation was demolished by a murder he didn't commit, I think it's important to have the truth come out."

"Well," Elisha said, her lips compressing into a grim line. "His reputation was already in tatters when he came back from Vietnam a crazy man. Adding murder to it didn't change much." Before Beth could object, Elisha added, "I suppose, at this point, it would be useless to bring up the question of selling your house?"

"I have been thinking about it, despite my preoccupation with the past. I plan to go back to New York City, but I may hang onto this house a little longer."

Elisha took one last swallow of coffee and set her cup on the counter. "I'd better be getting back home. Places to go, people to see. Thank you for explaining what you've been working on these past weeks. I can see now why you haven't had time to think about the house. I wish you luck in your inquiries, but I hardly think they will make any difference. As Sam always says, 'The past is the past, and you can't change it, so it's better to let it go.'"

She left, head held high, and Beth watched her walk to her car. As soon as she turned on the engine, Beth could see her lips moving. She must have been on the phone already to Sam Conklin. Beth watched her car pull away. Now to see what events unfolded since the hook is baited, she thought.

Chapter Thirty-Six

B eth didn't know what she expected as she slid into bed. Well, actually, she did. She had expected Sam Conklin to come charging over, and she'd confront him with the evidence. Then Kyle and Dom and the rest of them would take him to the police station. That didn't happen, nor did she hear from Elisha again. Hearing nothing was more disturbing. She wrinkled her brow and rubbed her eyes. What were they planning?

She turned out her bedside lamp, glancing at the clock. Eleven o'clock. Kyle had called about an hour ago saying Ken reported the lights going out at Sam Conklin's. According to Ken, the Senator's lights had gone off downstairs, and now they were off throughout the house. Beth laughed. "The boys," as she called them, had come up with names for the "perps." Just like junior FBI agents, thought Beth. Sam Conklin was "The Senator" and Elisha was "Clickity Clack." They had ascertained that Justin was out of town on a business trip. Kyle had called Jerod off from the airport in Eckley, since they had figured Sam wouldn't fly out of town. However, Kyle said he would stay outside on the street in front of Beth's house in an unmarked car for the rest of the night.

Smiling, she thought, boys and their toys. She tried to hide her disappointment. She had figured Elisha would go straight to Sam and call Justin with the news about the reopening of the case, although they'd probably read it in the morning paper. At the very least they must have gotten together for a meeting about what to do. Maybe she wasn't such a good planner or problem-solver after all. She yawned and could feel herself drifting off to sleep.

She tossed and turned through the early hours of the night, waking up briefly and looking at the clock. 2:38. Then, from a sound sleep, she sensed that something was wrong. She opened her eyes, trying to get them to focus in the dark. Little by little she smelled the sweet scent of Chantilly, but she couldn't figure out if she was awake and smelling it or asleep and dreaming. She started to get up and check her mother's room when something or someone pushed a heavy cloth over her nose and mouth and everything went black.

*****

Beth sensed that she was moving, but she was so groggy she couldn't keep her eyes open. When she did open her eyes slightly and began to understand she was awake and not in her bed, she also realized she was lying on something. She tried to sit up, but she couldn't. Slowly consciousness returned, and she realized her hands were tied with a rope that was connected to something on the other side of the seatback of a car. She was lying on a hard surface with her hands tied in front of her. She couldn't separate her feet or legs. They were tied, too. Heaviness seemed to be weighing her down. Must have been whatever they drugged me with, she thought.

She became aware of voices talking quietly. One was a man's, one a woman's.

"We must be able to do something else with her," said the woman's voice.

The man answered, "Don't get lily-livered on me now. We have too much to lose."

Beth heard the woman sigh in disgust. "This will be a real estate deal gone wrong. Seven years I'll have to wait to have a missing person declared dead."

Missing person? Beth thought. Real estate. Elisha?

"This is the last time I save your skin, Elisha. If you hadn't been so stupid and angry that day, none of this would have happened."

"I was being loyal to you, Sam. When she told me about their plans, I just blew up. I couldn't let her do that to you. I couldn't let her run off with Brian Nash. What a waste. What a terrible waste."

"And I appreciate your thoughts about my honor and reputation. However, that is what has landed us in this mess. If we hadn't thought fast, Justin and I would have ended up with a record for moving a body, obstructing justice, conspiracy, and smoking weed. We might have gotten away with the last one since our families could have gotten that erased, but the rest would have meant college down the drain and probably prison time."

"I didn't mean to hurt Melanie. It was an accident. I shoved her, and she fell and hit her head."

Beth's eyes were now wide open, and her thinking wasn't quite as foggy. Elisha? Elisha killed Melanie Tippitt?

"Besides," said Elisha. "How did I know her brat was going to appear forty years later and bring up the whole mess? I blame it on Melanie. If she hadn't flirted with everything in pants, none of this would have happened."

"Are you sure you relocked the door to the basement?" asked Sam.

"Yes. But taking the motion lights out yesterday afternoon is going to be a huge clue that something is wrong."

"I think I can get them back in early in the morning once the sun comes up," replied Sam. "That way she'll just disappear, and no one will be the wiser about how we got her out."

When did they do that? wondered Beth. Is this just Monday night? She vaguely remembered hearing Elisha moving around when she took the phone call from Gabby. She must have unlocked the pantry door then. Why didn't I check it before I went to bed? she fumed. Beth refocused and strained to listen. She appeared to be on the back floor of an SUV. She was facing the back window, the second set of car seats at her back. A pile of old rags was near her head, but nothing else that could help her. Listening to the sound of the wheels, she could tell they were on a highway of some sort because the road was smooth.

She pulled at the ropes on her wrists. Maybe they were a little loose and she could get her hands out. After a few minutes, she knew that was hopeless. Maybe she should pretend to still be asleep until she figured out what they were doing.

Beth felt the car make several turns. It slowed down, stopped, and then someone opened a window. She heard some electronic noises like Sam or Elisha entering a security code. Were they going to his house? He probably had a gated entrance with a security code. No, they had driven too long for that, she thought. The car started again and seemed to coast very slowly. It stopped. Then she heard Sam or Elisha get out while the other one waited.

Whoever it was got back in the car and Elisha said, "I'll shut them behind us." They moved several yards farther, stopped, and then Elisha got out and closed a door that sounded as if it were moving on a track of some sort. Very heavy doors. Bright lights came on outside the car.

"Keep an eye on her," said Sam. "I have to go through a list of safety instructions before we can take off." A car door opened and slammed shut. Then it was quiet.

Take off? thought Beth. They must be at the airport in Eckley. Sam, she knew, had a small plane there from what she had heard at that New Year's party. Maybe Jerod is still here, she thought. Oh. She remembered Kyle said he'd called everyone off. She kept her eyes closed, not sure if Elisha was watching her. Where are they taking me? Why hasn't Kyle or anyone else shown up? Maybe they're waiting for Sam to do something so they can catch him in the act. She tried to open her eyes a tiny slit. Sam. His plane. Talk about her being missing for seven years. She couldn't quite wrap her mind around that. Why hadn't Kyle or Dom tracked her necklace?

She could move her hands a little because the rope had some slack to it. In small, furtive movements so as not to attract Elisha's attention, she inched her fingers toward her neck. The necklace with the tracking chip was gone!

Chapter Thirty-Seven

Now Beth began to panic. Who knew where she was? Elisha or Sam must have taken her necklace. She slowly pulled her hands back down, but as she did, her fingers worried her PJs, only to discover she had something else on. She could tell she had her pajamas on because she could feel them on her legs. But they had put something else over her PJs. She could hear Elisha sighing in the front seat.

If no one is coming after me, she thought, I'm going to have to somehow get away myself. At some point, they're going to get me out of this car. But how to get my feet untied so I can run? Why do I feel like something heavy is weighing me down? She moved her fingers again, very slightly. It felt like she had a jacket on. She could feel a zipper down the front. Moving her fingers, ever so slowly, over to one side of the jacket, she could feel a pocket. It felt like rocks or gravel or heavy pieces of something were in the pocket. Moving her fingers to the other side, she discovered the other pocket felt the same.

Then it dawned on her. Airplane. Rocks. Hands and feet tied. She would go missing at the bottom of a lake or pond, weighed down and unable to kick or move her hands. Oh my God, how could they do this to me? As she realized what they were planning, she suddenly felt like she couldn't breathe. Her mouth was dry, and she tried to swallow to no avail. This was Sam Conklin, who had sat beside her at the wine store and charmed her? This was Elisha Davis? Her mother's best friend? How could they plot such a horrible thing?

Beth began to panic, her breathing tight and short, her hands

211

struggling at their bonds. No matter how hard she tried to loosen the ropes, she could not get free. What could she do?

Stopping her efforts, she considered other possibilities. Her only hope would be to get free when they tried to move her. Sam was still gone. She had a little time.

She thought about Gabby, Sarah, and Alyssa back in New York. If she couldn't get loose, she'd never see them again. They'd never know what happened to her. Beth almost sobbed but caught herself when she realized Elisha would hear her. What have I done to deserve this? And Brian Nash—never to see him again or find out what he is really like. At least she knew he was innocent of killing her mother, but no one else would ever know, including him. Never to spend another hour on earth with him, she thought. Suddenly, that seemed terribly important. She still had things she wanted to do in her life, places she wanted to see. And Kyle—she should have been kinder to him. She should have told him she liked him and wanted to spend more time in Sweet Iron. Why didn't she say those things? She felt tears in her eyes and realized Elisha had turned around and was looking at her.

"So, you're awake, sleeping beauty," Elisha said, trying to sound nonchalant. She didn't know how long Beth had listened to their plans.

"Elisha, please, why are you doing this?" Beth pleaded.

Elisha didn't say anything for a few moments. Then she turned farther around in the seat and looked in the back. "You've left us no choice, Elizabeth. If you hadn't come back and meddled, none of this would have been necessary."

Sam Conklin opened the door in the back seat and looked in. "Oh, you're awake. Maybe I'd better drug you again. Might be easier to get you out and onto the plane."

Beth stopped struggling and waited. No drugs, she thought. She needed her wits about her.

"Elisha, you're going to have to help me get her onto the plane. She'll be like dead weight trying to get her up the stairs, especially with that vest on." Sam untied the ropes that anchored her in the car. "You get her feet and I'll get her shoulders."

Awkwardly, they half-carried, half-dragged her out of the car through the trunk opening and moved her over to the steps of the plane. Then, with a great deal of heavy breathing and swearing, Sam walked backward up the steps, pulling her along. Her back hit the metal steps several times, causing her to groan repeatedly.

"Don't worry," Sam said. "You won't be in any pain ever again before too long." He left her on the floor in front of the passenger seats and retied the rope on her wrists to the leg of a seat. Elisha climbed over her and got into a pilot seat.

Once she was on the small plane securely, Sam left again. After he returned, he looked at Elisha and said, "You're next, Elisha."

"What? What do you mean?"

"It's time you see what your stupidity has led to. You can be the one to push her out the door once we're over Carsdon Lake."

"Me?" Elisha whined.

"If you hadn't quarreled with Melanie and shoved her, none of this would have happened." He climbed over Beth and stepped into the cockpit.

Now Beth was lying on the floor, and she could see out a square window on the side wall above where her feet rested on the floor. They were still in the hangar. Sam and Elisha were in the two pilot seats, their seat belts on and a barrage of buttons and levers between them, in front of them, and over their heads. They both had earphones on. Sam pushed buttons and the engines came to life.

Beth took deep breaths, trying to ease the anxiety in her whole body. Her legs were shaking, and she could hear the engines start to get louder, but still the plane was stationary. Then she felt the plane taxi out of the hangar and turn. It moved slowly, probably to the end of the runway, and then it stopped. Sam was evidently checking some gauges. It must have been a few seconds, but it seemed like minutes. She blinked her eyes, brushing away the tears. They'd be airborne in only a few seconds.

Tears streamed down Beth's face. Nothing to be done, she thought. The engines began to get louder again, and the plane moved forward. The engines revved up to a fever pitch now just before taking off.

Suddenly, Sam Conklin shouted, "What the hell? Who is that?"

Beth could hear him unsnap his seatbelt and then just the sound of the engines. "What fool would park a truck in front of my plane?"

"Plow through it," shouted Elisha.

"Elisha, you idiot! Are you kidding? It would damage the plane and once we got off the ground—if we got off the ground—we'd be in a world of trouble."

Then Beth heard a huge banging noise, and the plane seemed to shudder and move backward. Again, she heard a loud noise and the plane bumped backward again.

"That insane truck driver is charging us!"

Beth heard Sam cursing and pushing all kinds of levers and buttons. The engines began to slow down to a stop. He threw his door open and lowered a set of steps. As soon as he disappeared out the door, Elisha got up and came back to Beth, untying her hands.

"Not in cold blood. I am not a cold-blooded murderer. I don't care what Sam says. Carsdon Lake is one of the deepest lakes in the Midwest." She helped Beth untie her hands and pulled off the weighted jacket. Then she helped her to her feet and into a passenger seat.

Beth began untying her feet as she heard voices shouting. She looked out the window but couldn't quite take in the scene. Her father, Brian Nash, slugged Sam Conklin several times and decked him. Sam didn't move from the tarmac. She heard sirens in the distance. Overwhelmed, she put her head in her hands.

Elisha was shaking, and Beth figured she thought she was next. Then the plane door flew open, Brian Nash's face appeared in the open doorway, and he said in a deadly quiet voice, "Where is my daughter, Elisha?"

Elisha stared at him in shock. "B—Brian?"

When he saw Beth slumped over the passenger seat, he yelled, "Get the hell out of here, Elisha, or you're next, and don't think I wouldn't hit a woman!"

Elisha grabbed the door handle on the wall next to her, throwing the door open, and launched herself, falling several feet onto the tarmac with a loud scream. Brian Nash covered the distance to Beth in two strides and pulled her into his arms.

Chapter Thirty-Eight

B eth looked around the living room at Tippitt House. She was nestled against the corner of the sofa, pillows behind her sore back and a comforter over her. The ER had cleared her after cleaning the scrapes on her back and giving her some ointment to help them heal. The bruising would hurt for some time. But she was alive.

She smiled and looked at the faces she never thought she'd see again: Ken Muir, laughing as he said something to Dom, Jerod arguing with Kyle about a football game that had been played the day before, and Molly, walking in from the kitchen with another bottle of wine in her hand. Only one person was missing, and now Molly and Ken knew Brian was alive, too. She cleared her throat and, getting their attention, asked them to recount what had happened the night before. Their versions.

Ken said, "I guess I can start. Jerod is the one who called it right. He saw Sam and Elisha headed toward Eckley just as he was coming into Sweet Iron from his stake-out at the airport, and since he knew we had called off the stakeout at Sam's house, he turned around and started making calls. Kyle first, then Dom and Molly, and finally me. We all took off. We are so lucky Jerod was on top of things."

"Thank you, Jerod," Beth said. "You saved my life. I hate to think where I'd be today without you—actually, at the bottom of Carsdon Lake. Since I saw my entire life flash before me on that plane, I'm sorry I got so angry with you over the desk in your office." She swallowed and added, "I think I owe a lot of statements like that to people."

Jerod laughed. "Nothin' like coming near death to remind a person of what's important, right? Apology accepted. After all, Dom and I kept you out of the loop, and if you hadn't seen that desk you still wouldn't have known Brian was alive."

"But how did Brian know about last night?" Beth asked.

"My fault," said Dom, his hands up in the air. "I know, I know—he figured something was up. Couldn't keep a poker face with him, so I had to come clean and confess we were watching Sam and Elisha with you for bait. He was *not* happy. Oh, man! The things he said when he realized you were the target. Brian didn't believe Sam would let it go by. When I told him who was where on the playing board, he decided to park and watch the area where the tunnel came out.

"Sure enough, he saw them bringing you out, and he followed them, but got stopped by a freight train on the outskirts of Eckley." He put his head down. "Brian may not speak to me ever again."

"But you told me, Dom, that he was such a quiet, laid-back kind of person now," said Beth, laughing.

"Not since you came to town. He's discovered parental responsibility." All of them laughed. His face took on a wry look and he shook his head.

"What will the police do now to clear Brian?" She turned to Kyle. "Do you know? Will they somehow exonerate him?"

Kyle nodded his head. "They'll have to get all the details of the story first. Sam, Elisha, and Justin are all in jail until their lawyers show up. Justin was out of town ditching the car he used to run Shelly down, but we got him on his way back and now we have the car. He is in deep trouble. Once we find out the details, Brian's murder charge will be vacated. Sam is willing to sing if it helps him with a shorter sentence. Once Brian is cleared, he'll have a clean slate."

"Except for the fifteen years he spent in jail," Molly said softly. "He won't ever get those years back."

"Yes," Kyle said. "That's right. It's too bad. I was shocked to see he was even alive. What an unbelievable story."

"And one we will be recounting for Abigail Sandstrom in an exclusive for the *Sweet Iron Sentinel*. It's payback for the story she put in about reopening the case, but we'll keep Brian's location out of it," said Molly.

Jerod motioned to Molly to pass the wine his way. Then he asked, "So what happened, Beth, while I was keeping an eye on Eckley Airport?"

"First, they drugged me. They must have torn off my necklace, and I don't understand why. I woke up, uh, for some reason, and someone was putting a towel with something—a drug to knock me out—over my face." She took another sip of wine. "You know, the more wine I drink, the less my back hurts. Once I became conscious again, I heard them talking in the car or on the plane. Can't remember which now. Elisha had stopped by the house, and while I was in the foyer, she checked out the pantry door and opened the deadbolt. Later that day, Sam removed the motion lights in the basement. Stupid me. I didn't even think to check the pantry door before I went to bed." She shook her head.

"I'd say you had enough on your mind," said Dom. "Besides, you came up with a good plan. It should have worked."

"The necklace was a great idea, but I know why they took it off. It would have identified you if your body had somehow been found," said Kyle. "They were taking no chances."

"They were going to deep six me in some place called Carsdon Lake," she explained. "Elisha stayed true to form. She was concerned that she'd have to wait seven years to have me declared dead before she could sell my house. That's what she was worried about while they discussed killing me."

"Elisha, by the way, is talking," said Kyle. "She was the one who killed Melanie. It was an accident. They were arguing. Shelly took the body and put it in Tippitt Pond, thinking she could make it look like a drowning. She didn't realize the autopsy would negate that."

"Was Sam there when that happened?" asked Molly.

"He and Justin did go into town earlier that day, but after they returned to the pond Brian showed up and got into it with Sam over Melanie. They fought—hence the scratches on Sam's arms—and Justin finally managed to pull them apart. Brian left for town, and Sam and Justin went to town to clean up, change clothes, and get more beer. The fact that Brian totaled his car and couldn't remember was an unplanned plus," said Kyle.

Ken added, "They blamed it on Brian, and he was so depressed and ill with PTSD that he just gave in and took the blame."

Beth, who had been quiet through the discussion, asked, "I still don't understand why Melanie died. I still don't understand why they were arguing"

"Sam and Justin were in town when she died," said Kyle. "Unfortunately, Melanie made the mistake of telling Elisha that she and Brian were going to take off the next day and get married. I guess she had to tell her best friend. Brian already had the wedding rings, and Melanie had them safely tucked away. Elisha was incensed. She had this intense loyalty to Sam, who had helped her out of plenty of jams. She was also doing a slow smolder because she thought Melanie had been flirting with Justin, Elisha's boyfriend. Actually, it was the other way around. When she heard Melanie was going to run off with Brian, it was the last straw. She and Melanie got into a pushing match, and Melanie fell and hit her head on a huge piece of wood, a log that was behind her on the beach," said Kyle.

"I've seen Elisha in an emergency," said Beth. "I can't imagine she dealt with this very well."

"Not at all," said Ken. "She was hysterical, according to Justin. Shelly kept the level head and tried to help. She's the one who checked Melanie's pulse and realized she was dead. When Sam and Justin returned, they concocted the story about Brian coming back and the girls walking to the mill while Brian talked to Melanie. Remember, Beth, I mentioned their stories were all too pat?"

"Yes. You were right. But I imagine their loyalty as fellow conspirators in this lie kept them together." She paused for a minute. Then she added, "Until I came back. I believe that was why Shelly's conscience finally got to her. I guess I look a lot like my mother. It brought that day barreling back into her mind—memories she thought she'd forgotten. She probably saw what they were doing to try to find those rings. It became too much for Shelly."

"Elisha broke into the house twice, looking for the wedding rings. The scrapbook was just an afterthought to grab. I'm sure she panicked," said Kyle.

"What I don't understand," said Beth, "is why Sam and Justin helped conceal the murder and blame it on Brian. Elisha was the one who killed Melanie, even if it was an accident."

"That's clear to me," said Ken. "Remember I told you Sam and Justin had big college plans—to go to Ivy League schools out East. They were just kids at that time, and smoking pot would not have looked good on their records. Weed was a criminal offense that often ended in prison time. Once they decided to help conceal a murder, they were in it for the foreseeable future. Shelly might even have been paid off by Sam with money that helped start her business. What he didn't count on was her resentment over his treatment of her. She was always second-class. It was Melanie who had been kind. That must have gnawed on her conscience."

"My understanding is that she also liked Brian and perhaps felt guilty about what they'd done to him," said Beth.

"I'd agree," Jerod chimed in. "They all knew about the tunnel in this house, and they helped confirm the lie that Brian was angry and high that day, and that he was driving erratically."

"It was you, Beth," said Dom. "If you hadn't shown up and insisted on finding out the truth, Brian would still be considered a murderer."

"You were able to do what I couldn't," said Ken.

Jerod added, "Maybe Brian can come out of the shadows now. He'll know he didn't commit that murder. But I have a feeling he will deal with this a little bit at a time."

"So now," said Molly, "my library is at your disposal. We're ready to take on whatever projects interest you. I hope you'll think about staying here."

Beth looked around at their faces. Dom, Jerod, Ken, Molly, and Kyle. Most of all, Kyle. She paused, considering the one face that wasn't there.

"I don't think I've ever had so many friends in my life," she said. "I need to rest up a little, and then I'll figure out what I can or can't do. I have some talking to do with Brian, too. We'll see."

Chapter Thirty-Nine

After everyone left, Molly stayed on at Tippitt House during the rest of the day to keep away the media that was parked out front and answer the newspaper reporters that kept calling on the phone. Beth slept for several hours, trying to let her brain process her horrible experience at the airport.

Now it was evening, and only a skeleton crew of reporters waited outside. Beth had eaten dinner, checked the lock on the pantry door, and was about to go up to bed. As she turned off the lights, she thought she heard a knocking sound. It wasn't at the front door. Walking back to the kitchen, she realized the knocking came from the pantry door.

"Who's there?" she demanded through the locked door.

A pause ensued and then, "Brian."

She opened the door and stepped back.

"Thought it might be easier to evade the reporters out front if I came in through the back way." He closed the door and turned toward Beth. "That tunnel is actually in better shape than I thought. Left a flashlight down there."

Beth led him out to the living room, saying, "It's such a piece of history. I'd like to find out which ancestor built it."

"The Tippitt family is a formidable one in many ways. If you researched your ancestors, I imagine you would find jaw-dropping stories. Maybe you should consider doing that."

"Maybe I should," she replied.

They sat in a companionable silence.

Beth said in a quiet voice, "Thank you again for saving my life. I thought for sure that it was over."

He sat back in a wing chair and said, "Other than Melanie, I've never had anyone to watch over—and I did a terrible job of keeping her safe." He paused and added, "Dom told me what happened that day at Tippitt Pond." He thought about how to continue. "I always knew Sam had a cruel streak. He didn't treat Melanie well. But abetting murder?"

"I think he saw me as a living reminder of Melanie. Maybe he never really had her love—only you did—so he was getting rid of everything from that time by killing me."

Brian nodded slowly. "What will happen now?"

"Elisha is in the hospital with two broken ankles. Probably the end of her four-inch heels. She'll be charged and tried, and so will Sam and Justin."

Brian digested that bit of information. Hesitantly, he said, "I didn't think it would matter, but you were right. It did. I—I had lost her memory—the ability to remember so much. It was fading, and I didn't care anymore." He slowly shook his head and dropped his gaze. "All my feelings, my emotions, went into my creations. All that was good and hopeful, all that was loving… lost. And then you came back and now, between you and what you did, Melanie's back. I'm grateful."

Beth smiled, thinking he had no idea how true that statement was. "Would you like a cup of coffee?"

"No, but thanks. I just wanted to see you again, to tell you how much it meant to me to have my memories of Melanie back. And you. Times I thought about ending it all. Maybe seeing her in another life. Maybe you. But something always stopped me—the possibility of seeing you in this life. You're the thread that binds us all together."

Beth thought she saw tears forming in his eyes, but he turned away. He cleared his throat and looked around the living room, his eyes settling on various objects. "It's weird. I haven't been in this house for decades, and that was mostly in the kitchen. Shirley Denny used to save me some of her peach cobbler. I can still taste it."

"Were you ever in Melanie's room?"

"No," he said. "The upstairs was off limits."

Beth thought for a moment. "I think you should see it. But be prepared for a huge shock."

She led him slowly up the main, mahogany staircase, turning for a moment and taking his hand. When they reached the door to Melanie's room, she turned on the light switch and held on to his hand a little tighter. Her father gasped, a look of shock spreading slowly over his face. His hand went up to his mouth, and he simply stood there.

"All of her things were left as they were when she died. It's like going back in a time capsule," said Beth. She watched him stand perfectly still. "It's all right. You can walk in."

He stepped slowly into the room, looking all around.

"I'll leave you to look around. Her hope chest—the one you made—has held up beautifully. I sometimes feel her presence here, and it's so calming to me. You take your time. I'll be downstairs," Beth said.

Returning to the living room, she thought about her father's pain. She'd never considered anyone but herself. Oh, she'd felt hurt about her mother's death and wanted to know what Melanie was like. She had simply been so angry at her father, thinking he was the murderer, that she'd never considered any other possibility. How selfish she'd been.

She thought about trials for Elisha, Sam, and Justin. Going to New York City would mean she would have to come back here to testify at their trials. That would be a long time from now, though, since the justice system moves so slowly. Her father was right; it had been a good thing to sweep away the cobwebs and let the truth shine out. Now maybe he could go on with his life, realizing he had not killed the one woman he loved. And what should she do? Maybe she would hold on to the house here long enough to find out about its past and deal with the trials when she came back. I'd love to stay here longer, but my life is in the city, she thought.

She sighed as she considered her two lives. It was becoming easier to think of Brian Nash and Melanie Tippitt as her parents. They would never replace her adoptive parents, but all four had played a part in her life, she realized. She was just thinking about this new revelation when she heard Brian Nash coming slowly down the stairs.

"That is amazing," he said. "It's as if she's still there—even her

222

perfume. I've never forgotten that scent. It brings back so many memories."

"Did you smell it in the air?" asked Beth.

"Very gently, lightly. It's amazing how your sense of smell brings such a strong memory to your brain. Chantilly. It opened the door to so many things I'd forgotten, as did her clothes and her photograph, the jewelry box I'd made her, and the—the hope chest."

"She kept scrapbooks and photo albums from back then, and her diary is in the secret drawer to your hope chest. I plan to take it back to Long Island and read it. Then I'll bring it back because maybe someday you'll want to read it, too. It should be yours." Beth rose and walked out to the foyer, finding the small black bag with the wedding rings and handing it to Brian. "These are yours, too. They helped free you. I think it's apt that the very symbol of your love for each other is what set you free."

He turned and hugged her a bit awkwardly. "Sorry," he said. "I'm out of experience with hugs. It's been a long time. What will you do now? I was hoping you would stick around so I could hear about your life in the city."

"That's a good question. I'm not sure. I think I'll keep this house for a while, but I need to get away from this month of living in another time and place. New York City. That's really where I belong. I still need to do some thinking about all that. I'll be around for a little while, and then back for the trials. We'll talk before I go and when I'm back," Beth said. "I think it's time we got to know each other."

He looked out the doorway of the foyer, avoiding eye contact. "I hope you'll come back. I would like to get to know my only daughter." Then his voice changed, and he said, "Guess I'll brave the paparazzi this time. Besides, it's dark and they'll be so shocked to see someone come out the door that I'll be gone before they can get their cameras and mics on."

She lifted her arms and gave him one last hug, and he turned and left.

Beth watched him hurry down the sidewalk, fending off the news people. Then she resumed turning the lights off and checking the doors. She climbed the mahogany stairs, touching the smooth railing, and stopped in her mother's room.

"Did you see him, Melanie? He was here remembering you. Now at least we've met each other. I know he smelled your scent. Chantilly."

She waited for a response: the scent of Chantilly or lights going on or off. Nothing.

"Melanie?"

It was dark, quiet, peaceful.

*****

Spring was visiting the city in late April. Beth had arranged to meet Gabby at a posh New York City restaurant, and they were just finishing the yummy blueberry and lime tastes of Vacherin.

"And lunch is on me now that I have a larger budget," Beth said, laughing.

Gabby pulled her hair away from her face and leaned forward, picking up her wineglass. "And to think all of that happened because I convinced you to go back and check out this little town you knew you'd hate," said Gabby. "I think I can take some credit for that!"

"You can. It's taken me quite a while to figure out what I'm going to do about all that—you know, a residence and a decision about my next project. But my little apartment welcomed me back, and the Rose Reading Room is still there with my favorite reference books."

Gabby set her fork down, wiped her mouth with her napkin, and asked, "You know, I've only seen you a couple of times since you've been back. You're different. You seem so pensive. What's up with that?"

"I don't know," said Beth. "In some ways, I guess it's like I've had an epiphany at the age of forty-eight, and I'm still working through it. But I think I've decided what to do."

"What?" asked Gabby.

"Well—" began Beth.

*****

That conversation had happened the previous week after months of thinking about how the year began.

Now, Beth sat quietly and thought about the ideas she had considered over the last months. She had worked it out in her head, recalling the many pictures in her mind, the slides of her life that had seemed moments away from extinction in Sam Conklin's plane: walking with Ally to the school bus stop, her mother waiting for her after school, her father patiently teaching her how to shoot a gun, and meeting Gabby for the first time in grad school. Those experiences in the past would always be a part of who she was. She smiled to herself as she thought about Spring Harbor. To those memories she added the scary first road signs for Sweet Iron, the scent of her mother's perfume, the rounded swirl of the mahogany staircase banister, the faces around the dining room table agreeing to save her father, Kyle's tender kiss, and her father's gentle eyes and melodic voice.

One thoughtless moment that day at Tippitt Pond, and so many lives were changed forever. Elisha, Sam, Shelly, Justin, Brian, Melanie, and me, and that doesn't even include the collateral damage among families and friends. All of us caught up in a moment that would forever affect our lives. All this dumb worry about who her parents were. She'd decided she was fortunate to have two sets of parents. Remington Hatcher had been more accurate than he realized months ago when he said, "I must warn you. Your life is about to change forever." Now she had made her decision. Amazing what a moment of facing death could do to prod a person into reflecting on the years she had left. And, of course, she added to herself, some understanding of what was important.

Moments later, Beth closed the book that lay largely unread on her lap. She got up, gathered her things, and walked out through the airport tunnel. How different than her solitary journey to Sweet Iron just months ago. She searched the waiting crowd and picked out Kyle Warner's face. Just as she reached him, he held out his arms. She dropped her bag, moved into his arms, and whispered, "I'm home."

About the Author

Susan Van Kirk began her writing career with her 2010 creative nonfiction memoir, *The Education of a Teacher (Including Dirty Books and Pointed Looks)*. Her mysteries about the town of Endurance began with *Three May Keep a Secret* (2014, Five Star/ Cengage). *Publisher's Weekly* said, "Van Kirk's appealing mystery debut... introduces recently retired teacher Grace Kimball. Cozy fans will find a lot to like." *Marry in Haste* (2016) followed, along with an Endurance novella titled *The Locket: From the Casebook of TJ Sweeney* (2015). Her final Endurance mystery was *Death Takes No Bribes* (2017). She is a member of Mystery Writers of America, Sisters in Crime, and is on the Steering Committee of the Guppies, a subgroup of Sisters in Crime. Her books display her lifelong interest in the Midwest, history, and mystery. Educated at Knox College and the University of Illinois, she taught for forty-four years. Mother of three and grandmother of eleven, she divides her time between Illinois and Arizona. You can read more about her books at www.susanvankirk.com